Two or three degrees off plumb

Two or three degrees off plumb

Sam Venable's unique look at life

The Knoxville News-Sentinel, 1988
A SCRIPPS HOWARD NEWSPAPER

Printed in the United States of America
First printing
ISBN 0-9615656-3-2

Cover illustration: Martin Gehring
Back cover photograph: Michael Patrick
Book design and layout: Susan Alexander
Typesetting and editing: Mary Booher, Donna Colburn,
Bonnie Lynch, Bob Martinson

To all the Jim Bobs, Bo Jacks, Bubba Joes, Sue Fayes, tubbos, winos, weirdos, cornhuskers, 'mater belles, nerds, good ol' boys, yankees, hillbillies, brethren, sistren, white trash, geeks, Greeks, suspendered yuppies and shameless hussies who make 208 W. Church Avenue such an interesting place to work, this book is gratefully dedicated.

Contents

Introduction

Writing the introduction to a Sam Venable book isn't easy. Do you play it straight or attempt humor, knowing all the while that trying to match wits with him is a losing battle?

Three years ago we turned out our first Venable collection — "A Handful of Thumbs and Two Left Feet" — a compilation of his best outdoor stories. Sam either has a lot of relatives, or more friends than House Speaker Jim Wright of Texas (who sells books to associates by the caseload), or he is simply that popular. In any event, his first book is now in its third printing with nearly 15,000 copies sold. Now he'll probably ask for a raise.

This is another collection of Sam's best columns from the pages of The Knoxville News-Sentinel. In 1985, after 15 years as this newspaper's outdoors editor, he became our general columnist. That was either a stroke of genius on my part or a great case of salesmanship by Sam. I still haven't decided.

As this anthology of his writing well illustrates, Venable has an interest — and opinion — in a variety of subjects, not the least of which is food. In "Two or Three Degrees Off Plumb," you will soon discover that Venable enjoys other topics, too, and is never hesitant to activate his bizarre sense of humor when the need arises. Or even when it doesn't.

A special word of thanks and appreciation goes to News-Sentinel artist Martin Gehring who does the "Martoons," as we call them, that are used to illustrate many of Venable's columns. Also to Susan Alexander, The News-Sentinel's public service director, who compiled the columns for this book as well as for Venable's successful first effort.

And, finally, a fond word of appreciation to the staff of The News-Sentinel, especially those whose desks are near Venable's. They're the ones who must endure his bird whistles, duck calls, screams and other antics whenever he thinks the newsroom needs a little humor.

We hope you share our enthusiasm for Sam Venable and this collection of his columns as much as we enjoy bringing them to you.

Harry Moskos, Editor
The Knoxville News-Sentinel
August 27, 1988

My wife is a mathematician who specializes in high-tech computer instruction. I love her anyway.

Like all mathematicians, engineers, statisticians, computer wizards and other freaks who work with numbers, Mary Ann has taken a vow of orderliness.

She thinks in orderly terms. She makes plans in an orderly fashion. She bases all decisions on logic. She carefully reads written instructions and follows them to the letter.

Fortunately, she has me around to liven up her life with last-minute fits of panic and cursing. Otherwise, the poor child would probably die of boredom.

My problem — one of my problems, anyway — is with the system. The very mention of the term causes me to break out in hives. Anything governed by a system will be laid out in a rational, methodical pattern and should be avoided at all costs.

I don't function well in the face of plans, budgets, forms, rules, regulations, schedules, advice, instructions, directions, charts and computer terminology. These are mere play-pretties of the system and should be reserved for other people.

Bless their analytical little hearts.

Chapter I
A victim of the system

The art of excuse-making

September 6, 1987

I don't know the first thing about delivering a fastball from pitcher's mound to home plate, nor swatting it from home plate to the outfield. Still, there's a bit of advice I'd like to impart to Joe Niekro and Billy Hatcher:

If you're going to tamper with the rules, at least have the decency to give a reasonable excuse when you get caught.

As you may know, Niekro, a pitcher for the Minnesota Twins, and Hatcher, an outfielder for the Houston Astros, are enjoying 10 days without pay.

Niekro was nailed for doctoring baseballs before the pitch. Seems he was hiding an emery board in one pocket and a scrap of sandpaper in another. With sleight of hand Houdini would have envied, he was roughing the surface of the ball for better control. This is a no-no.

Hatcher earned his suspension at home plate. His bat splintered, revealing an interior crammed with cork shavings. This procedure gives the hitter more wallop in his swing. It also happens to be illegal.

So what did the lads have to say for themselves?

Niekro allowed as how his fingernails were always bothering him on the mound, so he had to stroke 'em regularly with the emery board. He also said the emery board sometimes got wet; thus, he needed sandpaper for emergencies.

Yeah. And the Queen of England sells Avon.

Hatcher maintained that all his regular bats were broken, darn the luck. So during a game with the Chicago Cubs last week, he inadvertently picked up a stick owned by another player. The bat shattered when Hatcher swung on a grounder and — what have we here? — a bored-out section was exposed. At least he could have blamed it on termites.

Sorry, boys. But a sixth-grader caught at the swimmin' hole on the first day of school could do better.

I am obliged to preach on this topic because I personally have brought excuse-making to uncharted heights. I have honed it and polished it to a brilliant luster. I have perfected a face of innocence unattainable even by the likes of Oliver North.

I hate to brag. But in matters of excuse-making, you prosper or you perish.

Unfortunately, after a childhood of successfully excusing myself from unfinished chores and mysteriously broken windows, I failed a big test in college.

This happened the night I walked into a Sigma Chi party at Deane Hill Country Club, breathed when I shouldn't have, and one of two half-pints tucked under my vest crashed to the floor, just as I passed the guard.

I uttered something about those awful sonic booms and whisked my date onto the dance floor. Even then, it was a perfectly miserable evening. Partly because my excuse reflex failed me. Partly because it hurts to dance with broken glass in your wet shoes. But mainly because it was such a waste of good liquor.

I rebounded a couple of years later during a fishing trip with Ray Hubbard. Ray is one of my dearest friends in all the world. He also is an expert fisherman, which explains why I have to cut corners just to stay even.

That particular afternoon, we each caught a good-sized bass. We couldn't agree on whose was the champ — I suspected mine wasn't — so we stopped at a country store to borrow the scales.

It was time for action.

As Ray strolled through the doors carrying his lunker, I lolled behind. By the time I entered, his bass had already been weighed. I plunked mine down and beat his by two or three ounces.

But the victory was short-lived.

Ray squeezed my fish. Then he shook it by the tail. Out dropped a handful of rocks. Rocks, strangely enough, the same size as those in the parking lot.

"How d'you explain them things?" he sneered.

I didn't even blink.

"Kidney stones."

The sounds of success

January 15, 1988

The dripping water faucet is no problem. Neither is the puppy whine, the growling stomach, the champagne pop, the trumpet or the 1962 Buick. Oh, and the rude sounds — the Bronx cheer, the old-fashioned raspberry and other unmentionables — have been in my repertoire for years.

But never, not even with Frederick R. Newman's help, will I be able to perfect the two-fingered whistle. This is my cross to bear in life.

If you are lost at this point, it may be because you've never heard of Frederick R. Newman. He's a master sound-maker, a man who can produce 70 distinct noises with his mouth.

Newman has written a book and cut a record. It's a package called "Mouth Sounds," which tells me he is more original with noises than titles. My brother and sister-in-law gave me the set for Christmas.

Aside from the fact that I tend to sit alone in the corner and make funny noises, one of the reasons Ronny and Lianne gave me this present is because I never learned to whistle like an all-American boy. The very mention of this embarrassing problem turns my face scarlet.

Sure, I can pucker whistle. Anybody can pucker whistle.

I can purse my lips and whistle a tune with the best of them. I have excellent range and control. I can even whistle both ways, exhaling or inhaling. But I cannot stick my fingers into my mouth and produce one of those ear-piercing blasts audible in 12 counties.

All I do is slobber and go "thufff."

It's awful. When I was a kid and attempted to play Little League baseball, everyone else on the team blew the two-fingered whistle. All I could do was slobber and go "thufff" and yell "C'mon babe!" and other stupid things baseball players yell at each other.

"It's no fun playing with Sam," the other boys would complain to the coach. "The guys on the other teams make fun of us 'cause Sam can't whistle. And that slobber — yeech! Did you ever try to throw a ball after he's touched it?"

The curse followed me into adult life. When I was an outdoor writer and made my living hanging around sporting dogs and their owners, I was constantly in the company of two-fingered whistle experts. When their bird dogs ranged too wide, they would emit a shrill blast (the specialists didn't even use their fingers), and their dogs would immediately close the gap.

"It's no wonder Venob's dogs don't pay attention to him," I overheard one handler whisper to another. "They don't know what 'thufff' means."

"Yeah," the other man replied, "but his dogs sure seem to love him. He slobbers as much as they do."

I can't even escape this pox today. When I'm in a big city and try to hail a cab, all I can do is wave and hope for the best. Cabbies see enough weirdos as it is; I know they aren't about to pick up some idiot who's standing on the corner slobbering and going "thufff."

I had high hopes for Newman's "Mouth Sounds." I listened to the record and read the text. I tried all the steps he had listed in Chapter Five: lip control, finger placement, tongue bending, air direction, the works.

I tried it again and again.

I got nothing but a bath.

"Experimentation is necessary in developing your whistle," Newman writes. "Adjust the lips. Try different air pressure. Move the tongue slightly. And always listen for hints of that elusive whistling sound. Once you begin to hear a faint whistle, you are close to home. It will then be a matter of fine tuning."

Yeah, sure. After 40 years of failure and 60 gallons of slobber, I have but one thing to say to Frederick R. Newman:

"'Thufff' to you, buddy."

Smithwick's finest hour

October 15, 1985

Some things in this world are simply meant to be defaced. There's no sense trying to argue.

If you visited a public restroom a few years ago, you found a dispenser of paper or cloth towels. Not any more. These days, it'll be one of those hateful electric dryers that never does the job for which it was made.

Manufacturers of blow dryers must figure we are dummies. They always print instructions on how to use their products. The federal government assumes any old fool can fill out an IRS form, yet we get detailed lessons on how to go about drying our hands.

When the dryer is shipped from the factory, the instructions read something like this:

1. Push button.
2. Rub hands gently under warm air.
3. Stops automatically.

But within 10 minutes after installation, someone will have taken a key or nail file and scratched revisions. So the instructions read like this:

1. Push butt.
2. Rub hands gently under arm.
3. Stop auto.

And then that immortal line is inserted:

4. Wipe hands on pants.

Such editing, no doubt, has caused great consternation among the kingpins of drydom. I can just imagine a bunch of them sitting around a conference table, puffing thick cigars and plotting retribution:

"Haarrummph! I tell you, J.B., it's a terrible situation. Those graffiti writers are ruining our dryers. Tell Smithwick down in Research and Development to come up with something new."

I was in a public restroom the other day and saw the fruits of Smithwick's labor.

Before me on the wall was a brand new dryer. Sparkling white. But instead of a list of written instructions, the message was relayed by a simple illustration. It showed a pair of hands being rubbed together under red, wavy lines. I assume the lines represented heat.

Strike one up for Big Business?

Not quite.

An artist already had been at work. He — I assume it was a he since I was in the men's room, but these days you never know — had scratched a diagonal line across the face of the illustration. It was like those new road signs that tell you not to do something.

And below, in neat block letters, he had printed:

"Wipe hand on pants."

That guy deserves a medal.

The schemes of mean machines

March 14, 1986

Machines and tools hate me and always have.

They scheme against me and lie in wait until I bumble along and fall into their trap for the 87th time. This has been going on since I was a child.

In the 1950s, it was chic for boys to build model airplanes and cars. These were detailed, working models, designed to help American lads hone their engineering/mechanical minds.

Every birthday, a boy could count on receiving a '48 Ford coupe or a Piper Cub. He was supposed to scream, "Golly, gee whillikers! This is keen!" and dash off to his bedroom to put the pieces together.

I got lots of models for presents, and I hated them all. Every time I picked up a gaily wrapped package and shook it and heard the unmistakable sound of plastic parts, my heart sank. It is better to get underwear and T-shirts for your 11th birthday than model planes and cars.

The few times I actually tried to build one of the despicable things, it was all I could do to figure out which pieces to break off the plastic form. What I thought was a Ford gearshift turned out to be a bumper. The wings to my airplanes were, in fact, part of the cockpit.

But as bad as I thought the situation was then, I had no idea what mechanical horrors awaited me as a teenager.

When other boys' bicycles fell apart, they fixed them on the spot with string and chewing gum. When mine broke, I pushed it home and beat it with a hammer.

When other boys' fishing reels needed to be torn apart and cleaned, they performed the task blindfolded. I learned to cast with a gritty, hammered reel.

It was years before I figured out how to operate a screwdriver. Wheelbarrows took longer. And to this day, the thought of sawing a board in two and having the pieces be exactly equal scares me into wetting my pants.

I'm telling you this so you will understand why I have a nervous tic. It is spring gardening time, you see. That means the garden needs tilling. It also means it is time for machines and tools to take advantage of me again.

You'd think I would know by now. After all, we have grown a garden for more than 10 years, and each year the machines and tools have conspired against me. I do not learn easily.

A few days ago, I borrowed a tiller. I rolled it into the garden and started yanking the starter rope. It coughed and laughed. I pulled some more. It belched white smoke and almost started. I pulled again. The rope broke and snaked into the bowels of the machine.

Once — surely I was slobber-jawed drunk at the time — I tried to repair a lawnmower when the same thing happened. I ended up with a terminally ill mower and a cigar box full of parts. All hammered.

So this time, I said "pshaw!" and drove to a rental shop. For $12, they loaned me a two-wheeled, six-horsepower grizzly bear. The bear and I fought each other into the bed of the truck, then out of the bed and then into the garden. At least it started when I pulled the rope.

But as I was being dragged around by the bear, something got hung underneath. I threw the gears into neutral and got on my knees to investigate.

The first thing I did was impale my forehead on a piece of metal protruding from the middle of the handlebars. I said "pshaw-pooh!" and turned my head to the left, where I banged it on a support for the left handlebar. I said "pshaw-drat!" and turned to the right, where my head hit the engagement doohickey and threw it back into gear.

Having dirt hurled in my face was bad enough. But when I jumped up to stop the stupid thing, the engagement doohickey got hung in the galluses of my overalls. Then the grizzly bear dragged me halfway around the garden until I dug in my heels hard enough and twisted free.

I started to grab a sledgehammer and beat the blasted thing into submission. But you know how machines and tools are.

With my luck, the hammerhead would have dropped off and smashed my toe.

The computer crisis

April 19, 1988

I knew we should never have listened to those computer experts. I just knew it.

The experts told us computers were nothing more than cold, emotionless pieces of metal and micro-chips. They said computers were electronic servants who could neither reason nor think. They said these machines had one function, and that was to serve at man's disposal. They said computers would never act like humans.

Well, the experts were wrong. As usual.

I know for a fact that computers are starting to behave more and more like the people who created them, and I find it frightening. If this trend continues, the uppity things are liable to take control of the world. Lord knows one computer can out-think any 10,000 smart people as it is. If they organize, it's curtains for the human race.

Just look at the evidence: Already, computers are starting to get sick. They catch viruses.

Technically, they don't "catch" a virus. Someone, a human, has to give it to them. But how do people catch viruses except from other people?

A computer virus is a glitch hidden deep within the software. It can cause an entire system to go haywire and destroy all or portions of the data which has been entered.

Viruses are secretly planted by "hackers." That's the name given to technological coneheads who relate to computers better than to women and get their jollies by tinkering with the software instead of going bass fishing, watching professional football or drinking beer with the boys.

I have enough problems keeping myself physically fit. So now I've got to worry about my computer's health as well?

I can just see what's going to happen one of these days when I sit down to write a column at my computerized word processor. I will punch in the command, "ne samcol" — which is computer jargon for "Let's get another one cranked out, Percy" — but it will just sit there, mumped up and moaning.

"I'm sorry," the computer will type back to me on its display screen, "but I'm not working today. I have a virus.

"I probably won't feel like working for at least two or three days. Maybe not until the first of next week. You'll have to make do with your old manual typewriter until I return.

"Oh, and keep the noise down, will you? My mainframe is hurting something awful. And while you're at it, bring me some chicken soup and a cup of hot tea. Lemon, no sugar. Now, get moving before I breathe germs on you."

But viruses aren't the half of it. Computers are acting like humans in a far more steamy, earthy way. They're into pornography.

Yes, porn. Skin and flesh and such as that.

A few days ago, I was summoned to the computer of a friend. He punched a few buttons, and up popped a program called "MacPlaymate." It featured this long-haired hussy who took off all her clothes and then, to the accompaniment of background groans, played an intriguing little game with an assortment of interesting objects.

I was taken so aback by this coarse display of raw sex, I had to rewind the program and see it again. Five or six times, in fact. I am a stickler for thorough research.

At least the exercise made me realize why young boys are so fascinated with computers. This "MacPlaymate" stuff beats the heck out of National Geographic and the bra section of the J.C. Penney catalog.

Computer viruses and computer porn. Incredible. I wonder what they'll think of next.

On second thought, don't tell me. Let me guess.

Computer condoms. I just know it.

Pad punishment

September 22, 1987

It's too early to fall on my knees and scream, "Hoooooo-ray!" just yet. The gods of fashion are oh-so-fickle, and once they find out how delirious with glee I am, they're liable to bring 'em back just for spite.

Shoulder pads, I mean.

Surely you have seen them — those puffy, half-acre rectangles women have been stuffing into the tops of their dresses the last couple of years. I have it on no other authority than Christine Anderson, fashion consultant for this esteemed publishing house, that shoulder pads are outta here and — in all likelihood — won't be back until well into the next century. We can only pray.

The last time this evil was visited upon Western civilization was during the 1940s. At least there was an excuse. A war was in progress back then, and people had to exist on the worst of rations.

But we have prospered in the decades since. Full-time production leaped into high gear, even though the clutch may have slipped temporarily. Except for little bumps in the road like Korea, racial injustice, double-digit inflation, Milhous Nixon, Watergate, Vietnam, polyester and AIDS, we've had it better than any other people in American history. So why did some zipperhead choose now to resurrect those clumps of sponge?

I know. It's one of those equal rights things. Several years ago, men were forced to suffer through the embarrassment of bell-bottomed trousers — another throwback to World War II. This time around, it was the ladies' turn to be made fun of by designers.

Or maybe this is all a Pavlovian response on my part. In the autumns of 1962, '63, and '64, I wore a set of shoulder pads four afternoons and one night every week and was relentlessly stomped into a quivering mass of human jelly. These days, I notice my bum knee and kinked neck really start to throb whenever I spy stacked shoulders.

Whatever the reason, I'm glad to see that the pads are exiting.

Before you say it, I am fully aware that East Tennessee women won't realize the rules of fashion have changed for quite awhile. But at least this is a start. Like when you have the flu and your fever finally breaks. Even though it'll be a week before you're hitting on all cylinders, you know the worst is over.

Since I don't wear dresses — not in public, anyway — why am I so happy shoulder pads are fading out?

Because I won't have to (1) look at and (2) feel the barfo things.

Fashion designers would have us believe shoulder pads give the illusion of slim hips on a woman. It's a relative thing, they contend.

Right they are. In relation to the USS Nimitz, the silo of a hog feeding lot is quite small indeed. And based on the size padding I have seen recently, a woman can own hips wider than Chef Paul's and still end up looking like a toothpick. Of course, she has trouble walking through double doorways, but haute couture has its price.

Feeling the horrid things is even worse. The first time Mary Ann wore shoulder pads and I put my arm around her neck, I recoiled in shock.

"Yee-iii! There's a dead cat under your dress!"

"It's not a dead cat," she answered dryly.

"Well, then, I know where my missing blue sock is. It musta got rolled up in there when you were doing the laundry. How come you're always losing my socks, huh? And by the way, I don't like the way my shirts have been turning out lately. I get you the newest iron and the best starch money can buy, and what good does it do?"

Mary Ann made a fist and double-dog dared me to say another word.

Which is another reason I hate shoulder pads. The women who wear them have absolutely no sense of humor.

Wearing o' the green

March 17, 1988

I will not be wearing my green jacket today.

You couldn't make me wear it, not even on a dare. I don't want to give any more wise guys the pleasure of saying, "Hey, Venob! You finally got it right!"

Truthfully, I have no business wearing a green jacket on St. Patrick's Day. Or anything green, for that matter.

That's because I am not Irish. We Venables are of French descent, as you can tell from my waxed and pointed moustache, my continental accent, my artistic abilities and my famous reputation as a lover. We French also are bad to tell lies.

I happen to own a snappy, single-breasted, kelly green blazer. It has been an important part of my wardrobe for the past three years.

I saw this blazer on the back of a handsome, muscular, slim, tanned model in a catalog. Realizing it would look exactly the same on me, I bought it.

Sometimes I wear this blazer with navy slacks, sometimes with tan slacks. But whatever combination I choose, I am the very picture of sartorial success when I have it on. Just ask me.

Come to think of it, there was one minor backfire. That was the Sunday morning I showed up at church to usher along with Larry Coomer. I had on my green blazer and navy slacks. Larry was wearing a navy blazer and green slacks.

It looked like we had just coming a'running from a vice squad raid at the No Tell Motel and had grabbed part of each other's suit by mistake. Larry and I are roughly the same size, and we debated about exchanging coats for the taking of the offering. But given the fact that people sprinting in and out of motels has become such a common scene around churches these days, we decided to leave well enough alone.

Nonetheless, the real problem I encounter on days I wear my green blazer is when I come face-to-face with any of the 1,593,417 registered smart-alecks in downtown Knoxville.

"Hey, Venob!" they shout from across the street or out of a window. "This ain't St. Patrick's Day!"

Then they go "arf, arf, arf!" like they are either tickled at their wit or else have started to choke on their tobacco. I never can tell.

Sometimes, these same pundits hit peaks of originality and drop the St. Patrick's Day barrage. That's when they shout, "Hey, Venob! Whad'ja do — win the Masters? Arf, arf, arf!"

It's not that these crude comments get under my skin. We French have heard worse. Besides, our mothers always told us that sticks and stones may hurt our bones but words would never harm us.

(Which is another one of those French lies. I called a guy a word one time, and he harmed me mightily.)

In any event, I have officially declared that my green blazer will remain in the closet this entire day. I realize this means I must walk around town today looking somewhat less handsome, muscular, slim and tanned than normal. Such are the demands of principle.

I also intend to boycott the wearing o' the green during the April 7-10 playing of the Masters golf tournament.

Not that this will stop any of the callous comments, of course. It's just that it gives me the opportunity for a good comeback later on.

You see, after the Masters is over and I'm wearing the green coat and I run into someone who shouts, "Hey, Venob! How'd you do in the final round at Augusta?" I will be able to raise a single finger and show him I scored a hole-in-one.

It's called body language. We Frenchmen understand things like that.

The trouble with waxing poetic

February 26, 1988

I have come to the gentle conclusion — a rude awakening is more like it — that I should never attempt to wax poetic.

Why?

Because I have a gorilla's sense of timing, that's why. No matter how hard I try to capture the essence of a moment and milk it for its philosophical worth, I am forever two beats off synch.

Keats and Shelley were never smitten by this demon. They merely had to think great thoughts, and all the characters fell into place. What transpired for them was a thing of beauty and a joy forever.

But when I try it, beauty turns into the beast. A killjoy forever.

Let's say I happen to be driving down a highway and see a gorgeous sunset, one of those orange and red panoramas that simply takes your breath. Does it behoove me to stop and admire this artwork of nature? Dare I let my mind run wild with great thoughts?

Of course not.

Sure as I pull off to the shoulder and drink in the splendor, a 75-truck caravan of National Guardsmen will rumble by the other way and block my view until midnight.

Or if I am walking alone on a mountain trail and come to a scenic overlook, you can bet this moment of wilderness bliss will be shattered when some jerk cranks up a four-wheeler. Or when, from way off down in the hollow, I hear, "Hey Vern! Ya'got them taters dug yet?"

I am telling you these things so you will fully appreciate the following story. As non-poetic waxing goes, it is my Olympic gold medal winner.

This happened last weekend when I was bird-hunting with some friends near Spring City. We were closer to Evensville, actually, but since Evensville is roughly the size of a 22-cent postage stamp and does not appear on many maps, Spring City serves as a better reference point.

We were hunting on Bowater Corporation property, some of the thousands of acres the company owns in East Tennessee. This is where Bowater raises trees for pulp. Pine trees.

Bowater grows pines on vast plantations. By the time these trees reach maturity, they form a dense, green pin cushion as void of animal life as a warehouse floor. Ah, but when the stands are young and choked with briars and brush, they are absolute havens for rabbits, quail and woodcock. Also rabbit, quail and woodcock hunters.

So there we were, a bunch of friends who don't see each other as much as we did in the old days, back together again.

We had enjoyed a fine day afield.

The dogs had performed admirably.

We each had taken shots.

There were quail and woodcock in the bag.

It was near the end of the day when I topped a hill and stared at the valley below me. Out there, by the tens of thousands, stood knee-high pine trees, each of them patiently soaking nutrients from the soil and energy from the sun and converting those nutrients and energy into fiber.

Fiber that will be used by Bowater to make paper.

Paper that newspapers will be printed upon.

Newspapers like The Knoxville News-Sentinel.

And so as I stood there in the gentle evening breeze, shotgun in the crook of one arm, I made the mistake of attempting to think another great thought.

"Fifteen, 20, maybe 25 years down the pike, all these little trees might become News-Sentinels," I mused. "Why, this young tree I am standing beside — this *very* tree! — might carry a Venob column some day."

And that, gentle reader, is when an English setter pranced up and hiked his leg on the tree.

Ain't it hell?

On the other hand, perhaps he is a better judge of writing than I am a waxer of things poetic.

Ma Bell's madness

February 21, 1985

As usual, I was running late.

I had leaped from the shower and broken the state record for drying and shaving. I had just grabbed my toothbrush, coated it with some blue gunk from a crumpled tube on the sink and was making history out of D.K. Germ.

The telephone began to ring.

No one answered it.

"Zumtoty phitt eee ooone!" I shouted around a mouthful of suds.

No success.

"Aaaay! Zumtoty phitt eee ooone, eeeez!" I repeated.

The ringing continued.

I spat.

"Hey! Somebody get the phone, please! If it's for me, get the number and tell 'em I'll call. . ."

Too late.

"It's Hiram," (that's a name change) said daughter Megan (real name). "He says it's important. He has to speak to you now."

I said pshaw (another change), wrapped a towel around my chubby little body and sprinted into the bedroom.

"I know you're in a hurry," Hiram said, "but you'll want to hear about. . ."

A gentle *dink-dink* came through the receiver just then.

"Hold on," Hiram said, "I got another call."

And there I stood — foaming at the mouth in more ways than one, listening to the receiver buzz every five seconds. I was about to slam it down when Hiram returned.

"Still there? Sorry. That was Bill (another name change). Now, as I was saying. . ."

What Hiram had to say was so unimportant, I swear I can't even remember the topic. But it did serve a good purpose. I resolved to never again be enslaved by one of those damnable call-waiting devices.

Next time, I'll hang up. I promise.

Despite what you see on the TV ad, I'm not so sure things weren't better back when we talked into tin cans tied to a string. Matter of fact, most everything about the new phone system these days is messed up.

What was so wrong with the way it was that the Feds had to bust it up?

Touch-tone dialing is OK. And even though the division between business and residential numbers in the phone book took some getting used to, I like it better than before. But those are the only improvements I've seen.

Previously, you got billed for long-distance calls. Period. The list was short and sweet. Now, with all the paperwork and lists they send, I gotta wear a truss to transfer the invoice from mailbox to den.

People have been calling me from AT&T, MCI, Call U.S. — probably CCC, FBI, LBJ, and TVA, for all I know — wanting to know whose services I desire.

Which one? I don't care which one!

When I buy shoelaces, I don't waste 10 minutes comparing brands. I just want something that holds my shoes onto my feet. Same with a phone. I just want to pick it up and have it work.

I don't understand all the promotional material I've been getting. One offers me x-minutes of free calls. Another is giving away bonus points. Like green stamps, I assumed; but then they sent me a catalog, and I couldn't figure out how to cash my points in.

I don't want a computer to call me, although some of my replies quite likely have blown circuits from here to Minneapolis.

I don't want to talk on those tinny little portables.

I don't want a recording to tell me to look up a number; if I could do that, I wouldn't be calling information in the first place. And I don't want to get the number from a mechanical operator.

I don't want recorded messages from people who aren't home.

I don't want call-waiting, call-forwarding, call-wakeup, or call-anything.

All I want is to find the government lawyer who engineered the AT&T breakup, plus the electronic genius who developed this call-whatever nonsense, and reach out and touch them both.

With a two-by-four.

Beauty and the beast

May 8, 1987

High-level scientific research always intrigues me.

I don't mean attempts to find a cure for AIDS or breakthroughs in new sources of energy or better ways to grow food so thousands of starving children don't die every day.

I'm talking about the real important issues.

Such as why 7.6 percent of the people in Kansas chew their nails compared with only 4.3 percent in Nebraska. Or why left-handed people take 6.9 seconds longer than right-handers to fry an egg. Gasp! Could you imagine having to endure another 10 years without knowing the answers?

Thus, it was with extreme interest that I read news of the latest research from the University of Texas at Austin.

According to the May issue of Developmental Psychology magazine, psychologist Judith Langlois and five colleagues say infants would rather look at attractive people instead of ugly ones. These findings, the researchers say, challenge the notion that standards of attractiveness are learned through years of cultural exposure.

To reach this conclusion, Langlois and her associates tested 30 infants whose ages ranged from 10 to 14 weeks. Sixteen were girls, and 27 were Caucasian, two Hispanic and one Asian.

Each infant was shown eight pairs of slides of Caucasian women. In each pair, one slide portrayed an attractive woman and the other an unattractive woman. The babies looked at the pretty faces for an average of 9.22 seconds, compared with 8.01 seconds for the hags.

The same experiment was then conducted on 34 infants, six to eight months old. Eleven were girls. Thirty-two were Caucasian, two Hispanic.

Wouldn't you know it; once again, the good-lookers were watched longer than the battle axes — 7.24 seconds to 6.59 seconds.

You mean to tell me it took a team of psychologists and God-only-knows how much money to prove this?

Did Langlois and her colleagues never have an Aunt Hazel with a mustache or an Uncle Floyd with tennis shoe breath? Were they never picked up by a blue-haired lady at church, an old cellulite queen who reeked of $4 perfume and loved to bury her drooling lips into their bellies and go "brrrrrrr"?

I am not talking about learned response. This is instinct. Babies know it the instant they draw their first breath.

It's like pain. A baby does not need to learn that it hurts when a safety pin is poked through the flesh. This is an instantaneous reaction. By the same token, the kid will scream loudly if some old snaggletooth who just polished off a mess of onion rings reaches into the crib to change its diapers.

Another thing: How did the researchers go about picking "unattractive" people for their study? Did they post announcements and conduct auditions? I can just see it now:

"Welcome aboard, Mrs. Pharquahr. You fit our needs to a T. Why, you virtually own the patent on ugliness. You're so ugly, my eyes are beginning to water."

"Oh, thank you, doctor. I'm so happy I can help with this important project. Is there anything I need to do besides look at the babies?"

"Yes, indeed. Be sure to keep a safe distance from all mirrors, windows, cameras and clocks. We don't want anyone hurt by flying glass."

But even as I jest about this project, I must admit it does have one valid point. One burning, aching valid point.

Now I know why babies always start to cry when I pick them up.

Forward to the past

January 16, 1987

Forgive me, Thomas Edison, but I've had it up to my data base with progress.

Ever since electronic journalism became the rage, newspapers have stumbled through a never-ending series of four steps forward, eight steps back. We love pain.

This month marks my 19th year as a writer. That doesn't make me a graybeard, but the timing has been unique. In the brief span of score-minus-one, I have bridged the gap between the old and new worlds of newspapering.

When I entered this hallowed profession in 1968, writers told their tales on typewriters. Heavy, metal, clickety-clack typewriters they were, some of which had seen daily service since Roosevelt — the first one — was in office.

It didn't matter if the writer made a mistake. After he (I'll keep this essay sexist, as there weren't many she's in those days) ripped it from the typewriter, he would go back over it with a pencil. Excess words were rubbed out, misspellings were corrected, and with judicious application of scissors and paste, entire paragraphs were rearranged.

It was a crude system. But it worked.

Things grew a bit complicated when the writer left town. That meant he had to carry a portable typewriter or arrange for one at the other end. When his story was finished, he had two options. The piece could be delivered to the nearest Western Union dispatcher, or else the writer found a phone booth and dictated his work, word by word, to a typist at the home office.

A little more difficult perhaps, but still very effective.

Then the computer age dawned, and my blood pressure has never stopped climbing.

In the mid-1970s, The News-Sentinel acquired a telecopier and several anvils called "portable transmitters." Yes, they were portable; at least in the sense they were not bolted to the floor. But if you wanted to actually move one, a team of oxen was required. I officially dubbed this The Monster.

According to the salesman, all the writer needed to do was peck out his story, attach it (one page of special paper at a time) onto a spinning cylinder in The Monster, hook it up to a telephone and send it back to the office.

I seem to recall that it actually worked. Once. The rest of the time, the hateful thing split pages, sent garbled messages or quit working altogether.

Which meant, of course, that after 30 minutes of fumbling with The

Monster and cursing violently, the writer ended up dictating his story. Just like before.

Around 1978, The Monster was retired. But in its place came a paper-fed computer, The Conehead, designed solely for Harvard-educated engineers. The Conehead was so complicated I had to compile a cheat sheet of instructions to carry on every trip.

The cheat sheet was my lifeline. I guarded it like a sick child. A thief could have stolen my wallet, my plane tickets or my clothes and I would not have blinked. But if my cheat sheet had vanished, I'd have turned into jelly.

In addition to being complicated, The Conehead was stubborn. It, too, worked off a telephone. And it, too, sent garbled copy. At least it did with me. I cannot recall ever successfully transmitting a clean manuscript. I would write my story, send it two or three times, then wind up dictating. Just like before.

All of which brings me to the present.

News-Sentinel road writers now carry a lightweight word processor, The $'&*%. I call it The $'&*% because that's the way my stories look after The $'&*% has garbled them. It's also the color of the air around me when I attempt to use the awful thing on deadline.

One technician tells me the problem lies in the telephone couplers. Another says it's the receiving unit at the office. It really doesn't matter. What does matter is the fact that, despite 15 years of technology, I invariably wind up dictating my stories. Just like before.

"New and advanced" equipment? There ain't no such animal. I propose we burn everything and go back to carrier pigeons and stone tablets.

Bashing the bugs

July 18, 1986

Why are we so mean to bugs?

I got to thinking about this a few nights ago while watching television. During one commercial break, an advertisement for Raid bug spray came on. It was a nice, cutesy cartoon sort of thing. The bugs — evil, nasty beasts — were hunted down, trapped in a crevice and gassed to death.

Gross-o-reeno!

The only thing missing was Vincent Price's "huuu-hooo-hahaa!" cackle in the background. Then the commercial would have made "Psycho III" look like a Mother Goose story.

Raid isn't the only culprit, by any means. Hot Shot, Rid-A-Bug and all the others use commercials that show their products not only eliminating the problem but having a grand ol' time in the process.

The bug doesn't merely crawl off and die. It has to be smashed, squashed, stomped, flattened and torched. Then nuked, just to make sure it doesn't come back to life.

Even products that don't actually kill bugs are presented as heavyweight mobsters in striped coats. Think back a few years ago when the people who make Roach Motels started a big TV blitz. Who do you think they hired as a spokesperson?

A housewife who demonstrated how easy it was to stick a Roach Motel on a shelf and let the little vermin wander in and get stuck on the paper inside? Nope.

A baker or cafeteria worker who lauded the absence of poison? Try again.

A studious-looking entomologist in a white lab coat who pointed to charts and reported the latest scientific results?

Wrong, wrong, wrong.

They got Muhammad Ali, the boxer. His pitch led you to believe he would personally come to your kitchen when your Roach Motel was full and pound the stuffings out of each and every inhabitant.

Please understand that my heart holds no more love for cockroaches, houseflies, silverfish, termites or mosquitoes than yours does. I just want to know why the ads have to look like they were filmed at Auschwitz.

Maybe it would be different if a cockroach had big brown eyes like a cocker spaniel. Could you look at a face like that and hose it down with poison?

Or what if houseflies rubbed against your leg like a cat and purred when you tickled under their chins? Would you spend your money on a product that promised to squash their brains into oatmeal?

Or how about if termites ran to meet you, their cute little tails wagging, when your car rolled into the driveway? Or if spiders came to the feeder at your window? Or if ants sang pretty songs in the tops of trees? Would you still want to grind them into the dirt with the heel of your shoe?

Whew! This is heavy thinking. Far heavier than I'm accustomed to. And it doesn't help the situation that there's a hateful ol' mosquito buzzing around my face while I'm trying to type.

Go away, varmint! Shoo! Scram!

Excuse me, dear reader. I've got to take care of this thing. That sonufagun has sucked the last sip of blood he's ever gonna get from me. I'll just sit r-e-a-l still for a minute.

And the next time he lands, I'm gonna slap his guts out!

Then I'm gonna take his little body in my fingertips and squeeze him till he splits apart!

And then I'm gonna grind his ragged carcass across the fabric of my jeans, just to make sure he's DEAD-DEAD-DEAD!

Huuu-hooo-hahaa!

Insanity by degrees

November 26, 1985

I don't care what scientists and government officials and the collected masses of Eastern Europe have to say about the matter. The metric system is just plain weird. So is everything associated with it.

Those eggheads can argue all they want about metric's uniformity and natural progression. I will stick to Americanese, thank you.

Riverbottom farms are supposed to be measured in acres, not hectares.

Distances come in inches, feet, yards, and miles. Not millimeters, centimeters, meters, and kilometers.

If you catch a largemouth bass weighing 8 pounds, you proudly carry it to a taxidermist. If you catch a largemouth bass weighing 3.73 kilograms, you throw it back and wash your hands immediately, because it probably was tainted with PCBs.

When you purchase aged, brown water, the bottles should be sized in pints or portions of a quart. Not those god-awful liters.

So much for weights and measures. The people who deal in metric numbers also are prone to take temperatures with a Celsius thermometer. That's where I get off.

When winter arrives and the temperature starts to drop, we should be able to look at our thermometers and know the road will get slippery when the mercury hits 32. Not zero.

I am particularly sensitive about the Celsius scale because tomorrow is the birthdate of its founder. On Nov. 27, 1701, Anders Celsius drew his first breath. This was in Sweden.

I guess it was only natural that little Anders would end up piddling with the thermometer, for he came from a long line of thinkers. Both his father and grandfather were mathematicians, and an uncle was a botanist.

Anders went a different route. He studied to be an astronomer. In 1730, he became a professor of astronomy. Ten years later, he was put in charge of a large, new observatory in his hometown of Uppsula.

But even though Anders did some important research into determining the magnitude of stars, it is in the field of thermometry that we remember — and revile — his name.

If you ever had a course in chemistry, you were introduced to conversions from Fahrenheit to Celsius. The Fahrenheit scale, by the way, was developed in 1724 by Gabriel Daniel Fahrenheit. Gabe was a German, but he must have been an American good ol' boy at heart because he knew water freezes at 32 and boils at 212.

Conversions are a nightmare. To convert Fahrenheit to Celsius, you must subtract 32 degrees and multiply by 5, then divide by 9. To convert Celsius to Fahrenheit, you must multiply by 9, divide by 5, and add 32 degrees.

You think that's tough?

Well, let me let you in on a little secret. A no-joke, it's-a-scientific-fact, if-I'm lying'-I'm dyin' secret: In 1742, when Anders developed the Celsius scale, he had it backward from what it is today. According to his original scale, water boiled at 0 degrees and froze at 100. It wasn't until a year later that the scale was reversed.

If you don't believe me, go to the library and look it up in "Asimov's Biographical Encyclopedia of Science and Technology." See page 272.

It's bad enough that Anders developed his crazy scale in the first place. But the people in charge of the scientific community back then should have taken a hint. When Anders uncorked that 0-boil, 100-freeze theory, they should have tossed him out into the cold.

And given him a Fahrenheit thermometer to read while his teeth were chattering.

GREAT MOMENTS IN SCIENCE.

THINK! THINK! THINK!

February 22, 1987

The late E.T. Bales tried to teach me this lesson years ago. But I was too stubborn to learn.

Bales, longtime sports editor of the News-Free Press in Chattanooga, used to shoot his own photographs. No matter what his agenda happened to be, he rarely left the office without strapping a camera around his neck.

Not just any camera. In an era when most photographers had switched to small, compact 35-millimeter packages, Bales clung to his ancient Speed Graphic. It was one of those bulky black film boxes you see in B-grade movies about reporters. You know, where the men wear baggy pants and stick press cards in their hats and run around shouting nerdy things like, "Right, Chief!" and "Stop the presses! I've got a scoop that'll blow this town apart!"

But that's not what I remember most about E.T.'s camera. It was the message he had taped across the top, a note he had written to himself in big block letters:

THINK! THINK! THINK!

"What's that all about?" I asked him.

"You'll find out for yourself one of these days," he replied. "No matter how much you fool with a camera, it will trick you. It's so easy to forget or overlook something. If you don't make it a point to THINK! THINK! THINK!, you're gonna mess up."

Two months later, I was on an out-of-town assignment. I switched from black-and-white film to color and forgot to adjust the ASA dial.

Didn't I know better? Of course I did. I just didn't THINK!

Thus, when the three rolls of spectacular color pictures I shot came back from the darkroom, they looked like I had spent all afternoon filming black cats in a coal bin.

The next day, I taped THINK! across my own camera.

But that created a new problem. I grew so immune to seeing THINK! that I started to ignore it. The next thing I knew, I was forgetting that spiteful ASA dial or failing to synchronize shutter and flash or committing some other grievous sin of photography.

I bring you this message to explain why I occasionally freak out into fits of rage. It usually occurs seconds after I realize I've done something stupid. Something I know better than to do in the first place.

The last time it happened was a few days ago. This was shortly after I had removed some clutter from my desk.

Not "clutter" as in papers and folders and empty coffee cups. It was computer clutter. What I was doing was erasing electronic copies of news stories, anecdotes and snippets I had stored in my word processor.

I came across a wire story I had been saving since last summer. Instantly, my brain became a battleground between Venob the housecleaner and Venob the junk collector.

The housecleaner spoke first.

"Go on. Kill it," he said. "You haven't looked at this story in eight months. If you haven't used it by now, you never will. Erase it and make room for more important material, you idiot."

The junk collector in me argued violently.

"Don't listen to him," he said. "THINK! This is a tasty gem of information. THINK! Some day you can work it into a column. THINK! Don't get rid of it under any circumstances. THINK! THINK! THINK!"

With one push of the button, I overruled the junk collector and sent the story to computer heaven.

That occurred on a Saturday. The following Monday — so help me — I had a chance to use the information. But it was gone, leaving that awful pain in the pit of my stomach, the pain all computer operators feel when they see those terrifying words "file not found."

I am starting to believe I don't need a THINK! reminder at all. Instead, I need one that says FIST!

The kind that activates itself when I start to do something stupid like clean up computer clutter.

End of the line, please

August 25, 1987

Just once in my life, even if only for a day, I'd like to be an M.

If not an M, then a K. Or an L or an N or any of their ilk. It really doesn't matter which. All I want is to experience what it's like not to cringe when I hear the words "alphabetical order."

All across America this week, kindergartners and first-graders are being taught a lesson in discrimination they will retain the rest of their days.

Well, most of them. Some of the girls with last names like Vincent, Williams and Young will eventually move to the front row by marrying boys named Adams, Baker and Campbell. Traitors.

Like it or not, we V's learn early that life is not fair. It only takes a day or two of school to realize that A's, B's and C's are favored in our society.

A's, B's and C's get to go to the bathroom first.

They get to have cookies and Kool-Aid first.

They get to go to the playground first.

By the time we V's (and, bless their hearts, the poor W's, X's, Y's and Z's) come around, all the toilets are stopped up, there's nothing left on the cookie tray except dry Fig Newtons, the Kool-Aid is warm and teams have already been chosen for softball.

Somewhere, I know there's a study proving that V-W-X-Y-Z's have a higher incidence of persecution complex than any other group of people. There's probably another study that shows how early in life we become skilled at solitaire.

Don't hand me that argument about reverse alphabetical order, either. The only time kids are told to line up Z-through-A is when a loathsome task is in store. I learned this cruel truth in the fourth grade when the health department treated us to polio shots.

In all fairness, I must admit that A's, B's and C's do break a substantial amount of new ground.

They always have to diagram the first sentence in English class.

They are the first to sing in chorus tryouts.

They are the first to demonstrate the side-straddle hop in phys ed.

But when the task is particularly irksome, count on the adult in charge to shift into reverse. It never fails.

Once when I was a fledgling Boy Scout, I accompanied a bunch of other guys to the YMCA for a final lifesaving exam. We were put into a room together, but told we would be tested individually.

Perfect. I figured the A's, B's and C's would go first. When they got back, they could tell the rest of us what to expect.

Nope. The hateful lifeguard started at the bottom of the list — and there was not a Weems, Xuan, Yarbrough or Zachary in the house.

I walked to the side of the pool and stared in disbelief. The "victim," who was casually treading water, could have passed for a Green Bay linebacker.

Then he started thrashing. A jolt of panic surged through my body. Somehow, I shucked shoes and clothes, leaped into the water and wrestled him to the side. I was filled with pride.

Then the lifeguard said, "Why did you go through all that? You wasted a lot of time."

He pointed to a pole leaning against the wall, then to a rope coiled nearby.

"You should have used one of those."

I walked back to the room feeling three feet tall. By the time the rest of the boys completed their test — all bone-dry, of course — I could have hidden under a leaf.

That's why I'd like to be a K-L-M-N for a day.

No matter how the roster is written, those people always wind up in the middle — eternally far enough from the front to escape the first trip to the blackboard, but never far enough back to miss the chocolate chip cookies.

On second thought, I bet they lead horribly dull lives.

No dice for 'Miami Vice'

August 20, 1987

I watched my first episode of "Miami Vice" the other night.

Well, almost an entire episode. I came in a little late, but as veteran cops and robbers watchers know, it doesn't take long to get caught up on the plot. And I might as well confess that the only reason I was watching was because my plane was behind schedule, I had finished my magazine and "Miami Vice" was blaring from the TV above the bar.

Reon Carter, The News-Sentinel's television critic, says "Miami Vice" is about to celebrate its fourth anniversary on NBC. Do tell. After watching Sonny Crockett and Ricardo Tubbs in action, I'll wait until the 10th anniversary before tuning in on a regular basis.

Forgive me for behaving like a Geritoler, but based on what I saw the other night, they just don't make good guy-bad guy shows like they used to. Mike Hammer comes close. But where is Joe Mannix when we need him?

Mannix. Now, there was a real man.

Once every week, from 1967 until 1975, Mannix would get the teetotalin' wad stomped out of him. Bad guys would kick him in the guts. They would pound his head with a tire tool. They would knee him in the groin — although you had to imagine what the creeps were doing. In those days, it wasn't polite to broadcast an attack on such an intimate portion of the body.

And what would happen to Mannix?

Nothing.

The next time he appeared, he might have a Band-Aid over one eye. Two minutes later, even that would be gone. Mannix was made of strong stuff.

Same thing with his car.

Ol' Joe could run it off a cliff or smash it into a concrete wall or wrap it around a tree. Next scene, it'd be back on the road with nary a dent. I think Joe Mannix taught the Dukes of Hazzard a lot about automotive resurrection.

So what do the stars of "Miami Vice" do best?

They sweat.

They take a normal, albeit noxious, bodily function and make us think it's the rage. Thank God only the senses of sight and sound are required for TV. If scent ever comes into play, I'm selling my set.

Tubbs and Crockett stake out a cocaine drop, and sweat trickles down their cheeks.

They work at their desks, and sweat soaks into their shirts.

They chase a crook, and sweat drips off their chins.

They look at gorgeous women, and sweat cascades off their chests.

Mannix could do all that plus wreck his car and get beat up and stay drier than day-old toast.

Perhaps I'd be more interested if Crockett and Tubbs moved out of Florida and took their crime-fighting skills to a cooler location.

"Bangor Vice."

Say, that *does* have a nice ring to it!

With the exception of vacations, out-of-town assignments, a summer job with Uncle Sam's Forest Service in Idaho and a tour of newspaper duty in Chattanooga, I have lived in Knoxville all my life.

This makes me a homebody.

In many professional circles — newspapering, for one — being a homebody is considered a severe drawback. People who remain in their hometowns are sometimes made to feel like they should wear a red "N" on their foreheads. For native.

But if being a Knoxville boy is a drawback, nobody bothered to tell me. On the contrary, I think it gives me a unique perspective about the happenings in our city.

I was living in Knoxville when Tommy Hope, sneaking a cigarette in his daddy's flower shop, set off the fire which burned down the Market House and launched downtown redevelopment; when City Councilmen Cas Walker and J.S. Cooper dispensed with parliamentary procedure and punched it out during a council meeting; when Chattanooga shellacked Tennessee in football and the resulting riot shook Neyland Stadium down to its very foundation; when anyone with a body temperature of 98.6 could get a job with TVA; when Jake Butcher wore three-piece pinstripes instead of one-piece prison stripes.

When you're a homebody, you've seen it all.

Chapter II
Knoxville, my hometown

Slices of history

March 2, 1986

It took seven minutes and a chain saw to erase 110 years.

That's what happened a few days ago when Larry Ramsey felled the giant American elm behind First Presbyterian Church, 620 State St.

Don't blame Ramsey for the deed. He was merely a paid executioner performing his duty. The death sentence was decreed months ago when church officials authorized a $1.4-million addition. When trees and building plans collide head-on, trees inevitably come in second.

Seven minutes and 110 years. Think about that for a moment.

In the eyeblink of 420 seconds, the airplane was invented, two world wars were fought, atomic fury was unleashed and men walked on the moon. Yet throughout those years, the tree stood firm.

It took a minute or two to prepare for the final rites. It always does in tree cutting. A wedge of wood must be excised so the victim will drop on target.

Once that was out of the way, the sawing began in earnest. As the whirring teeth of Ramsey's tool sliced through the bark and bit into the wood, the years began to melt away.

The saw began at 1986, the 100th anniversary of the newspaper across the street. It did not dwell there. In an instant, it cut through 1983 and the worst banking failure in the city's history. Then 1982 and the World's Fair.

Ramsey squeezed the throttle, and 10 years evaporated.

Now, it was 1972, when liquor-by-the-drink was approved by Knoxville voters. Then 1969, when a young, politically ambitious cop named

Randy Tyree was busting drug users under Operation Aquarius. Then 1964, when President Lyndon Johnson referred to a slum neighborhood, three blocks to the east of this tree, as the worst poverty he had ever seen. Then 1962, when Fountain City was annexed. Then 1960, when the Market House was destroyed by fire.

Ramsey goosed the throttle once more. Again, the years vanished.

The teeth cut into 1956, when politicians Cas Walker and J.S. Cooper made international headlines by fist-fighting during a City Council meeting. Then 1951, when the University of Tennessee football team won 10 straight games before losing to Maryland in the Sugar Bowl. Then 1946, when author John Gunther called Knoxville "the ugliest city I ever saw in America." Then 1942, when a top-secret government project was developed at a neighboring town. Then 1937, when the Knoxville airport opened.

The saw bit deeper toward the heart of the tree. As chips flew from within, history continued to unfold.

Next came 1936, when 50,000 jammed the downtown area to glimpse President Franklin Roosevelt as he passed through en route to the Smokies. Then 1930, when the city's population swelled to 105,602, a 36 percent gain in 10 years.

Still, the teeth bored in. They chewed through 1923, when evangelist Billy Sunday closed a six-week campaign with earnings of $29,054. Then 1919, when a race riot ended in the deaths of several blacks and a National Guardsman. Then 1917, when horses were abolished by the Fire Department. Then 1909, when Will Price was struck and killed as he walked near Woodlawn Cemetery, making him the city's first fatality caused by an automobile. Then 1903, when famed desperado Harvey Logan broke out of the county jail.

The saw was gnawing at the tree's youth by now. Back to a time when the First Creek area in which it grew was known as The Bowery, a rough and tumble red-light district.

The teeth crossed 1898, when spinal meningitis took the lives of 35 Knoxvillians. Then 1897, when the east side of Gay Street between Union and Commerce was destroyed by fire. Then 1893, when the paving of Gay Street with brick began. Then 1886, when Broadway Baptist Church was organized. Then 1877, when President Rutherford B. Hayes visited the town to help heal wounds remaining from the Civil War.

The blade would not be denied. Two feet into the massive trunk, the core of the tree was about to be breached.

It was 1876, a very good year.

That was the year when Knoxville let a contract for the construction of a viaduct on Gay Street over the railroad tracks. The year D.M. Rose Lumber Co. was organized. The year C.B. Atkin Co. began to manufacture furniture. The year Knoxville Street Railway Co. began the first streetcar for passengers — a mule-drawn affair with tracks between Main and Jackson Avenues.

And 1876 was the same year when an American elm seedling, 1½ blocks east of Gay Street, sent down its first roots.

Now, the buzzing teeth had done their mission. The trunk creaked, cracked, shook, swayed. Then, with an earth-pounding crash, it toppled from its four-foot stump.

Seven minutes, start to finish.

One-hundred-ten summers of shady, green foliage. One-hundred-ten winters of a wide, naked crown spreading toward the heavens.

Gone. Gone the way of what, ironically, is called progress. Gone forever.

"I just hope," sighed one church member as he viewed the fallen hulk, "that God doesn't punish us for this."

How to spel rite

September 30, 1986

I hope there is a thief in the distinguished leadership of Knoxville's cultural/civic affairs. I'm talking about a real highwayman. Someone who can look the victim square in the eye, smile, do the deed and never blink.

If that person will please step forward, I have a mission to propose:

Go to Hartford, Conn., and talk to the people involved in the First and Original Illegitimate Spelling Bee. Learn everything you can. Then bring the information back to Knoxville and stage a similar event here.

Do it during the Dogwood Arts Festival or ArtFest or whenever you choose. We'll call it the Good Ol' Boy Bee or even the Non-Original Illegitimate Spelling Bee, if the folks from Hartford insist. After all, it was their idea.

But by all means, let's get it done. Ever since "D. Boone cilled a bar," we have been famous for our ability to tamper with the dictionary. I say it's high time this talent was recognized.

In case you missed the news a few days ago, residents of Hartford and West Hartford got together to spell colloquialisms from the works of Mark Twain and Harriet Beecher Stowe. It was, as one observer put it, "a spel'n bee without a compere."

"Mark Twain was an excellent speller," said Wynn Lee, director of the Mark Twain Memorial in Hartford, "but he also had an ear for dialect and the talent to use it effectively. In 'Huckleberry Finn,' for example, you can follow progress down the Mississippi River just by watching the change in dialect.

"Twain once said it was too bad we Americans felt hamstrung to spell one particular way, because our language is so interesting and varied."

Agreed. And there's no better place to find examples than in Southern Appalachia, U.S.A., where Dixie drawl and hillbilly twang collide head-on.

Only here can a two-syllable word be reduced to one ("I gained so much weight, the doctor put me on a dite."), and a one-syllable word be ballooned to two ("Can you hale-yulp me with this problem?") Oh, and I dare not forget our unique method of pluralizations ("The teacher made us sit at our deskis and take testis.")

In case someone honors my request for a colloquial spelling bee in Knoxville, let me offer a primer for prospective contestants. Try these on for size:

■ Cheers — furniture for sitting.

■ Laig — part of the human body used for walking; also, the piece of a cheer that holds it off the floor.

■ Thang — an object, event or circumstance.

■ Atter — occurring at a later time.

■ Hale — where evil people go atter they die.

■ Far — what burns in hale.

■ Fartar — structure used to spot forest fars.

■ Bobwar — material used to keep cattle in and people out.

■ Cadlack — car driven by rich people.

■ Warsh — to remove dirt.

■ Arn — a heavy metal; also, what you do to clothes atter they have been warshed.

■ Taters and punkins — vegetables eaten fried or in pies, respectively.

■ Quare — anything unusual, especially of a sexual nature.

■ Aigs — the thangs hens lay.

■ Taldaga, Panmawciti — places to visit on vacation, especially if you don't own a Cadlack.

If you spelled all 16 correctly before reading the definitions, consider yourself a shoo-in for victory.

Twelve through 15 is good, but you still need to learn a thang or two.

Eight through 11 means you ain't lived here real long.

Four through seven indicates serious cultural anemia.

Three and below? Hale far, son! You better be gettin' on back to Brooklyn.

A tale of two cities

February 20, 1986

I simply must reply to Allen Norwood.

Allen is the columnist for The Charlotte (N.C.) Observer who got bent out of shape last year when I referred to his town as "podunk." He replied with a column that made fun of Knoxvillians and called us rednecks. Then I replied with a column that made fun of Charlottians or Charlotters or whatever name the people who live in that city go by, and called them bluebloods. Then he replied with a column that made fun of the fun I had made.

Now, it's my turn again.

Allen's latest missive contained a plethora of scurrilous anecdotage which, though intended to cast East Tennesseans in a most unjust and unpropitious sphere, ultimately revealed a basal inerudition of the mannerisms and customs of hillfolk because of its immoderately fictional nature.

(That's the way he would have written it, which gives you a taste of the tripe I've had to wade through in his columns. What I mean is that Allen repeated some jokes he'd heard about East Tennesseans, but he didn't tell them right, leading me to wonder if his quiche is fully baked.)

Allen tried to beg off responsibility for the tales, saying he heard them from somebody in Jefferson City, Tenn. I have a hard time believing that, because anyone from Jefferson City would know better. Except maybe someone from Charlotte who was evicted for stealing horses and ended up on this side of the mountains.

I quote from his column: "How do you tell if a fellow from East Tennessee is level-headed? There's tobacco running down both sides of his chin."

Again: "What do East Tennessee girls give their boyfriends at Christmas? Syrofoam spit cups."

Now, don't that beat the hens rootin' and the pigs peckin'?

Allen, it's not tobacco that runs down both sides of the chin. It's tobacco juice. Or "ambeer," if you want to get technical. I'm surprised someone from North Carolina didn't know this already.

The tobacco itself doesn't run down both sides of the chin unless the chewer accidentally swallows the ambeer. And that only happens to bluebloods from Charlotte who try to chew.

Then I must triple-chastise you about spit cups.

First, the Styrofoam people don't make cups or coolers. I've gotten enough letters from their patent lawyers to know this for a fact, and I would assume you've also heard from them by now.

Second, cups — foam or cardboard — make terrible spit containers. Just breathe on 'em and they tip over, spilling ambeer on everything from the Sunday morning paper to your 1040 tax form. A Bush Brother's bean can is better suited for the job.

Third, a gal would never give her man an old bean spit can for Christmas. Not on your life! She'd give him a full can of beans, then offer to cook 'em up alongside a piece of hog meat and serve 'em with a pone of cornbread.

Sorry to embarrass you once again, Allen. But facts are facts.

One more thing. After these interstate barbs began flying, I went to the library and looked up some information about your city. I found this in U.S. News and World Report: "Charlotte has more banking resources than any city between Philadelphia and Dallas. The area's $26 billion in reserves compares with Atlanta's $16 billion."

So what's the big deal? All you have is banks full of money.

Over here, we've got jails full of bankers.

Roots

October 11, 1987

NORRIS — Roots run deep in Southern Appalachia.

They burrow into the rich humus of north-facing slopes along Clinch Mountain. They bore into the grassy flats of sun-splashed Cades Cove. They snake beneath limestone bluffs overlooking the laughing waters of the Nolichucky River.

Yes, they run deep. They must run deep. Without them, Southern

Appalachia has no anchor. Indeed, without them Southern Appalachia has no being at all.

It is a network of roots that feeds life into Southern Appalachia, actually. A massive network that has been burrowing, digging, weaving for hundreds of years — each strand adding its own individual characteristics, one filament at a time, until the framework is complete.

Roots are on display this weekend at the Museum of Appalachia. Cultural roots, that is. Stroll the grounds during the annual homecoming festival, and you will sense their presence in a very tangible way.

Some of these roots have been around for quite a spell. They are seasoned, tougher than dry hickory.

You can feel their strength when you talk to the likes of Margaret Lyons Smith of Johnson City who, at 88, has completed a book about her grandmother. "Miss Nan — Beloved Rebel" is the true story of Nannie Kinkead, who lived on Cave Hill Farm near Rogersville during the Civil War.

Smith pieced the book together from a treasure trove of letters, notes and personal remembrances of a brave woman so committed to her cause that she once dismissed a Union officer with the terse comment, "I am a private citizen of the Confederate States of America, and you are standing on ground that belongs to my country."

Or you can enjoy the humor of Southern Appalachian roots when you sit beside 73-year-old Jesse Butcher, watch him split white oak slats for baskets, and listen to his tales as a Union County game warden more than 30 years ago.

Butcher carries a packet of old photos from that era. Among them is a classic he calls "Mountain Justice." He presents the picture for your inspection and relates its story in his raspy mountain drawl:

"Ah'd arrested this ol' boy for huntin' squirrels outta season. Took him before Judge Carl Seymour, who was a-cuttin' tobacco. He held court right there in the field. Ah read the charges, and he passed judgment. Fined the ol' boy $10. That was big money in them days."

Smith, Butcher and other homecoming exhibitors are hand-me-down specialists. They are the splicers who link us, one to another.

I know not what calling prompts these people to capture the skills and the stories of their forebearers, to preserve these priceless heirlooms, to keep them alive for future generations. All I know is that I am forever grateful.

I'm talking about folks like Tim and Linda Beets, who turn hog lard and hardwood ashes into lye soap.

And Jacquelyn Bedwell, who creates beautiful baskets from strands of honeysuckle and grapevine.

And Rick Stewart, grandson of legendary cooper Alex Stewart, who still makes churns and buckets the old-fashioned way.

And Bill Henry, woodcarver, who breathes life back into chunks of yellow poplar long after the tree has crashed to earth.

And Red Rector, monarch of the mandolin, and Dorsey Williams, dean of the dulcimer, who see to it that mountain music continues to ring through the ridges and hollows.

And native son John Rice Irwin and adopted son Alex Haley, both of whom have an extraordinary sensitivity for roots, both of whom help teach us about ourselves.

The roots of Southern Appalachia will never wither as long as these people, and countless others of their breed, remain in charge of the cultural lifeblood of this region.

Yes, the roots on display run deep. Deep into the heart and soul. And that's the way it should be.

For these are strong roots.

Proud roots.

Our roots.

Southern commandments

June 26, 1987

Dear Brother Jim and Sister Tammy:

Welcome to East Tennessee.

I don't blame you all for coming here. Not one bit.

If I had been hounded by the press for four months and been the butt of jokes from Maine to California and needed a place to find peace and solitude, I would be hard pressed to come up with a more beautiful, relaxing site than Sevier County, Tenn. With no offense to the Good Book, the term "Promised Land" will take on new meaning after you've had a chance to nestle your feet in Sevier County soil.

I wouldn't rely on the Welcome Wagon during summer, this being the height of the tourist season and all. But if I know Sevier Countians — and I do — I bet it won't be long before some of your neighbors come calling with a jar of pear preserves or some bread and butter pickles. That's just the way us ol' home folks operate.

The two of you had better be prepared to shift gears. Literally. Palm Springs, Calif., is flatter than a blown-out tire. (That's "tar," as I'm sure you'll soon discover.) On our hairpin curves, you'll want all the second gear and clutch-riding your pickup truck can take.

Even more so, you'll need re-adjustment from the societal standpoint. Perhaps that's where I can help.

First, there's this business of your old group, the PTL. I don't care whether it used to stand for "Praise the Lord" or "People That Love." That's all over now. Here in East Tennessee, PTL means "Plow the Land" or "Pass the Lard."

Also, we need to talk about your own names. "Tammy Faye" will be quite acceptable among the natives. But plain ol' "Jim" sticks out like a watermelon in the tater patch. I suggest something more natural. "Jim Bob," maybe.

Those duties out of the way, let's look at a few other important matters. I've compiled them in a language you understand best.

1. Thou shalt not make graven images of thyself, neither with gold, nor with silver, nor with Maybelline.

2. Thou shalt not look with lust upon thy church secretary, nor lay hands upon thy church secretary, lest thy church secretary's daddy cleave thy head asunder with a pole axe.

3. Thou shalt not divulge the location of thy neighbor's likker still, nor thy neighbor's trout stream, nor the route thy neighbor travels when he sneaketh his coon dogs into Cades Cove.

4. Thou shalt not take the name of Dolly Parton in vain.

5. Thou shalt not speak evil to visitors from the shores of Toldeia, Akronita and Jersey Citarium until a fortnight hath passed and they are no longer heavy laden with traveler's checks.

6. Thou shalt not conduct mass baptismals at Ogle's Water Park, neither shalt thou speak in tongues from the parking lot of Christus Gardens.

7. Thou shalt not ride thy four-wheel drive on Smoky Mountain trails, nor cast down thy Budweiser can, unless thy park ranger's back be turned.

8. Thou shalt not desecrate the Rebel Corner, the Space Needle and other sacred temples.

9. Thou shalt not skinny dip, nor abandon thy flip-flops, in the holy waters which part this land.

10. Thou shalt not — whatever thou dost — gather people about thee and poor-mouth about having only $37,000 to thy name.

There. That ought to get you started.

Please read over these passages, commit them to memory, and act accordingly. Before you know it, you'll be weeping tears of joy.

I trust your stay in our mountains is safe, comforting and happy. But not the least bit profitable.

Lord have mercy on us all,
Brother Sam

Metropolitan madness

March 4, 1986

I might as well tell you right from the top that I'm not going to use real names.

It won't make a bit of difference anyway, because the guilty parties all live out of town. Their names wouldn't mean a thing to you.

But their associates in Knoxville certainly know who they are, and if word got back to the big city that "John" and "Joe" made fun of "Frederick" and "William" in a Tennessee newspaper, it would kick the struts right out from under their megabucks dealings. So you're just going to have to trust me when I say this is the truth, the whole truth and nothing but the truth.

John is a successful Knoxville businessman. Frederick is one of his clients, a $150,000-a-year chap who lives in New Jersey but keeps an office in downtown Manhattan.

Frederick occasionally travels to Knoxville, and when he does, he likes to flaunt his urbane ways in front of John. They were enjoying a post-meeting drink the other night when John mentioned he lived three minutes from his office.

"Three minutes?" blinked Frederick. "That's impossible!"

"No it isn't," John replied. "Takes me exactly three minutes to drive from my house to the parking lot at my office. If something's wrong at home and my wife needs me, I'm just a phone call away. But what's the big deal about living so close to your work?"

"It can't be done in New York," said Frederick. "It takes me an hour and 45 minutes one way."

Then he detailed his daily regimen. By the numbers:

Up at 5 a.m. Leave home at 5:45. Drive car to bus station. Ride bus to train station. Ride train into New York. Walk from train station to office.

In the afternoon, he backtracks.

It takes Frederick until 8:30 p.m. to get home. That leaves just enough time for supper, a bit of reading or TV, then to bed. He performs such a routine 5 days a week, 12 months a year. This is called progressive yuppie living in a northern suburb.

But hold on to your overalls, folks. You ain't heard nothin' yet.

Joe is another successful Knoxville businessman. William is one of his out-of-town associates. Another New Yorker.

William was in Knoxville not long ago for high-powered dealings. When the meeting adjourned, Joe took William to his farm on the Knox-Sevier county line.

We are not talking about a doublewide on cinder blocks with chickens pecking at the door. This is a gentleman farmer's spread. It features an expensive, yet rustic, home with a panoramic view of the Smokies out the front window. Acres of green pastures. A herd of high-dollar beef cattle. Get the picture?

So there they were, sitting on the front porch, savoring a gorgeous sunset. All was quiet, save a chorus of spring peepers down in the hollow. Just the scene that makes one sigh contentedly.

Unless one is a William from Big Apple, U.S.A.

"I hate to be rude, Joe," he said, "but I must be honest with you. It's too quiet here. I'm about to go crazy!"

And so — if I'm lyin', I'm dyin' — Joe drove William to the airport, where he sat in hustle-bustle, push-shove, people-pocked peace until his flight was called.

Incredible.

Call us rednecks, rubes, hillbillies, bumpkins, if you please. We stand guilty as charged. But at least we know a good thang when we see it.

A burning issue

November 6, 1987

Twenty, twenty-one, twenty-two . . .

Sorry. Can't talk right now. Be back with you in a jif.

Twenty-three, twenty-four, twenty-five.

There. That's got it. I didn't mean to be rude, but I knew if I stopped counting, I'd lose my place.

What I was doing was totaling the plastic bags piled in front of my house. If my figures are correct, there are two dozen plus one. They're all lined up like penguins, waiting for the garbage man to usher them into plastic bag heaven.

These bags are filled with leaves. For the last two afternoons, the kids and I have spent a lot of time beneath the maples and dogwoods in our yard.

Actually, those 25 bags represent only a fraction of the total deposit. I have already dumped the equivalent of 18-20 other bags on the garden and worked them into the soil. More will go into the compost pile. But our small garden and compost pile can only hold so much. Then they scream, "Enough!"

Not all of the leaves have fallen, either. One silver maple in the front yard, the larger of twins, still holds about half of its cargo. Another round of raking, piling and bagging will be in order before we can put a wrap on the fall of '87.

Those two big maples always disagree this time of year. In spring, both send out leaves in unison. But come autumn, the one on the eastern side of the yard cannot wait to drop its load, while its twin to the west holds on until the very last minute. I have actually seen the faster maple standing naked when the slowpoke is still green. I'm sure there is a botanical explanation for this behavior, but I like to think of it as friendly bickering between two old men.

In any event, we are talking about the equivalent of 50 to 75 black plastic bags of leaves from one suburban lawn. Multiply that by the number of homes in my neighborhood, then by the number in Knoxville, then Tennessee, then across the country, and you get an idea of how rich the plastic bag people must be getting. I'm not greedy; I'd just like to have the twist-tie franchise. That alone oughta be worth millions.

I do not mind raking leaves. In fact, I rather enjoy it. But the aggravating part of this ritual is knowing those hateful leaves have to be bagged. Knoxville outlawed burning some years ago. Pollutes the air, they say.

So instead of filling the air with the perfume of burning leaves, we buy hundreds of millions of petroleum-based plastic bags, fill them with leaves, and send them to overflowing landfills on trucks which, collectively, burn hundreds of thousands of gallons of gasoline. Sounds a lot like the guy who took extra-long steps to save wear on his $35 shoes and wound up splitting his $40 trousers.

Clearly, the theory of no leaf-burning has merit — especially at a time like this, with the sun-parched earth as dry as a powder house. I could not agree more in principle. But principle and practicality occasionally butt head-on.

I find it hard to believe that once-a-year burning of leaves by homeowners comprises even one-tenth of one percent of the junk American industries pump into the atmosphere. What's more, I don't understand

why it is legal to burn logs in my fireplace if I cannot burn the limbs and leaves previously attached to those logs in my back yard.

There's this matter of aesthetics, too. From a purely scientific standpoint, the scent from a pulp mill is just as foreign to the environment as that from a bakery. But to the nose, one is repulsive and the other delightful. I classify leaf-burning near the top of delightful.

Still, it's not to be. We shall bag our leaves like good little suburbanites and line them up on the curb to await the garbage truck.

Sheesh. It all seems so unnatural. Next thing you know, they'll make squirrels sweep up their acorn hulls and birds sing in three-part harmony.

Fair-skinned beauty

September 17, 1987

Her name was June. I knew that because the barker told me so — me and the other teenaged gawkers standing outside his tent.

"Shooow-time! Shooow-girls!" he spoke with nasal monotone into the microphone strapped to his sweaty neck.

"They're all here for you on our stage tonight. You'll see April. You'll see May. And you'll see June, who's busting out all over."

I forget how much I paid to see June and the other, ahem, dancers that September evening so many years ago. Probably a dollar. But I do recall it was money well spent.

That's because the dear Miss June had a marvelous talent, a skill she unleashed upon the audience when the program was in its waning moments. She untethered her bra (which was about all she had on by then; that plus a G-string and a smile) and let it all hang out.

Then, she rotated what was hanging out.

In opposite directions.

At the same time.

I don't know where a woman receives training for that type of vocation, but wherever it was, June graduated summa cum laude.

You don't see girlie shows these days when you visit the fair. At least not the Tennessee Valley Fair. I spent several hours wandering around the midway a few evenings ago, and the only females I saw on display were Tracy the Headless Woman and Angel the Snake Girl.

Admittedly, Tracy and Angel possess unique drawing power, but they leave a lot to the imagination. That's something June never did.

Besides, when was the last time you looked at the women's underwear section of the Sears catalog and fantasized about a girl with scales down her back and fangs in her mouth?

Girlie shows and the fair have had a roller coaster existence around here for years. In his book "Meet Me At the Fair!" Knoxville historian Stephen Ash notes that the only amusements missing from the original Appalachian Exposition of 1910 were "gambling, liquor and girlie shows, all strictly banned by the Exposition officials."

But as the idea of a fair caught on, strip shows found their niche. By the late 1940s, the niche had evolved into a cavern.

According to Ash, the city's Board of Review — which already was busy banning men's magazines from newsstands — turned its guns on fair stage shows in 1949. One hootchy-kootchy act "so offended the ladies and gentlemen of the Board of Review that they walked out in the middle of it."

Lordy, would I have loved to have seen that! The review board, I mean. I bet there was so much harrumphing by the men and forehead-dabbing by the women, the onstage antics would have paled in comparison.

Nonetheless, the degree of heat in girlie shows fluctuated with the marketplace. And the times. By the late '60s, things were rocking again.

"A lot of 'em were billed as dance shows, but they eventually became strip shows," recalled Crosby Murray, secretary-manager from 1965 until 1973. "I heard one or two complaints about 'em, but I told folks I didn't know what was going on in those tents — and didn't want to know! Anyway, they were pretty tame by today's standards."

Indeed. As one fair official dryly observed: "The amateur strippers have put the professionals out of business."

But who knows? Maybe it's time for a striptease revival — with appropriate updating. Given the recent success of the Chippendale dance revue, a male strip show would pack the tent with whooping, hollering, money-waving women.

And I bet not a one of them would walk out in disgust at intermission.

Goodbye, Young High

June 4, 1984

What's all the fuss about losing an old building? Isn't this the way a city is supposed to grow — tear down the old, build up the new, cut the ribbon and smile for the camera?

Perhaps.

But when the bulldozer is tearing out a piece of your life each time it bites into the bricks, you view the situation in a different light. Such is the case with Young High School on Chapman Highway, which is being leveled to make way for a shopping center.

Walk around the grounds with me for a minute. Let me tell you what it means to see Young High in ruins.

See what's left of the main hall, up there where the office used to be? That's where I was standing Nov. 22, 1963, the day President John F. Kennedy was shot. Perhaps no other memory of Young High School, 1961-65, is branded so deeply into my mind.

News of the assassination hit during a change of classes. It spread through the student body like measles.

"The President has been killed . . . haven't you heard? . . . somebody shot him in Texas. . ."

Except nobody believed a word of it. Kids were laughing and joking and trying to figure who had masterminded the hoax and pulled it off with such perfection.

Then John Hicks, the principal, came on the public address system and stopped us in our tracks.

In seconds, the noisy hall went silent as a tomb. A few students and teachers began to weep. Just thinking back upon the moment, a shiver still runs down my back.

Let's move across the yard and look down into The Hole — the old boiler room. You can't tell it now for all the standing water and broken glass, but that's where our Key Club used to gather. We busted out the old furnace and sold it for scrap and made us one fine meeting room.

Mrs. Rogers' algebra classroom is behind us. (You may remember her as Mrs. Leonard Rogers, wife of the mayor) . She could work absolute wonders with logarithms and graphs and math theory. But one glance at the way I keep my checkbook illustrates how often her messages fell upon deaf ears. Far better that we journey on to the English wing.

Two very happy, lasting events occurred in these classrooms. On the bottom floor, where Miss Anderson held sway from a rocking chair in the corner of her senior classroom, the notion was first put into my head that maybe I could write for a living. And upstairs, in Mrs. Runion's sophomore room, I met a brown-eyed girl named Mary Ann.

I walk around these grounds and kick at the rubble and let my mind wander through a montage of memories:

■ Football practices where I sweated; football games where I watched from the bench.

■ The high crimes of skipping line in the lunchroom, rolling pennies in study hall, torching a cigarette anywhere but in the smoking area and running Mr. Austin's chair up the flag pole.

■ Crazy nicknames — Squire, Flintstone, Rat, B.O., Wildroot, Flathead, Bosco, Deesh, Dooge, Biz — and contemplating how some of our crowd's biggest hell-raisers are ministers today. The Lord, indeed, works in mysterious ways.

■ The intense, often bitter, rivalry between Young and South, and chuckling at the thought that today's students at South-Young High

School probably have more important matters to worry about.

We came through in an awkward era, we kids of the '60s. We were too late to wear flat-top haircuts, too early to be flower children. Like high schoolers everywhere, we underwent the metamorphosis from juvenile to adult in 48 months. We arrived together as youngsters and departed on separate journeys toward careers, higher studies and a hell-hole called Vietnam.

Enough of nostalgia. The people who own this place bought it fair and square. Let them bulldoze and rebuild as they see fit. I won't even take a brick. With a nitric acid burn from chemistry class on my right arm and two bum knees from the football field, I surely don't need another souvenir to remember my days at Young.

But someday later on, when you see us at the new shopping center, pointing this way and that to our children, please understand what we are trying to recollect. A very real part of South Knoxville and the people who lived there will be buried under all that asphalt.

The game spoilers

November 19, 1987

I have come to the conclusion that there is not a perfect seat anywhere in Neyland Stadium.

Maybe longtime season ticket holders would argue that point, especially ones who own an entire block of seats and can choose their Saturday afternoon neighbors. Ditto those who are perched in those big-dollar stratosphere boxes, even though the height surely has strained their eyes by the end of each game.

But speaking as one who has viewed Volunteer football from the field, from both end zones, from the student section, from halfway up on the westside 50, and from hither and yon as scalpers' prices dictate, there is not a spot in the entire joint where one can truly enjoy the game.

Why?

Because no matter where you park your buns, you are surrounded by COBBRACARPs.

Surely you've encountered one of them — the Coach, Optimist, Boo Bird, Ref, Analyst, Critic, Announcer, Reporter and Prognosticator who have attended every game since UT began playing football.

COBBRACARPs foul the environment in a variety of ways. In the parlance of jockdom, let's look at their thumbnail sketches.

■ COACH: Has forgotten more about the sport than Robert Neyland, Bear Bryant and Bobby Dodd ever knew. . .says he used to "play a lot of ball," but forgets to add it was golf. . .direct relationship between size of girth and volume of voice.

■ OPTIMIST: Sickeningly cheerful. . .when UT trails opponent 45-2 in fourth quarter, keeps hoping for big play. . .smiles a lot, but occasionally sports a black eye — especially during prolonged losing seasons.

■ BOO BIRD: Chants "booooo!" at everything and everybody: UT coaches, visiting coaches, Vol players, opposing players, both bands, peanut sellers, low-flying pigeons. . .frequently laces his Coke with Maalox. . .changes chant from "booooo!" to "How 'bout them Vols!" at game's end.

■ REF: Amazing physical specimen. . .has eight sets of eyes and X-ray vision. . .seated on top row of upper deck, can spy otherwise-undetected holding (by UT opponent) in 22-man pile-up. . .from same vantage, can clearly see Vol runner did not step out of bounds at the 5, despite call of striped-shirt idiot four feet away from the action. . .often flies in same flock as Boo Bird. . .despite extraordinary vision, has trouble seeing chili stain on orange tie.

■ ANNOUNCER: Suffers from rare vocal disease, *Wardonta den-*

tonis . . .feels compelled to repeat every play for the benefit of those unfortunate enough to be sitting around him. . .when Reggie Cobb goes up the middle for seven yards, he announces, "Cobb goes up the middle for seven!". . .when Sterling Henton drops back to pass, he yells, "Henton's dropping back to pass!". . .mating call includes bursts of "Give him six!" and "Please, pay no more!"

■ CRITIC: Opposite of optimist. . .when UT rallies from 45-2 deficit in fourth quarter and wins, calls it a fluke and vows to drop season tickets he has owned 35 years. . .repeats, "They just ain't got it anymore" at 30-second intervals throughout game.

■ ANALYST: Perhaps most irritating of all COBBRACARPs because of fog-horn voice. . .has compulsion to describe theory behind each play to spouse and closest 150 people seated nearby. . .is passionately hated by all, even Optimist.

■ REPORTER: Mostly female. . .often found in company of Announcer, but deals in non-game topics. . .when Wave starts, reports, "Look! The Wave has started!". . .when band comes onto field, reports, "Look! The band is coming onto the field!". . .needs to eat corsage she's wearing and hush.

■ PROGNOSTICATOR: All-knowing seer of the future. . .accuracy rivaled only by TV weather forecasters. . .starts every season making holiday plans for French Quarter, but quickly settles for a stroll down Peachtree Street.

See what I mean?

COBBRACARPs are everywhere. If 93,000 people funnel into Neyland Stadium on a given Saturday afternoon, you can count on 92,998 of them to be COBBRACARPs.

What about the other two?

Why, they're sane, ordinary people. Just like you and me.

Except I ain't so sure about you.

So what's a few years?

August 21, 1987

Keep a stiff upper lip, Knoxville. Remember that every dark cloud has a silver lining. If at first you don't succeed, try, try again. The only difference between a champ and a chump is "u." Rome wasn't built in a day. We have nothing to fear but fear itself. These things take time. When the going gets tough, the tough get going.

There. I've exhausted every "be not discouraged" motto I can recall from my childhood. I've written them down so you will feel a lot better about the sad state of Knoxville affairs — especially since it looks like plans for redeveloping the World's Fair site will be deep-sixed. Again.

What's that? You say you've read my list — twice, in fact — but you still don't feel any better?

Hmmm. Well then, let's try another route:

"Sometimes, you have to laugh to keep from crying."

Laughter is about all we have going for us these days. We might as well get used to it, too, because Knoxville is fast becoming the laughingstock of the Southeast.

Oh, and despite what your momma used to tell you, those other folks aren't laughing with us. They're laughing *at* us.

One of the prime selling points of the 1982 World's Fair was the wondrous downtown redevelopment that would take place after the Fair closed. Five years, two mayors, two developers and a lot of money later, we're still waiting for it to occur.

Aaah, but what the heck. Let's go on and laugh.

We can dust off those old stories about bringing a giant flea market to the state amphitheater — "Tube Sox and Taters at the Tennessee."

Or perhaps we can have folks rolling in the aisles with suggestions for a carp farm or PTL baptismal font in Waters of the World. Those are good ones, for sure.

Or how about donating the Sunsphere to the Golf Hall of Fame as the world's largest tee? Whee-doggies! I can't take it anymore!

So while I'm dabbing my eyes and trying to regain what's left of my composure, let me remind you of a city that suffered an even worse case of on-again/off-again than Knoxville — and lived to tell about it.

This city, somewhat to the north and east of our fair village, brought fits of laughter to an entire generation of Americans before it finally buckled down and completed a major downtown project.

As usual, the issue became a political ball, a toy to be tossed back and forth across town with every change in administration.

Work would stop for a while. Then it would start. Then it would stop again.

The heat of political battle grew so intense, one faction even went so far as to physically capture the project site for a time.

Months turned into years. Years turned into decades. The site evolved into a caustic eyesore. There was a move afoot to simply tear the blasted thing apart and end this foolishness once and for all.

But proponents prevailed.

Twenty-eight years after the cornerstone was laid, a concerted thrust for completion was undertaken. Still, another nine years would pass before the ribbon was cut and dedication ceremonies were held.

It wasn't until 1885, a full 37 years after construction began, that the Washington Monument became a reality. These days, more than 1.3 million tourists in the District of Columbia visit the site every year.

So hang in there, Knoxville. Chin up. Be of good cheer. Smile, darn ya, smile.

We've got 32 more years before it's time to panic.

It wasn't until I started compiling material for this book that I realized how much space I had devoted to food.

There is an obvious reason for this. I love to eat.

Or at least I did until a nurse tried to draw blood for a cholesterol test one day, and the sample was so waxy it jammed the syringe. In medical circles, I am now referred to as The Crayola Kid.

Part of the blame lies in the fact I grew up in the South. This is a region where every occasion, special or otherwise, must be celebrated with food. Preferably fried. When Southerners come of age, they are given a frying pan and a vat of hog lard and sent into the world to conquer heathens.

In recent years, the Knoxville Academy of Medicine has attacked my body like a band of settlers exploring a vast expanse of uncharted territory. My flesh has provided research material for God-only-knows how many projects, and my billfold has funded a record number of fur coats and European vacations.

These efforts have not been in vain, however. I have listened to the doctors and followed their advice. I am eating less and exercising more. My weight is down, and so is my cholesterol. I am, quite honestly, the very picture of health.

Which means I'll probably step off a curb tomorrow morning and get run over by a bread truck.

Chapter III
I'll eat to that

Taster's choice

March 18, 1988

This is one of the toughest confessions I've ever had to make. But if Jimmy Swaggart can tell all, so can Venob.

I entered a wine tasting contest the other day and accurately picked the finest vintages.

Go ahead and laugh. I deserve it. As Brother Jimmy would say, "I have let you down, my children, and I am soooooo ashamed of myself."

You would think a man who grew up believing haute cuisine was a jar of Penrose smoked sausages, a pack of peanut butter cheese crackers, a 16-ounce Blue Ribbon and a triple-decker Moon Pie would know better. Especially one whose taste in wine runs along the lines of Mad Dog 20/20 and Boone's Farm. At least this proves one thing. After four decades of culinary abuse, my battered old tongue can still separate the wheat from the chaff.

This tasting — or "wine evaluation," as we connoisseurs prefer to call it — was part of the annual Tennessee Wine Festival at the Hyatt Regency. The people in charge contacted a bunch of us media types and asked us to try our hand at professional judging.

They did this for two reasons. First, they know media people will do almost anything for free likker. Second, they also know that once plied with free likker, these same media people will go back to their offices and write/broadcast nice things about the Wine Festival.

See what I mean?

When I showed up at the Hyatt, a number of people were already seated around dozens and dozens of glasses. Some of these people were swirling wine under their noses. Others were taking sips and gargling like they were using Lavoris. Others were spitting into a bucket on the floor.

Quite frankly, I was grossed out by the entire spectacle and turned to leave. I have seen better manners from the Saturday night crowd at Giles Grill. At least they have the decency to spit outside.

That's when someone in charge informed me professional wine tasters are supposed to behave in such a crude fashion. Then I found out these judges had been sampling the grape for over six hours and had tried something on the order of 300 wines. Each. The very fact that they were still sitting upright impressed me to no end, so I said OK and agreed to stay.

We media types did not sample 300 wines. We only had eight, four each of a chardonnay and a cabernet sauvignon. We were asked to judge them according to aroma and bouquet, appearance, taste, aftertaste and then give an overall rating.

Confused, I told one of the experts I generally didn't encounter aftertaste until, oh say, 10 o'clock on the morning after a big party. He sighed and turned the other way.

About the judging: They asked us to rate the entries under guidelines of the American Wine Society. In other words, according to terms like "outstanding and complex bouquet" and "mouth-filling and overwhelming."

This was difficult for me. I was more comfortable with terms such as "smells like Third Creek after a heavy storm" and "the last time I encountered this taste was in Newport."

Anyhow, when the scores were tallied and labels revealed, I discovered to my horror that I had chosen the most expensive and oldest wines as my favorites. They were the Rodney Strong chardonnay (1985) and the Sebastiani cabernet sauvignon (1982), selling, respectively, for around $18 and $12.

One of the wine experts congratulated me on my fine taste.

"Ha-yell far," I replied. "That stuff was good enough to make me want more. You better believe I'd plunk down 18 bucks for a case of it."

He groaned and wandered off.

A touch of gas, perhaps. Or maybe he couldn't stand being exposed to so much culture all at once.

Fry it — you'll like it

July 16, 1985

I have this friend named Bernard. Except he doesn't answer to Bernard. He uses Kelly, his middle name. It goes without saying that Kelly is not overly fond of the name Bernard.

"I hate it," he once told me. "I hated it when I was a kid, and I hate it now. Parents do their children a terrible injustice when they give them stupid names. Children should simply be numbered. Then when they reach the age of 21, they can choose a name they like."

I hold somewhat the same theory about green vegetables.

Green veggies are far too valuable to be wasted upon children. Let alone forced upon them. Nonetheless, this dinner table warfare has gone on since the dawn of creation.

"Eat your ferns, Ikbot!" Carl Caveman would say. "They taste good, and they're good for you. They'll give you strength to outrun saber-tooth tigers."

"Yuck!" Little Ikbot would reply. Then he'd stick out his tongue.

"Young man! You can just stay in your cave until the new moon!"

You would think that now, jillions of generations later, parents would learn. No way. Peek into the nation's dining rooms any night, and I promise you'll see the same scene.

The truth of the matter is that green veggies do taste good — except for brussels sprouts — and are good for you. But truth matters not. Kids are born to hate green veggies and won't acquire a taste for them — except for brussels sprouts — until they approach adulthood. Ask Dr. Spock if you don't believe me.

The reason I know so much about this topic is that I once (1) was a kid and (2) had green veggies rammed down my throat.

Especially okra.

I was raised on okra. My folks always grew it in the garden. We ate the stuff — three meals a day, plus midnight snacks — from July until September.

And we ate it boiled.

A bowl of boiled okra is the most nauseating thing you can set before a child, regardless of the child's state of hunger. It might as well be a bowl of boiled, green, garden slugs. Boiled okra goes down like spaghetti, except spaghetti is not hairy and gooey.

"Eat your okra," Big Sam would say. "It is good and good for you."

"Yuck!" Little Sammy would reply and stick out his tongue.

"Young man! You can just go to your room for the rest of the evening!"

I slipped and slid through years of boiled okra. And as I did, I vowed to never, ever visit this horrible monster upon my own children. Assuming I should live so long. It is a proven fact that children forced to eat mountains of green, hairy goo rarely attain puberty.

Then one day shortly after we were married, Mary Ann returned from the store carrying a large plastic bag. It was full of okra.

"Good wife," I said. "I am a kind, considerate, compassionate, forgiving man who loves you dearly. I truly want this marriage to work. But if you don't get that !%'$!&*! hairy, slimy stuff outta here in 30 seconds, we're through!"

"Slimy?" said Mary Ann. "Fried okra is not slimy."

"Fried?" I said. "You don't fry okra. You boil it."

"Boil it?" said Mary Ann. "Yuck! I bet that would taste like a bowl of boiled, green, garden slugs."

That's when I knew I had picked the right woman.

Mary Ann whupped up a pan full of fried okra, and I was converted on the spot. It was more dramatic than St. Paul's episode on the road to Damascus. I went from an okra persecutor to an okra lover. Take a glance at our garden and you'll know what I mean.

But I still hate brussels sprouts.

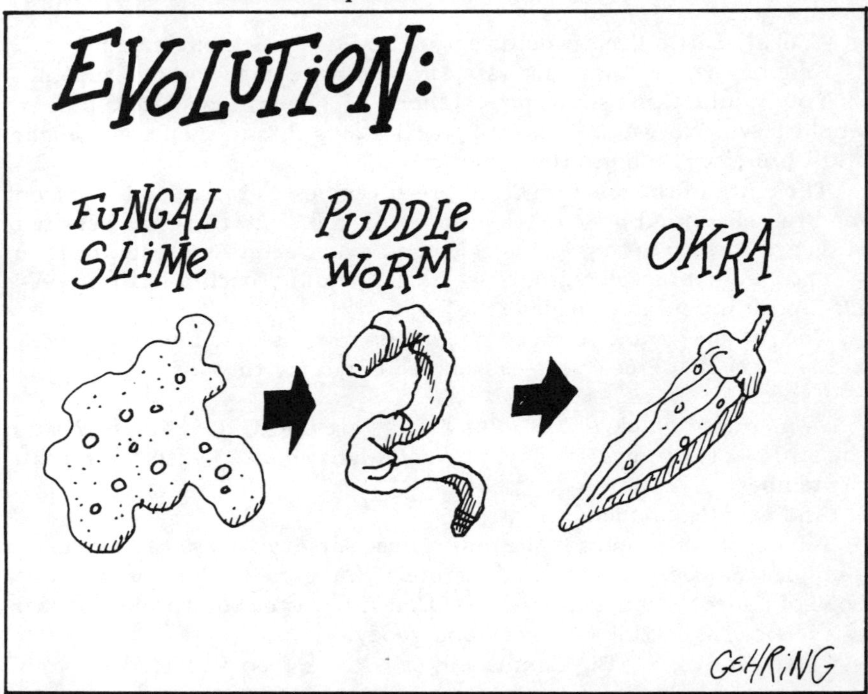

Bless this grease

February 11, 1988

I don't know how this Simplesse stuff is going to work out. A fellow from the South just has to be suspicious of grease that can't be fried.

Surely you've read about Simplesse. It's the new fake fat developed by the same people who make NutraSweet, the fake sugar. Hailed as a major dietary discovery for controlling calories and cholesterol, Simplesse contains ground-up protein from fresh egg whites and milk.

According to developers, this material breaks down into millions of tiny, mist-like spheres which literally roll across the tongue. Such a property gives Simplesse a rich taste and consistency that mimics honest-to-gosh fat.

But don't reach for the skillet. Simplesse can't be used in frying because heat makes it congeal. It's like what happens when you boil an egg.

I dunno. The part about skipping calories and cutting cholesterol does make sense. Ever since my doctor laid down the law about cholesterol, I have practiced so much dietary piety I can't stand myself.

It was a lot more fun in the days of B.C. — Before Cholesterol — when half the joy of culinary sinning was the knowledge I had bombarded my body with grievous transgressions.

You see, it's this risk, this danger, this quest for the unknown that we porkos truly crave.

Would a downhill skier travel to Switzerland and shove off the top of an alpine peak if he knew the next 30 minutes would be as tranquil as a stroll to the library? Of course not. He yearns for that surge of adrenaline. Otherwise, the experience is incomplete.

There's also this matter of aesthetics and doing what's right because that's the way God ordained it. Those of us with proper Southern upbringings know about these things.

Back when I did my typing out-of-doors and could get away with vocational murder, I used to spend most of each spring in the mountains, hunting for wild turkeys and fishing for trout. So did several of my friends. One of them, Ray Harper, would drag his old camper trailer into the forest and park it for the duration. We used this as our base camp.

I don't know how many platters of fried eggs, fried ramps, fried taters, fried trout and fried beef I have eaten at that camp. Dozens of dozens, at least. Each meal was cooked in a blackened, cast-iron skillet heavy enough to double as a Chinese ceremonial gong.

This skillet was, as they say, "well-seasoned." Which means it didn't get washed in the traditional sense. If you are familiar with black skillets, you know what I'm talking about. If not, eat your quiche and forget it.

Meals prepared in this manner demand liberal application of a lubricant. Most certainly, not something fake.

Instead, what you need is a big blob of hydrogenated grease — of animal origin or vegetable origin or both — containing enough saturated fat to clog every artery within 250 yards of the stove. Including those of the coons and mice that sneak in at night to eat the scraps.

Like Simplesse, this stuff would congeal. But in reverse order.

Simplesse turns to a lump when the temperature rises. Crank up the heat on our grease, though, and it would melt into a smoky liquid that would sizzle meat and taters alike to a delicate crisp.

Only after the fire was out and you had gone to the forest or stream for a few hours would it return to its former state. That's when it reminded me of a black skillet full of vanilla ice cream, dotted with the peaks of yesterday's hash browns and patiently waiting to be re-heated, and re-melted, once again.

That's grease what am, cousin. Real 10W-30 grease. Southern grease. The kind of grease the Good Lawd hisself uses in Heaven.

Which may explain why he calls so many of us Southern folk home at such an early age.

Piddling away the pounds

April 28, 1987

I am so happy, I may buy a pack of Twinkies to celebrate.

On second thought, I might buy an entire case of Twinkies, plus a dozen jelly doughnuts and a box or two of chocolate chip cookies. With all the weight I lose each day, I can pig out from now on and never show the effects.

That's because I am a fidgeter. A card-carrying, toe-tapping, finger-drumming, nail-biting, coffee-sipping fidgeter. And I've just read about a new study by the National Institutes of Health which says fidgeting can result in weight loss.

Researchers say nervous habits can actually burn upwards of 800 calories a day. In fact, some people squirm away the caloric equivalent of jogging several miles.

If you are a thoroughbred fidgeter, you can appreciate the importance of this revelation. It is a virtual Emancipation Proclamation for those of us who are slaves to piddling. At long last, our shackles of shame are gone.

And so are our excess pounds.

Blue-ribbon fidgeting is not the sort of skill you can acquire easily. Years of honing are needed if you expect to achieve perfection. The problem is those buttinski non-fidgeters who insist you are wasting time.

This can be particularly irksome for fidgeting children because grownups will fret and worry about them and try to find a way to rid them of their condition.

"Poor child," they say, "look at how he fidgets. He probably hasn't eaten his greens. I always say feed a child a good meal of greens, and that'll take care of his fidgeting."

It doesn't get any better as life goes on. Trust me.

For example, it is impossible for me to sit down at my desk and begin writing and not come up for air until a column is finished.

First, I have to get a cup of coffee. Then I must walk around the office and chit-chat. Next, I must drum my fingertips and crack my knuckles and chew on a few toothpicks and drink more coffee and bite my nails and drum my fingertips again and chit-chat again and chew on more toothpicks and look at some old notes and drink more coffee and twist my neck until it cracks like my knuckles and drink more coffee. I break this routine just long enough to visit the bathroom. Even champion fidgeters can only hold so much coffee.

Fidgeters recognize the need for this reflective, creative period of every working day. Non-fidgeters dismiss it as unproductive frivolity and shun you like a leper, tsk-tsking piously all the while.

Even Dear Wife, a terminally efficient person, chides me about this portion of the day. She calls it my "piddle time."

"How long will you be at the office today?" she asks as I peck her on the cheek and walk out the front door.

"Oh, I dunno," I reply. "I've got a column to write and some letters to answer and some other paperwork to do. It may be 8 or 9 o'clock before I get everything wrapped up."

"But if you'd just go in and get the work done and not piddle around, you would be finished three hours earlier. Can't you be home in time to eat supper with the rest of us?"

"We'll see. By the way, what are we having?"

"Greens."

Thanks to the new study, she and other non-fidgeters may now help themselves to a generous portion of crow. I'll have a Twinkie, thank you.

And then I shall tap my toes as the pounds melt away.

My cleanliness is downright ungodly

October 11, 1985

Uh-oh. It's autumn again, and that spells trouble.

Which is not to imply a dislike of autumn. Quite the contrary. With one exception, I enjoy everything about this glorious season.

I like the feel of autumn weather. I like the sight of mountains and valleys ablaze in color. I like the smell of wood smoke and the plaintive sound of geese against an orange October moon. Autumn means tattered brush pants and old boots from L.L. Bean, bird dogs with bells on their collars, and the smooth, metallic *clack-clack* of a pump shotgun.

But autumn also means apples. Truckloads of apples. Stop at a roadside market or stroll through a grocery store, and you'll see what I mean.

Neither the abundance of apples nor the consumption thereof bothers me. In fact, I am an apple addict.

The problem is what's supposed to occur before an apple is eaten. As any mother will tell you, it must be washed. The First Rule of Motherhood is specific on this point.

"Don't ever eat an apple that hasn't been washed" is a more serious commandment than "don't ever get into a car with strangers." It is leagues ahead of "don't ever go anywhere without clean underwear" and cannot hold a flame to "don't ever leave food on your plate because children are starving in China."

There is merit to this admonition. Certainly, food should be washed before it goes into your mouth. Especially food that might have been treated with pesticides. But sometimes, admonitions have a way of getting out of hand.

I hate to admit this in public, but I have outgrown many of my mother's warnings. I have accepted rides from people I didn't know. I have been known to start a trip without changing my undies. And if there is excess food on my plate, too bad for the children in China.

But to this day, I cannot put an apple into my mouth until it has been washed. The order of washing is immaterial. It's a form of vegetative baptism. As long as the apple is bathed at some point in its life, it is forever safe to consume.

It doesn't matter if the apple has rolled in the floor of my truck all morning or bounced in the game bag of my hunting vest alongside the bodies of deceased quail. Nor do I blink if I slice an apple with the same knife used to gut a deer two days earlier. Once washed, it is clean.

Let me tell you how bad this curse is.

One day last fall, I was driving home from Mooresburg after training bird dogs with Doc Baird and Ray Carter. I was sweaty and dusty as sin. That morning, I had bought a couple of apples and a Tab at a country store.

I extracted an apple from the junk on the front seat, rasped it across the beggar lice on my jeans and started to bite down.

No way. The apple had not been washed. My jaws refused to open.

This is a dire predicament when you are on a remote road in Hawkins County, no water within sight, and you desperately need to wash an apple. So I did what any thinking person would do.

I pulled to the side of the road and held the apple out the window by its stem. Then I poured hot Tab over it and dabbed it dry with my grungy handkerchief. Now purged of all unrighteousness, it was OK to eat.

Too bad Freud is dead. He could have had a field day with this.

The definitive dope on diets

October 12, 1986

OK, folks. Let's tighten up. Better get it done now before the rush begins.

Take a look at the calendar. It's just a little over six weeks until Thanksgiving Day — the official start of holiday pigging. This assault begins with cranberry sauce and a verse of "Come Ye Thankful People, Come"; peaks with a wedge of fruit cake and "We Three Kings"; then goes out in a fury with the last drop of pink champagne and "Auld Lang Syne."

All of which means you have barely enough time to get the ol' waistline whipped into shape before those calories come calling.

How to lose weight? Easy. When it comes to shedding excess baggage, I am a decided expert. I've done it hundreds of times. In fact, if you added all the weight I have lost in the past 20 years, you could easily match, pound for pound, the interior offensive line of the Carson-Newman football team.

Of course, if you added all the weight I then have regained in that same period of time, you could easily match, ton for ton, the entire roster of the Minnesota Vikings, including cheerleaders, mascot and pep band. But that's neither here nor there.

Most people start a diet with the same enthusiasm they have when they sit down to figure their taxes. This is a big mistake. They count calories diligently — 157 here, 206 there — and get all bent out of shape if they pile up one too many. This makes them sad. So they eat to drown their sorrow and the next thing they know, the belt goes out another notch.

What they fail to realize is that by picking and choosing their food carefully, they can forget calories altogether. Honest. It's like making a cool $1.5 million and then finding enough shelters to avoid paying taxes.

Ready to eat? Great. Lick those chops and dive in, honey, 'cause there are absolutely no calories in food if the following rules are observed:

■ The meal is free.

■ It's the kind of food you really don't enjoy.

■ You eat off someone else's plate, especially the plate of a child who has not developed a taste for fried chicken, gravy, rolls and cheesecake.

■ It's the last piece.

■ Someone insists you take a bite "just to see how it tastes."

■ The food is actually good for you, although I rarely employ this rule.

■ You make taste-tests of the food you are preparing. Especially desserts.

■ The meal is bottled and may be sold only to persons of legal age.

■ No one is around to see you eating.

■ You do not remember eating.

■ The food is consumed between midnight and 4 a.m.

■ You are in any of these emotional states: sad, happy, depressed, anxious, glad, cheerful, jolly, elated, dejected, disappointed or despondent.

■ There is leftover dough or icing.

■ Some foods actually have negative calories. For example, if you are forced to eat beets or brussels sprouts, you will run up a calorie deficit and may compensate to your heart's — or belly's — content. Figure on two Twinkies per beet, four jelly doughnuts per brussels sprout.

See? Just listen to your ol' Uncle Venob, and you'll be a completely different person by Thanksgiving Day.

If you work extra hard, I'd say two, maybe three, sizes different.

Goblin gut-busters

October 22, 1985

Anything created from corn syrup, sugar, salt, gelatin, resinous glaze, cream of tartar, artificial flavors and artificial colors has got to be good for you.

But don't take my word for it. Just ask your dentist.

For the ignorant in our midst, that's the recipe for the No. 1 Halloween goody, the creme de la creme of saintly sweets, the goblin gut-buster of October 31.

I speak, of course, of candy corn.

Eating candy corn during the Halloween season is patriotic. It's as American as eating turkey for Thanksgiving and watermelon on the Fourth of July. In small communities, gossip quickly spreads about "those people" (and they know who they are) who don't eat candy corn on Halloween.

The reason so much candy corn is consumed this time of year is because huge bags of it are stacked at every checkout counter in every store in the land. Escape is impossible. Once your eyes fall upon a bag, you're hooked.

"Gosh, Halloween's just around the corner," you say to yourself. "I might as well buy some candy corn to give out."

Which is a lie.

People don't give candy corn to trick-or-treaters. They eat it themselves, usually before they get home.

Walk into Target for a pair of blue jeans and you will come out with candy corn. Walk into Revco for aftershave and Q-Tips, and you will come out with candy corn. Walk into Kroger for some frying chickens and a six-pack, and you will come out with candy corn. I suspect that even if dear Aunt Hattie keels over shortly before Halloween and you go to Berry's to make arrangements, you would saunter back to the car munching candy corn.

In light of this predicament, what should you hand out to the kiddies?

Anything except popcorn balls, apples, peanut butter taffy kisses and miniature Almond Joys.

There is no sense going to the trouble of making popcorn balls, because kids won't get to eat them. Even if you are a deacon in the church, their parents will fear you're a closet ghoul who delights in lacing popcorn balls with Ex-Lax. So into the garbage they go.

Ditto apples — especially if your neighbor happened to see you purchase a pack of razor blades the same day you bought the apples.

As for peanut butter taffy kisses, the ones that come wrapped in black and orange waxed paper? Arrrgh! Gross me out! That's the worst excuse for Halloween candy known to civilization.

Which brings us to miniature Almond Joys.

I like the taste of Almond Joys, but I have never forgiven the hateful things for what they did to me long ago.

That particular year, Mary Ann and I had given miniature AJs to trick-or-treaters. Two hours before dawn the next morning, I slipped out of the house to go deer hunting. Just as I walked out, I scooped up a handful of leftovers to munch in my tree stand.

Around 8 or 8:30, I remembered the candy in my pocket. I unwrapped one and popped it into my mouth.

Within 10 seconds, the inside of my mouth was coated with melted chocolate, and shredded coconut was tickling my throat. I tried to cough silently, which is impossible.

At the same instant, a twig snapped behind me. I turned around to see a four-point buck, well within range of my arrow.

It is natural to get the shakes in such circumstances. That made my quasi-silent gagging even worse. And that is when the almond — the low-down, miserable almond — lodged in my throat.

There I stood on a three-by-three-foot platform, 25 feet off the ground, trying to draw a 50-pound bow, excited as whiz and about to choke.

By the time the arrow got halfway back, I was blue in the face. So I tried to draw a tiny breath.

Gaaaaaaaaaak!

The almond shot 20 feet, straight out.

The deer high-tailed it into the next county.

And I made a vow to boycott miniature Almond Joys evermore.

An exercise in excesses

December 10, 1987

The nerve of government meddlers! Where do those people come up with such outlandish ideas? And why does the press stumble all over itself to spread these lies to an unsuspecting public?

Take that garbage I was reading in this morning's paper.

I'd just unwrapped a jelly doughnut when my baby blues fell across a headline — "Tennessee residents have worst sedentary lifestyle record."

Munching the scrumptous pastry slowly, the better to coat my tastebuds with its gooey interior, I read on:

"ATLANTA — More than half of Americans get no significant exercise, according to a survey, and Tennessee residents have the worst record.

"In the 1985 survey, reported by the National Centers for Disease Control, more than 25,000 adults in 21 states and the District of Columbia were asked about their physical activities to determine whether they exercised three times a week, 20 minutes at a time. Fifty-five percent of the respondents said they did not."

I stopped reading long enough to grab a couple of biscuits. I carved a slit into the first one and inserted a thick slice of country ham. Then I found my place in the story again:

"'Less than half of the American population is physically active at a level likely to confer health benefits,' the CDC said. In light of the findings, promotion of exercise 'should be a national priority,' the Atlanta-based agency concluded."

Those alfalfa sprout health freaks are at it again, I fumed, ladling gravy over the remaining biscuit. When will they learn to mind their own business? I read on:

"The percentage of men indicating a sedentary lifestyle ranged from 44 percent in Idaho to 66 percent in Tennessee. Among women, the percentages ranged from 41 percent in Idaho to 71 percent in Tennessee."

Idaho-schmidaho. No wonder people exercise out there. If I dug taters all day, I'd stay on the move, too.

Besides, I do get lots of exercise. So do my friends. We played football back in high school. And every summer, we get together for a few rounds of golf. Why, I even have to climb 40 rows of steps, maybe 50, just to reach my seat at the new Thompson-Boling Arena.

The story angered me so, I decided to go to the news editor and raise a ruckus as soon as I got to the office. But when I turned the ignition key in my car, a dull dragging sound told me my plans had been changed. The battery was dead.

No sweat. There's a bus line several blocks from our house. So I called a cab to take me to the bus stop. Told the driver to radio ahead so another cab would be waiting to scoot me from the bus to the office. Y'gotta know how to handle cabbies.

Once I reached the office, I stormed up to the news editor's desk. But he wasn't there. Didn't matter, though, 'cause I got word of a big news conference over at City Hall. I hitched a ride with the photographer and made it in 10 minutes.

We'd have gotten there quicker, but you know how bad traffic is these days. Why, I swear the people who were walking seemed to be going faster!

Anyhow, I finished the press conference and hopped a cab back to the office. Well, not all the way back. The cabbie dropped me off at Smittye's Sweet Toothe Shoppe for the Thursday lunch special — quarter-pound cheeseburger, hand-cut fries and a chocolate shake. Deee-licious!

Thank goodness, the news editor was there when I returned. I gave him the cussin' he deserved. Then I finished my story and called my wife to pick me up.

So here I am back at the ol' homestead after a hectic day. Things have about returned to normal.

A guy from the filling station brought me a new battery. Installed it for free. He also fixed my riding lawn mower. Oh, and he says his boy will be glad to rake our leaves for $5 an hour.

Great. Even though it's a nice crisp day, I just don't feel like working in the yard. It's those nagging chest pains again.

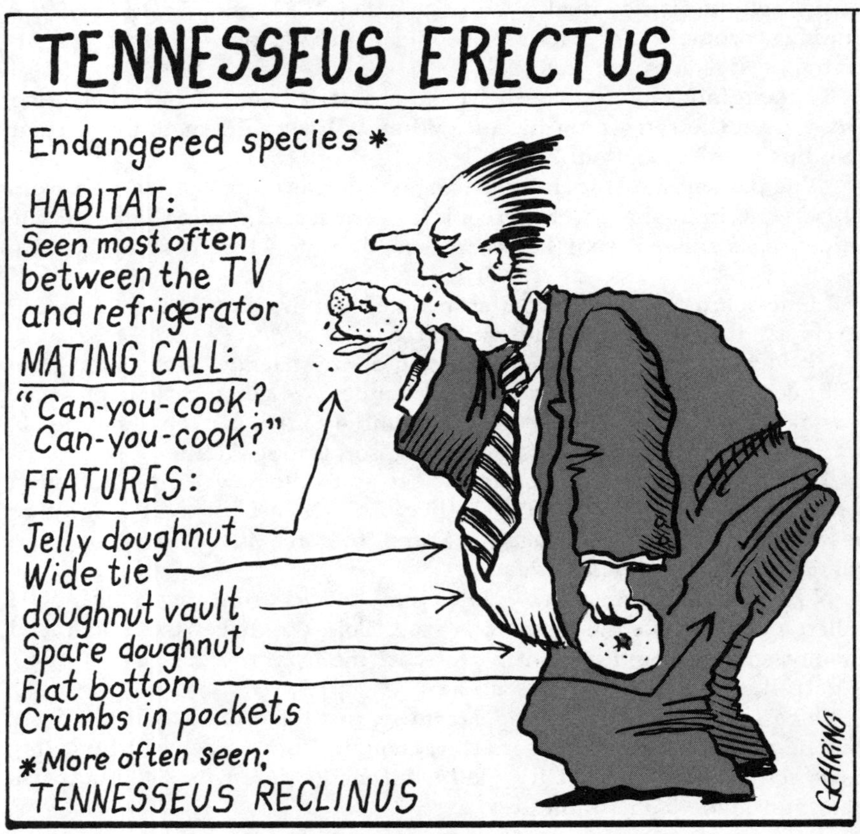

Candy Bar Diplomacy

August 12, 1986

I think Gov. Lamar Alexander may be onto something.

As you know, Hizzoner is a big friend of the Japanese. On a recent trip to promote economic and cultural exchange, he introduced the people of that nation to one of the most divine nectars known to mortals, the epitome of epicureanism, the true manna from heaven.

He gave them Goo Goo Clusters.

Sushi and country ham may never bridge international gaps, but Goo Goo Clusters were a hit. Standard Candy Co. — the Nashville-based manufacturer of this delectable mixture of chocolate, marshmallow, caramel and nuts — followed up with a 150,000-unit shipment and plans another for 300,000.

Amazing, isn't it? Forty years ago, we were nuking the Japanese until even their shadows glowed. Today, we're selling them Goo Goo Clusters.

There is a message in this for all statesmen: Why not try Candy Bar Diplomacy for a change?

It'd be far safer than Star Wars. A lot more tasty, too. And, for Pete's sake, cheaper by a landslide. I haven't checked the wholesale price of Hershey bars lately, but even at $10 apiece they'd be a wiser investment than a B-1 bomber held together with $650 bolts.

Right now, we are pumping millions of dollars worth of military equipment into Nicaragua to aid the Contras. But what if we shipped Moon Pies and Mars bars instead of rifles?

If I were secretary of defense or secretary of state, I would realign our thinking on these matters all across the board.

There would be Butterfingers in place of battleships, Teaberry gum instead of tanks, Reese's Cups and Rolos rather than rockets.

C'mon, now. Do you really think the Russians would be so persnickety once they sunk their choppers into a Three Musketeers or a Nestle Crunch? Why, they'd be putty in our hands.

I'm a realist, of course. I realize Candy Bar Diplomacy wouldn't work on all world leaders. The certified crazies could not comprehend this gesture of goodwill, no matter how hard we tried. But I've got a remedy for them, too.

It's called Candy Bar Wars.

Let's say you have an enemy. A real stinker. Somebody like Moammar Gadhafi or the Ayatollah Khomeini. There's no sense wasting good candy on these goons, so bomb 'em with the bad stuff. I am talking a regular attack of yucky sweets like Pay Days and Heath bars.

Think about this. How is Moammar gonna have time to meet with his terrorists and plan revenge attacks on the United States when he's picking Pay Day peanuts out of his shiny teeth?

And how could the Ayatollah froth and foam about the imperialist pigs of the West after he's bitten into a Heath Bar? Lordy, he'll gag for a month! Then he'll spend the next three weeks waiting for new dentures.

If we wanted to pull all stops and really go for a megaton assault, we could rain Bit-O-Honeys upon them.

Aaarrrrgh! The very thought makes my stomach churn.

Then again, this may fall under the Geneva Convention's guidelines against cruel and unusual punishment, even for enemies of the state.

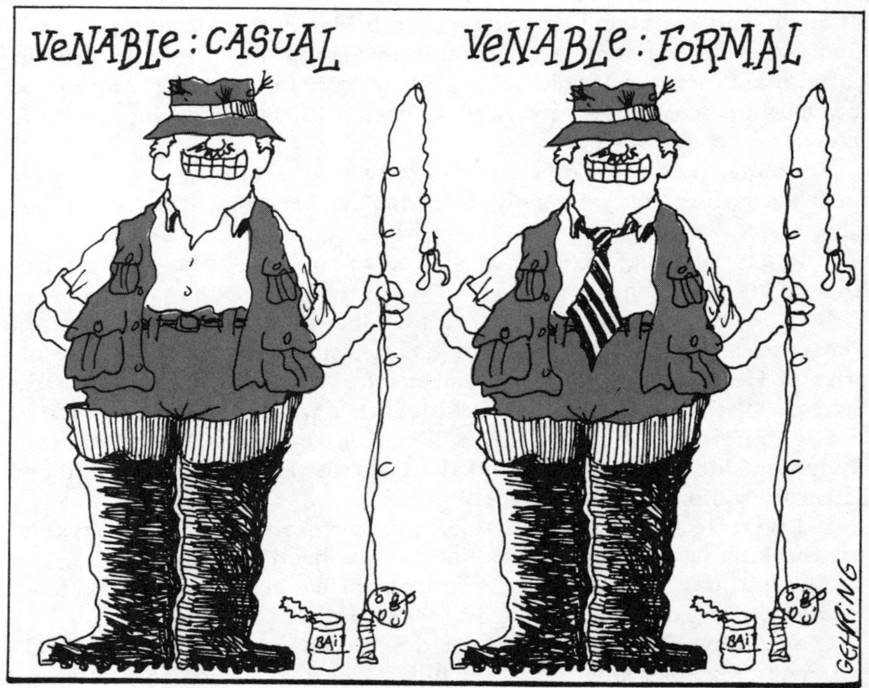

Shortly after I was hired as The News-Sentinel's outdoors editor in 1970, one of the big guys took me to lunch.

"What do you want to be doing 10 years from now?" he asked me.

"Writing outdoors for The News-Sentinel," I replied.

"Gosh. Don't you have any career goals?" he said. "Don't you want to climb up the ladder?"

"Sure, I have career goals," I told him. "I've always wanted to be outdoors editor for The News-Sentinel. And I am. As for ladders, the only one I'm concerned about is the one I use to climb into my deer stand."

He gave a pained look. I think it may have been the onions.

Careers have a way of changing, as you will see in the first story in this chapter. That was the first column I wrote after I exchanged my hipboots for dress shoes and came in from the cold.

Do I enjoy my present assignment? Certainly. It is just as much fun now as covering the outdoor beat was in the old days.

But just because I quit "officially" relaying news of woods and waters doesn't mean I don't occasionally sneak out with a shotgun or a casting rod and sneak back with a story to tell.

Of course, I never indulge myself in these wanton pleasures of the flesh until I have put in a full 2¼ days a week at the office. Work before pleasure, I always say.

Chapter IV
Room to roam

Changing of the guard

February 10, 1985

People have been asking me why I would give up a job I dearly love and how I can attempt to follow a man who has been revered in this community for decades.

I've been asking myself those same questions the last couple of months, ever since editor Harry Moskos decided I would follow Carson Brewer as the local columnist for this newspaper.

Funny. Here I am a writer, and I can't put it into words. All I can do is tell you I knew it was time.

A change of direction in one's career doesn't happen overnight. At least it didn't with me. It's like raindrops that keep tap-tapping into a barrel below the gutter. Or calories which silently, over a period of years, earn compound interest along your waistline.

You wake up one morning and realize the rain barrel is full and your belt no longer fits.

I have worked a lot of jobs in my life — from unloading freight to driving a towel truck to delivering milk (don't believe those milkman jokes) to fighting forest fires. Yet I've never enjoyed anything so much as writing. When it came to pass that I could combine my love for writing with my love for the outdoors, I knew what the preacher meant when he talked about the rapture.

I came to The News-Sentinel as outdoors editor full of confidence I would retire at the same desk. After four or five beats on two other newspapers, I now had The Job. At the age of 22, I was set for life.

I don't have to tell you that the last 15 years have been marvelous.

Really. It oughta be against the law for a man to have as much fun as I have had, to get in and out of the scrapes I have encountered, to run virtually unshackled, and get paid for it. Some would call it larceny.

But ever-so-slowly, those occupational raindrops and calories began to collect. One day, the rain barrel overflowed and the belt split.

It happened to me last summer in Atlanta. I was there for the American Fishing Tackle Manufacturers Association's trade show. This is a time when everyone who's anyone in fishdom comes forth with new products.

It was hotter than a depot stove as I drove to Atlanta. I didn't really want to go. I didn't care what was new. I was merely doing a job because it had to be done, and that was a strange sensation for me. I hit the showroom floor with note pad and camera and started talking to people. Numb, I wrote stories about what they said.

Dozens of press conferences are associated with a trade show like this. They're nice places to get a free drink and hear details about something you (1) already know about and (2) couldn't care less about. But one afternoon, I received an invitation to a huge press gathering. Something about the latest, most innovative, most revolutionary product in the world of outdoors.

With great fanfare — lights and music and everything — a company spokesman announced the development of a computerized reel.

Yes, a reel that thinks. And talks. And calibrates the distance of

each cast. And tells you the speed of retrieve.

That was the last straw. When reels start talking it's time to start walking.

Looking around the room, I saw perhaps 150 outdoor writers from all over the United States. Some of them were the dearest friends I ever had. Many of their names are among the most respected in outdoor journalism. They were taking notes and snapping photos and trying to digest every morsel of what was transpiring.

All of a sudden, I felt very alone.

I went back to the motel, wrote my stories and transmitted them to my office. Then I went to the bar and ordered the tallest glass of the brownest whiskey they had. And another. The next morning, I checked out of my room and left Atlanta. It was pouring rain.

I was on I-75, headed for Knoxville. That much I knew.

What I didn't know was where this new road in my life was leading. I still can't tell you now.

But it was at that moment I realized the glorious and exciting train I had been riding all those years, the train I had enjoyed for every second at every turn, had stopped. It was time to get off.

Wild on weeds

September 8, 1985

The trouble with names is they can be so deceiving. And so cruel.

Just ask the jelly belly who goes by Slim.

Or the chrome dome they call Curly.

Or the lean and lanky fellow who has to duck when he passes through a doorway. Nine times out of 10, he'll be known as Shorty.

So perhaps it isn't surprising to discover two of the most beautiful wildflowers on this earth are officially known as weeds.

Before you correct me, I know that technically speaking, the term "weed" is a subjective one. It can be applied to any undesired plant. Orchids and roses are weeds if they happen to sprout where you don't want them to.

Still, I find it incredible that plant taxonomists applied the handle to ironweed and Joe Pye weed, both of which are blooming in profusion throughout East Tennessee right now.

On second thought, maybe these two plants are "weeds" as far as traditional wildflowers are concerned. They do not remain hidden on remote mountain slopes. Nor do they flower briefly on cool, damp days in early spring. You will not have to get down on your hands and knees and paw through the litter of last summer's leaves to find them.

Quite the contrary.

Both ironweed and Joe Pye weed do their business in public. You can see them in pastures and along roadsides. They grow tall, often head-high or more. Best of all, this floral pagentry lasts from early August almost until Jack Frost starts whitewashing the Tennessee Valley.

Ironweed blooms come in small clusters that are so deep purple in color, you might as well call it violent violet. Joe Pye's clusters are larger, and en masse, they form a dome atop each stem. Their color is more subdued, however. Kind of a rusty pinkish-purple.

Wildflower writers don't have a lot to say about ironweed or Joe Pye weed. I combed through more than a dozen reference books at the library and discovered little I didn't already know about them.

For the record, ironweed was named because of the strength of its stem and root system. Joe Pye weed apparently gets its name from an Indian medicine man who used the plant to concoct a "cure" for typhoid fever. Another source said the word comes from an Indian word for typhoid, "jopi." Mountain people, who knew what was a weed and what wasn't, called it "queen of the meadow."

So much for technical verbage. What I like best about these two plants is they come into full flower during late summer, a time of year I really enjoy.

This is when the evenings are cool, when crickets are murmuring their sad swan songs, when the natural world finds itself torn between emotions — still yawning from the ho-hum of summer, yet quivering with excitement over the possibility of autumn. When you see ironweed and Joe Pye weed in bloom, you can rest assured you've beaten the rap of a hot, torturous summer one more time.

And that's why it riles me so to see them called weeds. These plants are far too regal for such plebian names. If there were a wildflower beauty contest, I know ironweed and Joe Pye weed would win it, hands down.

Or my name ain't Slim Venable.

Technology has its price

June 10, 1986

Forgive me if I sniff once or twice and dab at the corners of my eyes.

It's nothing. Really. Don't worry about me. I'll be all right in a minute. . .

There. My composure is back. Everything's OK.

These moments happen when you're a sucker for nostalgia. You'll be innocently daydreaming, recalling some special event from your youth. Then all of a sudden, it dawns on you that times have changed and you can never go back again. Next thing you know, you're reaching for a hanky.

A moment ago, I was all smiles, thinking about the delightful sounds of summer. You know — the chirping of crickets, the whistling of quail, the lapping of water against a rocky bank.

Then I read a press release from a major outdoor products company and grew misty-eyed, because I realized silence had befallen two ancient summer sounds. If you've ever camped or fished or hiked or done anything outdoors, you've heard them.

I speak, of course, of the "fuuumph!" when fuel ignites in a Coleman lantern. And then a split-second later, the "yeeee-iiiii!" emitted by the lighter of the lantern as he/she jerks back his/her arm and tries to turn down the flame, which by now is tickling the heavens.

These hallowed sounds of the season have been heard across our country for decades. Millions of times. They're as much a part of summer as the roar of an outboard motor.

The rudiments are best taught to youngsters. An adult — a scout leader with singed arms, usually — shows the kid how to fill the tank and pump the plunger and strike the match and hold it in place and turn the knob.

"Fuuumph!" goes the lantern.

"Yeeee-iiiii!" screams the kid.

"Great job, Willie!" says the scoutmaster. "Keep up the good work and you'll make Eagle before you know it! And with a little luck, the hairs on your arm will grow back out, too."

Any kid lucky enough to receive this education will never forget it. Twenty-five years later, it's still branded onto his brain.

"Ain't it nifty out here on the lake, Gladys?" Victor Vacationer says, snuggling up to his sweetie. "Nothing but us and the chirping crickets and the lapping water and . . . ."

"Fuuumph! Yeeee-iiiii!"

"And Willie Smith crankin' up his lanterns over at the next campsite," says Gladys. "Did'ja ever notice how his arms ain't got no hair?"

Oh, well. Enough of fond memories. Coleman giveth "fuuumph! yeeee-iiiii!" and Coleman taketh "fuuumph! yeeee-iiiii!" away.

The Kansas company, which has turned out nearly 40 million camping lanterns, has just introduced an electronic ignition system. All you do is push a button and the hateful thing lights itself.

Presto! Just like that.

No "fuuumph!"

No "yeeee-iiiii!"

All you have are two mantles aglow in brilliant white light.

How utterly boring.

This transition won't be immediate, of course. Extinction takes time. At this point, said a Coleman spokesman, electronic ignition is available only on propane lanterns.

But that's no consolation. Now that technology has reared its ugly head, it's only a matter of time before some yuppie engineer discovers a way to wed electronic ignition to the standard-fuel lantern.

And then, an era of Americana will be gone. Just like the buffalo.

Next thing you know, we'll be sitting around fiberglass campfires, sprinkling ashes on our hot dogs from little plastic bags and listening to owls on tape.

Kip

December 21, 1986

She is curled up in a bed of leaves next to the house, basking in the mid-morning sunshine.

It's a good place for an old bird dog to rest. It is warm and dry and sheltered from the wind. It's the place she calls home from the moment I turn her out of the garage at dawn until I whistle her in at dark.

But it's also the place I suspect she will die before the winter is out. One does not need a degree in veterinary science to know when an animal waits at death's door.

The old dog sleeps, but ever so lightly. Even my tiptoe approach to bring food and water is detected.

She raises her head, stares through vacant eyes and rustles her tail lightly in the dry leaves. Months have passed since I heard that tail thump wildly against the ground. It used to be a regular bullwhip.

I pat her on the head and scratch her ears, then gently pry her jaws apart and place the pills on the back of her tongue. She doesn't like taking them, and I can't say I blame her. It is a difficult task, completed only after periodic fits of wheezing. But it must be done if she is to stay alive.

Wait a minute; did I say "alive"?

What a mockery. In the context of this discussion, "alive" seems so awkward, so totally out of place.

"Alive" means to be running through the broom sedge, head up, tail flying. Not biding time until the curtain of death finally falls.

Old age has this awful habit of interrupting long, close relationships, and ours is no exception. Kip, a black and white English setter, has been in my kennel for a dozen years.

We have strolled countless miles together through quail fields and grouse woods and the damp creek bottoms where woodcock hang out.

She has grown up, literally, with my children.

She has not been a spectacular bird finder by any means — maybe 1 in 1,000 is — but of all the dogs I have ever owned, never has there been one with such a gentle, trusting disposition. Kip is the kind of dog you scold by clearing your throat and praise by smiling.

And now she curls up in the leaves outside the house. Frail. Feeble. Coughing. Waiting to die.

Heartworms? That's what I thought, too. But tests and re-tests proved negative.

It's simply a combination of old age and an ailing heart, the doc says. After the equivalent of 84 human years, her ticker is starting to misbehave something fierce.

So I give her pills twice daily. And she wheezes. And I wonder when it will be over.

This is not the way old friends should part. Not if I were writing the script, anyway. No animal, two-legged or four-, should be forced to leave this world coughing and wasting away, one pound at a time.

I'd have her simply drift off into peaceful sleep, dreaming of the days when we both were younger — a time when the hills weren't so steep and the heady scent of feathers and gunpowder hung thick in the air.

And yet I realize that I do, indeed, have control over the script. I can load her into the truck and take her to the vet and give the word and the peaceful sleep will come. I've done it before with old, suffering dogs. And I've known in my heart it was the right thing to do.

But this time, the decision is not nearly so easy. Each day, the emotions and options seesaw through my mind.

Ironic, isn't it? The ultimate cruel joke, you might say.

As teammates in the old days, these two partners specialized in death. Honed it to a science, in fact, and doled it out with merciless regularity, the way hunters and their dogs have done for centuries.

But when it comes time to make the same decision about a member of the team, the senior partner tastes bitter mortality in his own mouth. And he wishes life could go on forever.

The trashiest folks I know

July 10, 1986

One thing you can say about Americans: They really know how to throw a party.

Another thing you can say about Americans: Once the party's over, they really know how to leave an awful mess for someone else to clean up.

When the 100th anniversary bash for the Statue of Liberty finally ended the other night and celebrants staggered home from four days of whooping it up, tons of debris remained.

Hundreds of tons, to be exact.

In Battery Park alone, 500 tons of trash were collected during the first three days of the festival, said Skip Garrett, a spokesman for New York City's Parks and Recreation Department. In Central Park, where some 800,000 people gathered for a concert, an additional 300 tons were picked up. In lower Manhattan, cleanup workers collected more than 1 million cans and bottles.

The tab for this mega-maintenance operation was $1.05 million. That's roughly $200,000 more than the original cost of Liberty herself.

Amazing, isn't it? The same nation that so warmly welcomes the tired, the poor, the huddled masses yearning to breathe free also spawns the inconsiderate, the slovenly, the throwaway addicts yearning to buy anything that's disposable.

Sorry to be so glum in the wake of one of America's greatest birthday celebrations, but I'm especially sensitive about the trash blight right now. That's because I've just returned from a place where there is no litter. Or frightfully little of it, anyhow.

While you were sitting down in front of the television for Day Three of Liberty Weekend, I was strapping myself into my backpack for Day One of an overnighter to Mount LeConte. Up via Alum Cave Trail, down via the Boulevard. With every step away from civilization, I walked away from litter. With every step back, I found more of it.

It's the same every time I hike or take a hunting-fishing trip into the wild area. At the trailhead, papers, cigarette wrappers, discarded cans and bottles are everywhere. As the trail grows steeper and longer, the litter evaporates. On top, it's all but gone.

I'll bet you could search all day along the crest of Mount LeConte and not find enough rubbish to fill a sandwich-sized Baggie. Once you start back down, though, you don't need a sign to know the distance to the nearest parking lot. Just watch for the garbage to start growing.

What chaps me the most about litter is that it is one environmental problem that's 100 percent preventable without any great cost or sacrifice. If I can stomp a drink container and tote it in my pocket or backpack for six miles, then surely Tommy Tourist at Newfound Gap can carry his 100 yards and put it into a container.

Litter doesn't "just happen" any more than milk comes from bottles. Rather, a middleman is required — someone who takes a basic product and changes it into another form. Someone whose attitude can alter the looks of the landscape for years to come.

But you don't have to hike a trail in the Great Smokies to get worked up about litter. Driving into the office Monday morning, I happened to be behind a small car. Red. We were on Papermill Road, just east of the Boy Scout office. The guy on the passenger's side rolled down his window and heaved a bottle into the weeds. Then the car sped away.

If I had been close enough to get the license number, I'd have written it down. As it was, the only thing I could do was fume — and trust that justice someday will be served.

Perhaps that guy will roll over the jagged glass tossed out by some other litterbug and blow a tire.

With a little luck, his spare will be flat, too.

That sinking feeling

June 21, 1985

God does not want me to own a bass boat.

It is not part of the divine plan. Never has been. And now that I have his decision, perhaps I can get back onto the water.

I have owned boats and motors for almost 20 years. Nothing fancy. Just fishing boats, duck hunting boats, a canoe, johnboats, V-bottoms.

Except for zipping from Point A to Point B, I pretty much have gotten by with paddles, oars, push-poles and electric motors. For years, the meanest outboard I had was 20 horsepower.

There was no need, professionally or personally, for a larger boat. When I was writing the outdoor column and needed a story about bass fishing, I went with someone who owned a bass boat. If the script called for stripers, we went in a boat rigged for stripers. I often took my own boat on the job, but mainly as backup, or for dodging in and out for photos. On my own time, I was either floating rivers for smallmouth bass or hunting ducks on large reservoirs. Neither venture called for a fancy rig.

Then the kids grew older and were wanting to go to the lake more often. I started thinking about all the advantages of a bass boat, which is the best all-around craft afloat.

Bass boats might not have all the interior room of a runabout, but there's plenty for most families. They'll pull skiers from dawn until sunset. And, of course, they are superior fishing machines.

So a year ago last October, I bought a bass boat. Again, nothing fancy. Just a 16-footer, aluminum, 35-horse outboard. And a little black cloud that follows me everywhere.

On the way home from the marine dealer's office, I had a flat tire. I swear I did. That should have told me something.

Not long after that, I bashed the trailer. Despite two decades of backing in and out of launch ramps, I wasn't used to such a wide trailer as the new one. The first time I tried to park it in cramped quarters, I caught the corner of someone else's bumper and creamed a fender.

Within two weeks of the purchase, the electric motor died. Back to the dealer. He performed surgery and was amazed to discover that the brushes had been installed backward.

I wouldn't know electric motor brushes if they met me at high noon on Henley Street. But the dealer did. He inserted them properly, and the motor has hummed like a contented kitten ever since.

Still, the worst was yet to come.

The boat leaked from Day One. Not a gaping hole that let water gush in. Just a tiny fissure hidden under the carpet or in the livewell or dry storage area or somewhere else I could not locate.

I took it back to the dealer. He checked the boat from bow to transom. He couldn't find the leak, either.

Big deal, I reasoned. I've sloshed through leaky boats all my life. Besides, this one has a false floor, so the water never actually touches anything of importance. I decided to seal the dry storage area with caulking compound, then everything would be hunky-dory.

Or so I thought.

Despite caulk, the dry storage area still leaked. So did the rest of the boat. It was like Chinese water torture, driving me crazy, drop by drop.

Back to the dealer again. He wanted to call the factory and see what the next step would be. But we never got that far. Thieves broke in and relieved the dealer of thousands of dollars worth of merchandise. Included was my outboard, my electric motor and my depth finder.

The thieves did not take my leaky boat.

Everything was covered by insurance, so my loss is merely one of inconvenience. But I'm still not sure how, or when, I'll settle.

I oughta just take the cash and put it in the bank. And then go build myself a raft.

Etched in stone

November 7, 1985

I wish I could have known him.

There's no telling how long ago he stood where I am now standing. Five hundred years? A thousand? Maybe many more.

All I know about him are the arrowheads, left in his wake, that I have discovered on the backside of this ridge in southwestern Virginia.

These points of stone were not on display for all the world to see. In fact, they had been buried under leaf litter and humus for countless generations. But there is coal in these mountains as well as arrowheads, and an earth-moving machine, probing this hillside for carbon deposits, has sliced off a generous fillet of topsoil.

I suspected arrowheads would be found here, for already I had spotted several jagged pieces of flint. Find flint, the arrowhead hunters say, and you will find points. Since I was already tired from walking and hunting (fruitlessly) for wild turkeys, I sat my shotgun aside and whittled the point of a "flipping stick."

If you are going to search for arrowheads, it is necessary that you

first whittle a flipping stick. It is used to poke around in the freshly exposed dirt and flip out pieces of stone.

Most of the time, all you flip out are chunks of odd-colored stones and decaying wood. Aaah, but every now and then your eye catches a particularly interesting piece of rock and your flipping stick extracts it and — *voila!* — an arrowhead.

Which is what I now hold in my hand.

I am not a student of archaeology or anthropology. I cannot tell you what tribes of American Indians used to roam these hills, nor what era these points came from. All I can do is knock the dirt from these pieces of flint and let my mind wander with thoughts about the man who brought them to life.

I can just picture him sitting by his fire, patiently chipping stone with a piece of deer antler.

Neither of the arrowheads I am holding is what you'd call a perfect point. One is broken in two; the other is missing part of its base.

Maybe he wasn't satisfied with his workmanship and threw them aside. Or maybe he created these points elsewhere and used them to make a kill. And now — after sinew and flesh have rotted away — his projectiles remain for another hunter to find.

No matter. I hold his arrowheads in my fingertips and feel our link with each other, a link that transcends race and time.

We have our differences, for sure. I can leave my home in Tennessee before dawn and travel to these hills, courtesy of the internal combustion engine, and arrive as the sun peaks over the ridges. I am clothed in blends of cotton, wool and synthetic materials dyed to match my surroundings. My shotgun holds three rounds of awesome firepower.

Not so for my brother from long ago.

He likely never ventured more than a few miles from his base of operation during his entire life. His clothes once were worn by deer, bison, beaver. His weaponry consisted of a crude bow, handcrafted arrows and triangular pieces of flint.

Still, we share a common bond. And maybe eons from now, on another ridge where I have deposited the brass and plastic hull of a spent shotgun shell, some space age hunter will rest for a moment and whittle himself a flipping stick.

Maybe he will find the blackened, corroded remains of my shot.

Maybe he will knock the dirt off of it and roll it in his fingertips and let his mind begin to wander.

Maybe he will say to himself, "I wish I could have known him."

The Anchor Place

August 5, 1986

We used to call it the Anchor Place.

It was a steep, rocky point that snaked off the north shore of Island F and dropped abruptly into the clear, green water of Norris Lake.

We called it the Anchor Place for a very good reason. Most of the rocks on that section of bank looked as if they had been cut with a mason's saw. Each was about as large as a shoe box — the perfect size, shape and weight for a boat anchor.

I learned about the Anchor Place at a period in my young life when there was only one pursuit worthy of my time. Fishing.

And only one fish worthy of being caught. The smallmouth bass.

And only one place and one time to do it. Norris Lake at night.

I could not get enough of this marvelous, intoxicating elixir. At least two nights a week, sometimes three, I would meet the man who was teaching me his secrets. We would launch his tiny aluminum boat at Hickory Star Resort and drone up the lake under the power of a 20-horse outboard. We would spend the next six or eight hours in pursuit of smallmouth bass, bathed in the cool, moonlit splendor of a midsummer's night.

But before we made the first cast, we always motored to the Anchor Place and selected a stone from the thousands that littered the bank.

It would be secured to a rope at the bow of the boat, put to use during the night, then untied and sent to Davy Jones' locker when the eastern sky began to turn red. We never worried about not being able to find another stone on the next trip, for the Anchor Place was loaded. I suspect it still will be in the year 3000.

If you are wondering why I make a production of something so mundane as a lakeshore lined with rocks, you are relatively new to the sport of fishing. You see, all these events occurred before the term "bass boat" gained common usage in the language of the American sportsman.

There were no sleek, shiny boats back then. No high-powered motors. No graphite rods or digital depth recorders or big-dollar fishing tournaments. And no plastic-coated anchors from the marine supply store.

You didn't buy anchors in those days. At least the teacher and the kid didn't. Rather, we picked them up along the north shore of Island F on Norris Lake. At the Anchor Place.

Strange, isn't it, how the years change things?

At that time in my life, when the desire to go fishing burned within me as surely as if I were on fire, I owned one casting rod and a single-tray tackle box not much larger than a football. All the hooks and lures in my possession would fit into a coat pocket and hardly make a bulge.

Today, my basement is full of fishing equipment. A friend recently counted 19 rods in one holder alone. There are reels collecting dust, miles of line, and suitcase-sized tackle boxes stacked on top of each other. A bass boat is chained in the side yard. The children's water skis and knee board rest inside.

Like thousands of other anglers, my addiction has become vicarious. It has largely switched from lake to den. I am a mail-order junkie. I manage to find the time to actually go fishing not two or three times a week, but four or five times a year.

I drove past Norris Lake one night last week and got to thinking about how the years have evaporated since I used to visit it regularly. I got to wondering if there was another man out there somewhere on those clear, green waters, teaching another kid how to fish for smallmouth bass at night.

I wondered if they puttered up to the Anchor Place in a tiny aluminum boat and found just the right stone before they set out for the evening.

I wondered if they were using the same lures we used.

And drinking the same coffee we drank.

And telling the same stories we told.

And hearing the same owls and frogs we heard.

And I wondered if the kid had any appreciation, any remote appreciation, for the precious thing he was experiencing. And how empty he will feel when he realizes the thrill is gone.

Always keep one in your pocket

March 6, 1986

It's been two years since News-Sentinel management pulled me in from the fields and forests where I had spent 15 years harassing defenseless animals and getting paid for it.

In that time, I have refrained (as best as possible) from reverting to the ways of old and spinning a yarn like I used to do.

Yes, I have slipped on occasion. I still have feet of clay, and when the urge to tell a tale of ducks or deer flickers in my mind, not even a cold shower will dissuade it.

But throughout this period of indoor writing, not once have I fallen into the woods-and-waters trap of passing along tips.

Tips?

You know, helpful hints and sage wisdom. Outdoor people love tips, and outdoor writers delight in doling them out like candy. How to pitch a tent during a windstorm, how to work a surface lure to excite finicky bass, how to pluck a mallard using canning wax, how to recycle old tire weights into fly heads and decoy anchors. Stuff like that.

But now, I must yield to the urge.

Thanks to the rage of condom news that is sweeping the country, I am possessed to reach into my bag of outdoor tips and make little-known information available to you, the indoor public. So listen up.

All along, you thought condoms had limited purpose, didn't you? You thought they served only for the prevention of pregnancy and disease, not necessarily in that order.

Do I have news for you.

Outdoor people have been buying condoms for years because they have any number of uses, none of which involves, uh, harrumph — well, you know.

First, a condom makes a marvelous holder to keep your matches dry.

If you have ever tried torching a fire with wet matches, you can appreciate the protection a condom offers. Assuming, of course, you exercised certain precautions during purchase. If you bought the wrong kind of condom, you will know it the first time you attempt to strike the match and it falls apart in your hands. Please don't ask me to explain in further detail.

Second, a condom will keep rain from ruining your telephoto lens or dripping down the barrel of your shotgun or rifle.

I was not the originator of this idea. You can thank the Army for that. As long as Uncle Sam has been distributing condoms to fighting men, they have found bizarre uses for them.

Carson Brewer, the fellow who used to work here, told me infantrymen during World War II often waterproofed their M-1s with condoms. Carson was quick to point out he was in radar, not the infantry.

But the best alternative use I have ever seen for a condom is to make a wild turkey call. I do not lie. Cross my heart, hope to die, stick a needle in my eye.

What you do is take a three- or four-inch length of round PVC pipe, cut it at an angle on one end, and tape a rectangular piece of thin latex halfway across the opening. When you blow across it, the resulting sound is a perfect imitation of the *"kalk-kalk-kalk"* made by a hen.

The call is used when hunting turkeys in the spring. This is a time of year when turkeys and all other animals, wild or domestic, have the same thing on their minds.

The crafty hunter locates a gobbling tom (easier said than done, but possible), sneaks close to it, hides, makes a few seductive calls, and then blows the poor beast away with a magnum load of No. 4 copper-plated shot when it comes strutting to the innocent young lady it thinks just sounded off.

'Tis a bit cruel, perhaps. But somehow, using a condom to outsmart a guy with sex on his mind seems like the natural thing to do.

Call of the wild

December 15, 1985

There's nothing like a loon to brighten a dreary, rainy winter day.

Maybe some day, I can travel to Minnesota or Canada or somewhere else Up There and study loons at length. I'd like to see them with their broods and listen to their haunting calls on a cool, moonlit summer night. But for now, I'll have to make do with the handful of migrants that wind up in East Tennessee each winter.

In case you haven't guessed by now, loons are birds. Water birds. Kind of like ducks, but much larger. They've got red eyes and pointed bills and a wavy, black-and-white pattern on their backs. That much I know, because I have seen photographs and illustrations of them in books. Occasionally, I get to spy one in the flesh.

Better yet, I get to hear it.

The last encounter occurred a few mornings ago on Douglas Lake. I was hunting ducks.

Well, *technically* I was hunting ducks. If you want to know the truth of the matter, I did not fire a shot. Nor did any of my three buddies.

We were participating in the ritual of opening day of the duck season, a rite we have practiced together for years. We saw 30 or 40 birds. Mallards mostly. Also a few gray ducks. But the closest ones were 100 yards away. Which speaks poorly, albeit honestly, of our decoys and calling.

Anyhow, we were sitting there on a brown-speckled shale bank, covered with brown-speckled burlap, overseeing 75 decoys, retelling tales of opening days past and drinking coffee. That's when the loon sounded off.

It was a single, short yodel; loons never have much to say in winter. But for the trained ear, it was a symphony. I finally spied the bird across the lake. It was swimming alone, occasionally diving for a meal of shad minnows.

I wish I could write the sound a loon makes so you could enjoy it, too. But you'll just have to trust me when I say it is impossible. It's the same thing as trying to teach someone to use a duck call via the printed word. It simply cannot be done because, contrary to popular notions, ducks don't "quack." Instead, they give a high-pitched, "aink-aink-aink-aink" that looks dumb as I type it but sounds absolutely marvelous when executed properly.

Loons have a variety of calls. Loud, wailing calls. Yodels. Drawn-out calls and short, tart calls. I have heard them all, thanks to a 90-minute cassette recording of loon music.

But more than any other sound in the outdoors — with the possible exception of Canada geese on the wing or the gobble of a wild turkey on a spring morning — the cry of a loon is the most wild, primitive and beautiful sound you will ever hear. It is almost an emotional thing. Really.

The call of a loon is Maine northwoods and foggy mornings and rocky, windlashed shores lined with spruce trees, all brought to a muddy reservoir in East Tennessee on the wings of a bird. It symbolizes everything that is wild and free in this world, and I am envious as hell of it.

So forgive me, please, if I snuggle back under my cover of brown-speckled burlap, pour myself one more cup of coffee from the thermos, and pull up the hood of my parka against the rain.

Maybe the mallards will fly. Probably they won't. Even if they do, I'll surely miss.

But as long as there is a loon around to call every now and then, nothing else really matters.

A ranking editor of the first newspaper I worked for called me aside one day. He wished to impart some gentle sage wisdom.

"I think you ought to consider another line of work," he said.

In his estimation, there were two major hurdles, most likely insurmountable, blocking the path of my career as a journalist.

"First of all, you never take the news seriously," he said.

"Second, you're a smark-aleck."

Actually, he didn't say "smart-aleck," but you get the picture.

I thought about his advice for a long time. Ten, maybe 15 minutes.

"Suppose I am a little strange?" I said to myself. "So what? We're all supposed to be the same? And I'm supposed to grow up to be like him? Aaaaak!"

Thus, I came to the conclusion that I was going to stick with my chosen profession if for no other reason than to prove this jerk wrong. I was tired of going to school, and besides, getting paid to peck a typewriter sure beat working for a living.

I have mellowed considerably in the ensuing 20 years.

I no longer consider that editor a jerk. Not a first-class jerk, anyhow. In fact, I realize he was 100 percent correct in his assessment of my attitude.

I am, indeed, two or three degrees off plumb.

I rarely take the news seriously.

And I am a smarta. . ., er, whatever.

What's so weird is that this still beats working for a living.

Chapter V
Yes, I actually do this for a living

Let the record show. . .

April 25, 1986

The world sits precariously on the brink of war. The largest banking failure in this state's history continues to unfold. East Tennessee farmers are about to lose their shirts from a late-season freeze.

And what's the talk of the town?

Whether or not University of Tennessee sports fans can break the Guinness record for attendance at a spring football game, that's what.

At last count, the magic figure was 42,000. That's how many witnessed Minnesota's intrasquad game in 1984. UT and area businesses (including, ahem, this esteemed publishing house) are participating in all kinds of promotions to lure people to the otherwise-sleepy Orange and White game: free car, free vacation, fireworks.

Wouldn't it be funny if, despite all the hype, only 41,999 showed up?

This is like throwing a Christmas party on the first day of summer. You can import a tree from Canada, sprinkle fake snow on the carpet, turn down the air conditioner, exchange presents, and let Elvis's "I'll ha-have-ha-ha bluuuuue Christmas without you" float through the public address system. But it still won't feel like Christmas.

Same thing for football. Maybe the Vols will make it back to the Sugar Bowl sometime. That would be nice. But if you ask me, I say let's enjoy the rest of spring and eat some hamburgers and watermelon at the lake and listen to crickets and katydids before we leap into autumn and football once again.

OK, so no one asked me.

In that case, then, why not go for all the marbles? Why not break a record number of records?

In reading the 1986 edition of the Guinness Book of World Records, I have found several lofty goals Vol fans can shoot for during tomorrow's game:

■ Most hot dogs eaten: 23 (without buns) in 3 minutes, 10 seconds.

■ Most peanuts eaten: 100 whole, out of shell, eaten singly (record keepers are sticklers for detail) in 46 seconds.

■ Most ice cream eaten: 3 pounds, 6 ounces (unmelted) in 50.04 seconds.

■ Fastest beer-drinking: 1 liter in 1.3 seconds.

■ Longest clapping: 50 hours, 17 minutes.

That takes care of fans in the stands. But what about action on the field?

With a little planning, we can have a halftime extravaganza that would put the gaudy Orange Bowl to shame. Here's how:

Soon as the teams exit, sections of the field could be roped off.

In one corner, there could be a shot at the largest marching band (4,524 including 3,182 musicians and 1,342 majorettes, flag bearers and drill team members). Or perhaps the majorettes would go off by themselves to break the baton-twirling record (122-1/2 hours).

In other sections of the field, participants could challenge the records for tobacco spitting (47 feet, 7 inches), rolling pin throwing (175 feet, 5 inches), pipe smoking (126 minutes, 39 seconds), motorcycle jumping (212 feet over 16 buses), conga dancing (a "snake" of 8,659 people) and limbo dancing (6-1/8 inches). Oh, yes — and yawning (5 weeks).

The grand finale would be a cinch.

In their fervor to pack the house, UT officials have distributed some 180,000 free tickets. That's roughly twice the seating capacity of Neyland Stadium. If everybody shows up, they can collectively take a stab at Guinness' worst sporting disaster.

During the reign of Antonius Pius (138-161 A.D.), the upper tiers of the Circus Maximus in Rome collapsed during a gladiator match.

When the dust settled, 1,112 spectators were dead.

Where are they now?

December 2, 1986

John Gilchrist said a mouthful by never uttering a word. By merely taking a bite of cereal, he influenced the eating habits of Americans, spawned a catch phrase that lasted for years, and helped pay for his college education.

Not a bad day's work for a 3½-year-old kid.

Gilchrist played "Mikey" in the 1971 Life cereal commercial, one of the longest-running spots in TV history. The Quaker Oats Co., which knows every successful ad campaign deserves life after death, brought Gilchrist back this year by way of a guess-who-Mikey-is contest.

More than 300,000 people responded. Each correct answer qualified for a $100 prize, said Quaker, which then drew 5,000 names from the winners' barrel.

So where is Mikey, a.k.a. Gilchrist, these days?

He's an 18-year-old from Crestwood, N.Y., who attends college in Connecticut. He likes Bruce Springsteen's music, has a crush on actress Demi Moore, is studying communications and advertising, and dreams of becoming a pro golfer or film actor.

Oh, and just in case you're interested, Mikey's two brothers — the ones who goaded him into sampling the cereal and then uttered those famous words, "He likes it! Hey, Mikey!" — are Gilchrist's real brothers. Tommy is 23, Michael 21.

How neat. It's nice to know that somewhere out there in America, a boy can earn fame and glory by enjoying the taste of sugar-coated sawdust. In fact, Quaker's contest got me thinking about other commercial stars from yesteryear. I asked myself, "Where are they now?"

"Why not find out and write a column about them?" myself replied.

"Good idea," I said. "You mean do lots of research and make phone calls and talk to strings of public relations people and maybe have the story put together by the time Mikey is a grandfather?"

"Heavens, no!" myself snapped. "Do what you always do in situations like this. Make up something."

"Oh," I said, "You know me better than I realized."

Therefore, I am happy to announce the findings of Venob's Search for Famous Faces From Out of the Ad Past Contest. Quite by coincidence, I guessed every one of them correctly.

■ Aunt Jemima owns a cotton plantation in a remote corner of Argentina. She uses only white workers, and she insists they step lively and say cute things like, "Lawsy, boss lady! It sho' be pow'ful hot!"

■ Buster Brown stays in San Francisco these days. He is president of the Little Lord Fauntleroy chapter of Gay Americans in Advertising. His dog Tige and Morris the cat live in sin in the Florida Keys.

■ Speedy, who peddled Alka-Seltzer for years, is doing 10 to 15 at Leavenworth. Heroin. Said selling drugs was his life.

■ Right Guard deodorant's "Hi, Guy!" man, who popped out of the medicine cabinet, also is serving time. Police in Chicago caught him peeping in windows.

■ Elsie, the Borden cow, has had a rather rough time of it, too. Just last week, Alex the Butcher trimmed the fat off her loins and sold her for $1.79 a pound at Kroger's in Evansville, Ind.

■ Bucky, the Ipana toothpaste beaver, died six years ago at a flophouse in Denver. Seems he lost his two front teeth in a car wreck back in '64. Having no other body part to sell for money, he took to strong drink and wasted his life gumming pencils.

■ Johnny, who "caaaaaaaalled for Philip Morrrrrrrisssss!" was born again in 1959 and rakes in $1.5 million annually as a TV preacher in Bogalusa, La.

■ Colgate's Invisible *(knock! knock!)* Protective Shield was rescued from mothballs by President Reagan. It now serves as an integral part of the Star Wars defense system.

■ Timex's watch, which John Cameron Swayze beat, smashed, hacked, slashed and stomped upon, was sold to Piedmont Airlines. It is the official timepiece by which all the company's schedules are kept.

■ Prince Albert, the tobacco tycoon, is the saddest case of them all. He was the victim of a horrible murder in Winston-Salem, N.C. It occurred in 1967, but remains unsolved to this day.

All police will say is that they found his body in a can.

Bringing up the rear

April 14, 1988

I knew if I held out long enough, science and medicine would come to the rescue. I did. And they have. And now, after nearly 40 years of waiting, it is possible for me to own a perfect body.

I bring you this wonderful message after reading news from St. Joseph's Hospital in Atlanta. There, plastic surgeons have discovered a way to remove fatty tissue from the "saddle bag" area of a woman's thighs and use it to reconstruct her breast. The operation has only been conducted at St. Joseph's four times in the last few months, but doctors say it offers a bright ray of hope for women who have lost a breast to cancer.

Obviously, this breakthrough is a godsend for women who have suffered the physical and emotional trauma of breast removal. For that reason alone, let us hope the procedure is perfected and put into standard practice.

At the same time, let us encourage physicians to continue research in this important area of medicine. Now that there is a way to transfer fat from one part of the body to another, the chubbos of America can throw down their Spandex and leap for joy.

Few people are born with a 100-percent, picture-perfect physical frame. My personal albatross comes in the form of a convex belly and concave buns. This is a problem I have endured since childhood — although in all fairness I must confess that my gullet has grown decidedly more convex in the last two decades. The buns, alas, have stayed about the same.

If you are cut along the same lines, you know the humiliation I have faced. For one thing, it is impossible to buy trousers that fit properly.

If I find pants that feel comfortable around the waist, there will be enough excess cloth in the seat to hold a bushel basket of peaches, two footballs, a 16-pound country ham, half a loaf of butter crust bread and all four hubcaps from a '57 Ford.

On the other hand, if I try on a pair of britches that fits nice and snug around my buns, it will be impossible to snap the latch and zip up the fly without cutting off the supply of blood to my legs and feet.

Trust me. After experimenting with at least 4,296,471 pairs of pants in my life, I know whereof I speak. That's why I figure the plastic surgeons at St. Joseph's Hospital can help.

All they need to do is slice a layer of tissue from around my navel and slap it on my cheeks. Once the stitches are removed, I will be able to walk into any clothing store in this land and buy trousers off the rack like normal people are supposed to do.

The more I think about it, the more I realize this operation could revolutionize the way American men and women look. We are talking a complete evolution of the species.

If your arms are flabby but your legs look like those of a stork, no problem. Just get the doc to carve tissue from the upper extremities and weld it to your shins and thighs.

On the other hand, if your legs look like bowling pins and your arms are toothpicks, have the surgeon reverse the process.

Thick neck and weak knees? Same thing.

Fat feet and tiny fingers? Ditto.

Just pull the tissue switcheroo, pal. The opportunities are endless!

Of course, there is one serious drawback.

Once everybody starts looking like Arnold Schwarzenegger and Heather Locklear, there won't be anyone left to make fun of.

The big chill

January 10, 1988

Now let me see if I've got this straight.

If it's 16 degrees Fahrenheit (or -10 on the Celsius scale) and the wind is blowing at 20 miles (or 32.25 kilometers) per hour out of the north (or 10 degrees north by northeast), how cold is it really?

It's cold enough to send every brass monkey within 50 miles scampering for cover, that's how cold it is.

It's cold enough to freeze a witch's heart harder than Chinese arithmetic.

And it's cold enough to make me wish all those wind chill freaks would do something useful with their stupid charts. Like maybe make a bonfire out of them.

For millions of years, humanity got along splendidly without knowing the first thing about wind chill. Ground clutter too, but I'll save that debate for another time.

When it got cold, we bundled up. The colder it got, the tighter we bundled. There were no imaginary figures or what-ifs to compute.

But now, as sure as winter follows autumn, you can count on the wind chill experts to pop up like hoar frost once the mercury starts to plunge.

"The thermometer says it's 15 degrees outside right now," they tell us. "But because of the wind, it feels like it's 25 below zero."

It doesn't feel anything of the kind. It feels like 15 degrees with the wind blowing. Period. When it's 15 degrees and the wind is blowing, you're going to freeze your buns off, and it doesn't matter if it feels like 25 below or 125 below. It's just plain cold.

At least it is comforting to know other people are as vexed as I by wind chill calculations.

Dan Proctor, one of The News-Sentinel's resident lunatic artists, which is redundant, was sitting at his computer the other day when someone nearby began babbling about the wind chill. (Artists threw away their paper and pencils and learned to draw on computers about the time wind chill and ground clutter were invented.)

Anyhow, Dan began pecking on the keys. Out popped a series of charts that made a lot more sense than wind chill.

First, he devised the W.C. Fields table. It shows the apparent temperature of a wino based on the air temperature and proof of alcohol consumed. For example, if the air is 20 degrees and the likker is 120 proof, you can count on the wino to check in at -10.

Then there was the Big Chill table, designed to calculate the temperature of a yuppie. It's based on the AYI — average yearly income.

Next came the Big Ol' Coat table. Using the carefully metered AOC (age of coat in years), one can gauge how much wind will be felt through the fibers.

But my favorite was the Indoor Factor table. It works on the principle of ATS — the automatic thermostat setting.

According to Dan's precise projections, if the thermostat is locked on 68 degrees, the room will warm to 68 no matter how hard the wind is blowing outside. The same holds true for 69, 70 or any other setting. Amazing, eh?

Dan brought his charts over for my inspection. I was impressed. So impressed it took me 10 minutes to stop laughing.

I suppose I would have laughed even longer, but the editor walked by about that time. He told us to get back to work or else he was gonna kick us both out onto the street — where the air temperature was 15 and the wind chill was -25.

The terror of trademarks

September 5, 1986

I have sinned against corporate America, and may Madison Avenue forgive me.

I have used the "S" word.

Even worse, I did it in print.

I said (cover the childrens' ears, please) "Styrofoam." As in "Styrofoam plate" and "Styrofoam cup" and "Styrofoam cooler."

Writers who commit this sin cause the patent lawyers at Dow Chemical Co. to jump up and down and wring their hands and shriek, "No! No! No!" Then they mail a statement outlining what is Styrofoam and what isn't.

For those of you who don't know any better, the word "Styrofoam" is a trademark. It is owned by Dow. Thus, it may be used solely on products made and marketed by Dow.

According to the company, there are only seven types of Styrofoam brand products. They are insulation, decorative billets and boards, buoyancy billets, insulation mastic, foundation panels, foundation coating and lightweight roofing panel insulation.

That's it. Ipso, facto, over and out.

Dow Chemical does not make egg cartons, picnic plates, coffee cups, ice chests, shipping cartons or meat trays. Therefore, since Dow does not make these items, they cannot be called "Styrofoam."

Clearly, the company's reaction to trademark misuse is understandable. And justified. I'd do the same thing if I was sitting on top of millions of dollars in sales of a particular brand. Heaven forbid that my trademark would ever be eroded into a generic term.

Therefore, I am appealing to you good people to leave poor ol' Dow Chemical alone. After completing extensive research into this issue, I am now prepared to provide sage counsel on how to speak correctly when the occasion arises.

■ The next time you are sitting around a country store with the good ol' boys and you have a chew of tobacco in your jaw and ambeer is welling up inside your mouth, do not — repeat, do not — ask Bubba Joe to give you a "steerfome cup" so you can spit.

Instead, say, "Please pass me a molded, expandable polystyrene bead vessel."

■ When you come home from the grocery store some day and discover three broken eggs among the dozen you purchased, do not say ugly things about the "Styrofoam carton" in which they were packed.

Rather, curse the "thermoformed flexible polystyrene article."

■ When that 12-wide you've been eyeing at the mobile home lot finally becomes yours and you are proudly showing it off to your guests, do not refer to the ceiling decorations as "Styrofoam beams."

Just call them "stained, in-place urethane foam beams, molded to the desired shape and dimension," and all will be right with the world.

I realize these changes will not be easy. Old habits are hard to break. So here's another helpful tip:

Make a xerox of this column and scotch tape it to the frigidaire. Then whenever you go to the kitchen for a coke or a cup of sanka, you'll be reminded.

Planning ahead

April 15, 1986

OK, I'll admit it. I procrastinate something awful.

Venob's Sixth Law of Labor reads like this: "Always put off until tomorrow something you can do today. When tomorrow comes, hold out for more time."

We are talking about an elemental truth here. If God hadn't meant for us to postpone things, he wouldn't have given us the panic button.

There is no need to lecture me on this matter. Daddy wasted his breath years ago. Once, I started a list of all the reasons parents give for doing things on time, but I set it aside. I might pick it back up one of these days. Not now.

This blemish in my otherwise perfect character is my mother's fault. It began a full month before I was born. I was due in April, but she didn't get around to birthing me until late May. So there.

Being a procrastinator has its advantages. While other kids are studying, you can be playing. While other people are mowing their lawns, you can be fishing. While other shoppers are buying Christmas presents, you can be hunting ducks or sitting by the fire. While millions of taxpayers are punching calculators and digging receipts out of drawers, you can be watching TV and napping.

I am told there are drawbacks to procrastination, but they never seem to affect me. Doesn't everyone dash around madly right before deadline — sweating, cursing, kicking and swearing never to be late again?

The reason I am admitting this is to poo-poo all you snooty on-timers (and you know who you are) who have been watching Halley's comet since it first appeared.

When word of the comet surfaced last summer, I was just like you. I made plans to see it.

I read lots of articles on Halley's comet and learned the best times to see it and where the ideal locations were.

But unlike you, I didn't jump the gun. Astrological wonders take time.

Throughout the winter, I piddled. So what if I missed the comet? I knew it would be coming back in March and April. Why sweat?

By the first of this month, many of my friends had viewed Halley's comet at least once. They told me there really wasn't much to see; just a fuzz ball. But they said if I had any hope of putting my own eyes on it, I'd best get in gear.

Sure, sure. I'll get around to it.

As the full moon of April waned, I started thinking more often about Halley's. Once, I even got out of bed and drove to the lake and looked around in the sky. Nothing.

Ah, but then the panic button finally reared its head. It was time to get down to serious business. Last Friday night would be my final chance. The moon was down and I knew a place to get a good view.

"Oh, my gosh!" I suddenly shouted. "What if it's cloudy?"

"What if the kids get sick and we can't go?"

"What if we have a flat tire?"

"How do you get to Look Rock?"

"What if we can't find it in the sky?"

"Where are the $%¢$* binoculars?"

Everything worked out fine, of course. It always does.

We drove up Foothills Parkway, asked someone in the crowd to point out the comet and stared at it through the binoculars for maybe 10 minutes — just before a fog bank moved in and stopped the show.

Once again, procrastination paid off. I got in plenty of piddle time and still saw Halley's comet just as well as folks who fought for a glimpse in January. Now I can relax and not worry about a thing until it's time to start working on my income tax return.

Shucks, it's not even due for a full 10 hours.

Flash Gordon would have loved it

June 27, 1985

Holy heat shield! Have you seen what NASA has in mind for the men and women who make lengthy journeys into outer space in the 1990s?

Sex experiments. I'm not kidding.

"If we lock people up for 90-day periods," NASA spokeswoman Yvonne Clearwater says, "we must plan for the possiblity of intimate behavior."

Clearwater is leader of the agency's "habitability research group," which is a government term for shack-up artist. Her team, which includes psychologists, engineers and an architect, is in charge of designing a comfortable and efficient space station. One point they have discussed is how to build a soundproof "sleeping" compartment. For two.

Clearwater says sexuality is part of human nature and "we can't stop planning for healthy human behavior because of conservative reaction." She says, "It seems obvious that a group of normal, healthy professionals will probably possess normal, healthy sexual appetites."

Clearwater acknowledges that sexual relations between unmarried people in a space station is a highly controversial subject, "but it's not NASA's job to serve as moral judge."

I should say not. In fact, I fully expect NASA to seize this opportunity and turn it into valuable research.

Just think about those dedicated scientists, frolicking miles above the earth, pushing themselves to the limit in pursuit of answers to questions about extraterrestrial sex. Questions like:

- Do participants see the earth move, as well as feel it?
- If stars flash before their eyes, will they be real or imagined?
- Is there a relationship between G-forces and G-spots?
- With all that TV equipment onboard, will they be able to tune in Johnny Carson on nights when someone has a headache?
- Is this research applicable elsewhere in the space program? Like, say, alleviating motion sickness?
- If participants should take a cozy walk in space, will it lend new meaning to the term "full moon"?

I hate to tell NASA how to run its shop, but if those computerheads have any sense at all, they'll give Congress a sneak preview of this program. Maybe even a few sessions of advanced training. That way, full funding will be assured.

Just think. Back in 1969, the earth stood still as the words "one small step for man" wafted in from outer space. Maybe a decade from now, we'll hear another message from the wild blue yonder.

Something like, "Was it good for you, too?"

Arena football is un-Amurikan

May 19, 1988

I watched arena football the other night, and the experience left me convinced Americans have too much leisure time on their hands.

Perhaps Congress should expand the work week to 56 hours. If we have afternoons and evenings to piddle away on the likes of arena football, this country is in serious trouble.

Arena football is the latest gimmick sports weirdos have concocted in their never-ending attempt to make the football season last a full 12 months. Earlier attempts, like the ill-fated United States Football League, failed. And I suppose this one will, too.

Someone needs to tell these jockey strap addicts that football is a cool-weather sport, and trying to stretch it into the summer months is as futile as hanging your stocking for Santa on the Fourth of July. Check the U.S. Constitution. I'm sure it's in there somewhere.

Arena football is just what the name implies — a football game played within the confines of an indoor stadium. But it is not real, honest-to-gosh Amurikan football. Arena football is a fake, the blow-up doll of contact sports.

Everything about arena football is scaled down.

The field, for example, is only 50 yards long. Real football fields, the kind our founding fathers intended for men to play upon, are 100 yards long. What's more, the arena field is only 85 feet wide, half the distance of a National Football League playing surface.

There are other areas of shrinkage, including the end zone (eight yards deep) and goal posts (nine feet wide.) The goal post crossbar, on the other hand, stands 15 feet tall — five feet higher than NFL specs.

But that ain't the half of it.

The rules for arena football are so crazy, one is tempted to think they were devised after several long, snowy nights in a pub.

Since the field is only 50 yards from end to end, there is no need to punt. Instead, you always go for a field goal if you can't make a first down. Traditional field goals count three points. Drop-kicked ones are worth four.

Big nets are suspended behind the goals. If a field goal attempt goes astray and rebounds off the mesh, it can be fielded and returned by the non-kicking team. If it hits the ground, it is recoverable by the kicking team. Much the same principle applies to errant forward passes.

Furthermore, teams consist of only eight players, the clock doesn't stop on dropped passes and out-of-bounds plays (unless it's late in the game) and receivers only need one foot in bounds.

This means final scores commonly approach three digits each. What bunkum! Outcomes like 87-75 belong in basketball, not football.

Be that as it may, if arena football is destined to become a part of our summers, I propose these scaled-down regulations also be adopted:

■ Hot dogs and peanuts may not be sold at concession stands. Instead, viewers must snack on Vienna sausages and sunflower seeds, the latter of which must be sold individually.

■ Upon scoring a touchdown, players are not permitted to juke and slap one another with "high-fives." They must waltz (fox-trot optional) and then hook pinky fingers at waist level. This procedure will be known as "low-ones."

■ Fans are not permitted to display huge, foam fists with the outstretched index finger indicating "We're Number One!" Proper hand attire inside the arena shall be a pair of simple work gloves with the motto "We're Not Sure What We Are" tastefully stitched into the lining.

■ Marching bands are forbidden. Instead, a boom box, located at midfield on the home team side, will alternately play musical selections from rock 'n roll and easy-listening.

■ No extravagant halftime spectacles will be allowed. In their place, fans are invited to the playing surface to swap green stamps, recipes and grocery coupons.

If this doesn't shake America back to its senses, heaven help us.

Have you hugged your saw today?

May 23, 1986

We live in the Age of Abuse.

It's everywhere. Child abuse, spouse abuse, alcohol abuse, abuse of authority. You name it. But now, the consciousness arousers have gone too far. They are guilty of abusing abuse. In their zeal, they have discovered yet another type of abuse.

Tool abuse.

Cross my heart and hope to die.

According to the Hand Tools' Institute of Tarrytown, N.Y., lots of Americans are tool abusers. They're the ones who "use a screwdriver to pry, scrape, punch holes, stir or do anything other than driving or loosening a screw."

Huh? You mean there are people who own screwdrivers and *don't* use them to pry, scrape, punch, et al? Why in the name of Pete would they spend good money on a screwdriver? Don't they know you can turn screws with a dime?

"You would think tool manufacturers would ignore tool abuse practices," says William Cosmides, Hand Tools Institute spokesman. "After all, tool misuse and abuse lead to tool damage which, in turn, leads to increased sales.

"Not so. Institute members have spent millions of dollars over the years educating tool users on the proper and safe way to use many kinds of tools. Putting this information and training to practical use extends the life of the tool and prevents possible injury to the user."

The Hand Tool Institute people even sent me a test. They said it involved tools commonly found in American homes.

Could be, assuming all American homes contain shop teachers. I read over their quiz, and having never used such things as "aviation type cutting snips," I had a tough time even understanding the questions.

Still, their point is well-taken. So I made up my own list of do's and don'ts without all the technical mumbo jumbo. Read it and heed it, and you will live a happy life. Short, perhaps. But happy.

■ If you cannot find the leash or a length of rope, it is permissible to use an extension cord for walking the dog. Just be sure to unplug it first. Unless, of course, you don't intend to walk far.

■ If you see the head of a nail protruding from a board in the steps, do not try to stomp it back into place with the heel of your shoe. Don't use a brick or a piece of pipe or — gasp! — a hammer, either. Instead, leave it exposed. Then when the pop-top dohickey breaks off an unopened beer can, you will have something to push it open with.

■ Do not use a jigsaw to slice cheese or separate frozen Goo-Goo Clusters. The metal imparts an awful taste.

■ When bread hangs up in the toaster, never attempt to free it with a putty knife. The putty knife is for prying the lid off the jelly jar, fool.

Instead, turn the toaster upside down and shake vigorously. If you shake hard enough, you will not only loosen a mound of mini-croutons for your salad, you also will break small wires inside the toaster. Then you can take it back to the store and claim it was bum and they will give you a new one.

■ Pliers have unlimited uses — removing ticks from the dog, plucking dead goldfish from the aquarium, peeling gum off your shoes or turning steaks on the grill. Not necessarily in that order.

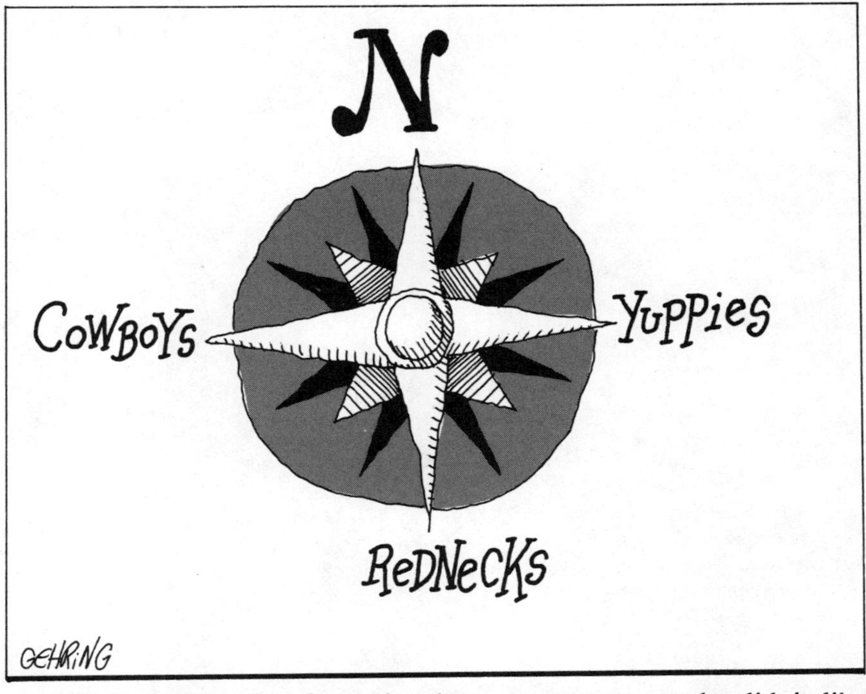

Will Rogers used to brag that he never met a man he didn't like. That is either a lie or else he had an incredible tolerance for pests.

Not only have I met some men (and women and children) I didn't like, I have encountered a few I would love to have thumped with a baseball bat.

Much of the time, though, I pretty much agree with Will's philosophy. People generally are fine folks. Especially one-on-one.

Writers have a habit of digging up offbeat characters. Or maybe it's the other way around. All I know is that it is a pure joy to sit down and talk to people who stray a tad off the norm.

Sadly, we writers sometimes don't get around to telling you about these folks until they die. Some of the characters in this chapter have gone on to their reward, and that is a loss for us all.

One marvelous quality about East Tennesseans is their lack of pretense. They're pretty much plain as toast, and that suits me just fine.

They've got their priorities straight, too.

I was among the hundreds of reporters who covered President Reagan's visit to McMinn County in 1985. I listened to any number of political speeches and interviewed dozens of people. I don't remember a word anyone said, except for one little old lady.

"Lord, honey!" she exclaimed, "this is bigger than when Elvis died!"

East Tennesseeans. I love 'em.

Chapter VI
The people of God's country

A bat and a dream

June 25, 1987

MORRISTOWN — They come from the factories, the fields, the schoolyards and both sides of the counter at McDonald's. In all likelihood, that's exactly where they'll be this time tomorrow, just like nothing ever happened.

But please forget that for the moment. For now, for this one precious day, let them cling to their dreams.

They are not hitting baseballs in tiny Sherwood Park in Hamblen County, Tenn. Rather, they are in front of 55,000 screaming fans at Shea Stadium. It's the seventh game of the World Series, bottom of the ninth. The championship rides on their bat. Confidently, they knock the dirt from their cleats, take their stance and face the mound. Here comes the windup and the pitch . . . .

"There's not a boy out there who hasn't imagined his name in headlines," says Joe Mason. "That's what keeps 'em coming. Even if things don't turn out, they can always think back and say, 'Hey, the Mets took a look at *me* once!'"

Mason looks at hundreds of them each year. He's a scout from Millbrook, Ala., assigned by New York to locate talent in the Southeast. He had come to Morristown to grade some 50 young players.

"Realistically, an older player's chances of being discovered are very remote," says Mason, 39, who was drafted by the Chicago Cubs after high school but found his budding baseball career nipped by military service in Vietnam. He later coached a college team before becoming a professional scout 10 years ago.

"Then again, another Danny Driessen may be out there. He was signed at a tryout camp and had a long career with Cincinnati."

The prospects he saw this time ran the gamut of experience.

There was 22-year-old Shane Adams, a Morristown resident who is studying to be a cook in trade school. Adams says during high school he didn't play baseball. But he pitches and covers a mean right field in church league softball.

Out at shortstop, one of the contenders was Vaden Landers, 17, a recent graduate of Gatlinburg-Pittman High who is headed for Lincoln Memorial University on scholarship.

"He has been dreaming of a baseball career since he was eight," said his mother, Earlynn, who sat in the stands and captured her son's performance on a videotape recorder.

"Vaden lives for baseball. For strength, he's been swinging a 10-pound sledge hammer — horizontally, just like he was hitting. The other night, he hit 600 balls from the batting machine and got blisters all over his hands. Sometimes he'll be up at 2 o'clock in the morning, throwing baseballs against the side of the house and fielding them."

Behind home plate was lean, muscular Larry Sauceman, 22, a graduate of Tusculum College who yearned to be picked up in the college draft. But a call never came.

"Larry's as good as any team could want," says his coach, Bill Smith. "He can play almost any position. He's got a great attitude. But sometimes, you wonder if he's one of those guys who's destined to be a year too old and a step too slow.

"That's the part that's so painful. All Larry wants is a chance. If a team sent him to Siberia, he'd go for room and board. He'd drag the field. He'd pick up balls and bats. Anything.

"I was talking to a Braves' scout the other day. He told me about a 17-year-old boy who'd been drafted right out of high school. He showed up to negotiate with two agents. Not one — two.

"Then you take a kid like Larry. He doesn't know anything about agents or salaries or negotiations. All he knows is saying, 'Yes, sir,' and playing baseball."

A different drummer

March 10, 1987

The first time I met Johnny Coleman was 12 years ago on the side of a ridge overlooking the South Fork of Citico Creek.

It was late on one of those gray February days that threatens snow at any moment, the sort of day that guarantees winter is a permanent fixture and you might as well accept the fact that spring will not arrive for at least two centuries. Maybe three.

For the previous eight hours, I had been climbing the Cherokee National Forest's steep mountains in search of ruffed grouse. Grouse hunting is perhaps the most physically demanding of all the shooting sports, and I was tired. Ragged, whipped, bone-aching tired. And my truck was still way on down the trail.

That's when I spotted Johnny sitting in front of his tent.

It is not uncommon to encounter backpackers in the Cherokee. During spring and summer, I mean. Even running into a few souls in the back country during the Indian summer days of autumn isn't out of the question.

But here it is the coldest part of the winter and I round a bend in the trail and something catches my eye and I look up to a little stretch of flat ground and there is a small nylon tent with a fellow sitting Yoga-style on the ground in front of it. And a pair of metal crutches is by his side.

Suddenly, my legs didn't feel nearly so tired.

"Johnny was one of those people who refused to let being crippled be a handicap," says Gary Dawn, a hairstylist and friend of Coleman's since their growing-up days in Burlington.

"I think he knew he'd never last a long time, so he lived every day to the fullest. He never complained; he just kept going."

Coleman was seven when he contracted polio. For the next 36 years, he would never be able to take a step without the aid of crutches.

"If Johnny hadn't gotten polio, he could have been an Olympic runner," Dawn continued. "When we were kids, nobody could keep up with him. He was the fastest person I've ever seen.

"Even with crutches, he refused to quit. Sometimes on hikes during our Boy Scout days, Johnny would knock me down with his crutches and pass me up."

Dawn and Coleman began backpacking together in 1968. For years, they combed trails in Tellico and Citico.

"The first time he strapped on a pack, he took one step and turned a complete flip," Dawn recalled. "I asked him if he was hurt, and he said, 'Only my pride.'"

But hiking was only one endeavor. Coleman was a skilled craftsman who manufactured dental crowns and bridges. He grew roses. He gardened. He fished. Using an auto-focus camera, he captured the outdoors on film. And he could absolutely knock the hide off a set of drums.

In the mid-'60s, Dawn and Coleman were drummers for the Bigger and Better Champs, a 12-piece rock and roll band. Later, Coleman played for Little Benny and the Stereos.

"Johnny couldn't use his feet to hit the bass drum pedal, so he learned to do it with his hands," said Dawn. "He'd come down with the stick, hit the pedal, then return to the snare drum without missing a beat. When other drummers would watch him, they couldn't believe he could do it so fast and never drop a stick."

The music died when a massive heart attack killed Johnny Coleman a few days ago. When his family and friends gathered for the funeral service, nobody had to ask why a pair of drumsticks and a bright red rose were tucked inside the casket.

I suppose there just wasn't enough room for his backpack.

The newest citizen

March 24, 1985

No, Virginia. Despite what you may have heard or read the last few years, the spirit of America is not dead. Not by a long shot.

It is alive and well and living in a man who was born half a world away.

If you can talk to Mark Mneimneh for a few minutes and not come away with renewed faith in the opportunities afforded by this country, perhaps you'd better check your pulse.

Last week was an especially happy time for Mark. On Tuesday, he received a master's degree in nuclear engineering from UT. A day later, he became a naturalized citizen. Next quarter, he will begin studies for a PhD. In a couple of years, he hopes to get a job with TVA or Martin Marietta. Pretty awesome statistics for a lad who could barely speak English when he came to the United States at age 19.

Mark is a native of Beirut, Lebanon. He remembers his homeland as quiet and peaceful, a good place to grow up.

That is, until he reached 15.

"Then the fighting started," he says. "We lived right on the dividing line. We could hear gunfire at night. You did not know if you would awake with a bomb over your head."

A person grows up in a hurry under those conditions. So Mark did like millions of others seeking refuge from war and oppression during the last two centuries. He set his sights on America.

He arrived in South Carolina in 1978. He started to college. He took a part-time job in a restaurant. Two years later, he married his supervisor.

Mark and Susanne moved to Knoxville. He continued studying for an undergraduate degree at UT. Susanne took a job in food services at the Hyatt Regency. Two degrees and two children later, he's still studying, and she's still working.

I first met Mark on Oct. 16, 1982. That was the day of the Tennessee-Alabama football game.

The most fans of that season, all 95,342 of them, were wedged into

Neyland Stadium. UT won in a fourth-quarter thriller, 35-28. It was Tennessee's first victory over Alabama in 11 years. Knoxville went totally berserk.

But Mark Mneimneh was not at the stadium. He was two blocks away, buried under a mound of papers and books at the UT library.

I had been assigned to the library that afternoon. It was my job to write a column about any students who happened to show up.

The project had been discussed in our sports department for days. "Go find you a bookworm," I had been told. "You know — a real Mr. McGoo, somebody who has no idea what football is all about. See if you can tear him away from his slide rule for a few minutes. This oughta be a lot of fun."

I found me a serious student, all right. But he sure didn't follow the script.

I found a man who had lost two brothers in his war-torn city. One of them had been killed by a sniper. Another, age 11, was among 250 who perished when terrorists blew up a theater. He had not heard from a third brother since the day he left Lebanon.

I found a Moslem who had been persecuted for his religious beliefs in his native country, who wondered aloud why all people — whether they are Christians or Jews or Moslems — cannot live together in peace.

I found an immigrant who knew he could never go back home. "If I get a job and a house in Lebanon, another war will come along and everything will be lost," he told me that day. "There will never be peace in the Middle East, no matter how hard the United States tries. I do not want to raise my son in war."

I found a man who put the whole silly spectacle of a college football game into its proper perspective.

So perhaps you will understand why I was delighted to see Mark standing in the courtroom the other day, raising his right hand with 54 other new citizens, and swearing his allegiance to the United States.

"Hopefully, this will give me good luck," he said in the marbled hallway of the Federal Building after the ceremony concluded. "Without United States citizenship, I could never get a job in the nuclear industry. This guarantees my future."

I asked Susanne how they planned to celebrate.

Nothing really special, she replied. When two people spend their days and nights rotating schedules of work and studies around children, it's celebration enough just to take a breather.

"This has been a long, hard fight," she beamed, looking at Mark's papers. "But it's worth it."

Mark kept staring at the certificate, too. He studied every line in infinite detail, making certain all the information was correct.

"I was never sure it would happen," he said. "There is always the fear you will be turned down at the last minute."

Leo Durocher was dead wrong. Nice guys don't always finish last.

In the beginning

May 5, 1985

The pace is less hectic these days. Larry Mathis snips hair in Maynardville, and Bud Brewster sells musical instruments in West Knoxville.

Both men are content with the cards life has dealt. They have sipped the wine of success and passed the chalice on. The way they've got it figured, there's no sense worrying about what might have been.

"Fact of the matter is," says Mathis, "we don't tell a lot of folks about the group. Soon as someone starts to hear the story, you can almost see 'em rollin' their eyes and sayin', 'Yeah, yeah. I knew Dolly, too. She went to school for six months with my brother-in-law's first cousin on his mama's uncle's side."

Then Mathis laughs.

"Well, maybe it isn't that bad. But it is hard to find anybody from East Tennessee who doesn't claim they grew up with Dolly Parton."

That certainly wasn't the case in the early 1960s when Mathis and Brewster were in the lineup of performers on Cas Walker's Farm and Home Hour. Five mornings a week, thousands of East Tennesseans awakened to their live pickin' and sangin' on TV.

"Besides that, we were on radio," says Brewster. "We also did supermarket openings, land auctions, anywhere Cas sent us. Even dog dunkings."

Say what?

"Dog dunkings. You know, where people'd bring their coon dogs and have 'em dipped for fleas and ticks. Those were real popular."

Parton was a high school student in those days. She'd get up at 4 each morning, drive to the studio, do the show, then head to classes in Sevierville.

"The fall of Dolly's senior year, a program called Hullabaloo started on TV," Brewster recalled. "It was folk stuff, real popular at the time. It was a big hit all across the country.

"Me and Larry and Dolly started singin' some folk songs. We got this little trio together. Dolly was a natural. I especially remember how congenial she was.

"She was a country girl, a little bit shy. But she could cut up and handle routines on stage like a pro. And when she started to sing, people would sit up and listen. The first time anybody'd hear her voice, they couldn't get over how strong it was and how much control she had.

"We cut a demo tape and had some publicity photos taken. Charlie Ledgerwood, a friend of ours, had an idea we could really make it big. He got the tapes and hopped on a bus for King Records in Cincinnati."

You can just see the scene now:

Here's a big city recording studio and in walks this fellow from

Knoxville-Wherever-That-Is, Tennessee. He's got tapes of the finest act you've ever heard. A-No. 1. They're destined for success. Better sign 'em now, Mr. Big Time, before somebody else beats you to it.

"The secretary told Charlie he could have two minutes with the boss," said Mathis.

"He started playing the tapes and the boss asked him to stay longer. Then he took Charlie to lunch. Before the day was over, he'd bought Charlie a plane ticket back to Knoxville and put three contracts in his pocket."

But this success story was not to be.

"Larry and I signed our contracts and drove to Sevierville to get Dolly's signature," said Brewster. "That's when she told us she'd already signed with an agent from Nashville. There was no way she could get into a contract with King. A few months later, she graduated from high school and took off to Nashville."

Musical success came to the three entertainers. But not in equal amounts. Nor did they enjoy it as a trio.

Parton, of course, teamed with Porter Waggoner, then split to find international fame on her own.

Mathis and Brewster left Cas Walker's show in the early '70s and formed a bluegrass group, The Pinnacle Boys. Their timing was perfect. Bluegrass music was the rage, and The Pinnacle Boys rode it to the top. They entertained crowds as large as 40,000. They cut seven albums. They appeared at the Grand Ol' Opry three times.

But by the late '70s, the popularity of bluegrass music was waning. The rigors of the road were taking their toll. The group played a few special engagements before drifting apart in 1983.

"If I had to do it all over again, I'd go on the road and dig it out like you're supposed to do," says Brewster. "Here, we had it made. There was a regular salary, a regular audience. That was nice and comfortable, but it didn't do anything for us outside of Knoxville."

Mathis would have taken another route.

"Playing on the road is tough. You're either traveling or performing. You've got to have a certain personality to make it. Don't get me wrong. Music was good to me. There were some wonderful times. But I reckon if I could do it all over again, I'd get a job at Oak Ridge or with the railroad and work until it was time to retire."

It's been years since the three have been together, but the friendship remains. Parton's biography, "Dolly" by Alanna Nash, includes a photograph of the trio.

"Oh sure, she remembers us," said Brewster. "We occasionally hear from each other through mutual friends."

"Why, I guarantee if we were to see each other on a street in New York City, she'd run over and hug our necks," said Mathis. "Dolly really made it big, and I'm happy as the world for her."

Then he winks and a grin creases his face.

"But you know, ol' Dolly sure missed a golden opportunity. There she is, singin' for a livin'. If she'd just stuck with me'n Bud, she could be cuttin' hair or sellin' banjers."

Home sweet home

May 29, 1986

JEFFERSON CITY — They're selling Ben Ballinger's old home.

It goes on the auctioneer's block Saturday morning, along with 53½ acres of forests and rolling fields near the banks of the Holston River. The old Clint Jones place, they call it.

Ben Ballinger lived here for 35 years, but not in your typical farmhouse. His place was neither brick nor board. It didn't have a white picket fence, a front porch swing or flower boxes in the windows. In fact, it didn't even have a front porch or windows.

That's because Ben Ballinger lived in a cave.

All those years, he stayed in a hole in a limestone cliff. It's just off Mill Springs River Road, not far downstream from Cherokee Dam.

Sometimes, Ben came out to work as a carpenter. Sometimes, people walked to his cave and sat on a stump and let him cut their hair. Others came merely to talk to Ben and see his simple lifestyle. No electricity, no plumbing, just a woodstove and crude furniture.

If you are a long-time News-Sentinel reader, you might remember Ben. He was a favorite subject of the late Bert Vincent, our "Strolling" columnist. Bert discovered Ben in 1938.

"He was a sight," Vincent wrote of their first encounter. "He was sitting up there at the cave mouth, his long beard down to his waist, like Moses, and chanting verses from a big Bible he held on his knees."

Every few years, Bert would visit his caveman friend and relay news to the outside world.

An example is this dispatch from 1956: "Ben's motto is 'Live Better for Less.' He has it over the door to his cave home. He really has been living that motto, too. Money hasn't interested him. Fellows who know this borrow from him. One fellow has borrowed more than $300.

"'I never ask them to pay me back. And, of course, they don't. When I see one of the fellows after the first of the year, I just write a receipt. That cleans the slate for the year, and they start borrowing all over again.'"

Again, this time from 1960: "Ben warred on mice at first. He set traps. He put out poison. Still the mice came, more and more of them. Finally, he quit trying to kill them.

"These mice wanted to live same as I, and the cave had been their home for thousands of years before I moved in. I don't want to kill anything now, or see anything killed. My nature has changed a whole lot since I've been here."

Once more, 1963: "Ben got rid of his beard. He's still a Bible reader, but he's not a recluse. He's not a hermit. He now puts on Sunday clothes every once and awhile and gets out and comes to Knoxville."

If Ben Ballinger had lived in the 1980s, it would have taken a team of psychiatrists to determine what ailed him and why he would adopt such a lifestyle. They would have studied him at length and then gotten together and puffed their pipes and nodded "mmmm-mmm" a lot and written all manner of scholarly works that would gather dust on a bookshelf until the end of time.

But in Ben and Bert's day, it was easier to plow to the root of the matter. The man simply wanted to get away from it all.

Ballinger had served in the military. He was nervous. He'd had enough of guns and people barking orders at him.

Oh, and there was one other reason. The only true love in his life had left him.

"We were engaged," Ben had said. "Then this fellow in a bright, shiny Model A Ford coupe started picking her up and taking her out right under my nose."

Ballinger said he thought about committing suicide, but kept postponing it. So he crept into the cave — "just for the winter, but I ended up staying."

After that, he never went out with a woman again.

In July 1969, Ballinger suffered a heart attack. A neighbor found him and took him to the hospital. He died a month later at age 64.

These days, there's hardly a trace of Ben Ballinger. His cot, stove and door are long gone. Tufts of delicate ferns grow around the mouth of the cave. The only evidence of permanent habitation are the smoke-covered walls. A few people have built campfires around the entrance. And there is litter and graffiti, the calling cards of our trashy society.

Etching and spray-painting tell you that Jenna and Jeff have visited since Ben departed. Also, C.S. and J.S., the River Rats, Robin Murray, Mike Walker, Gary Wells, Jungle Jim and Melissa.

Yet there's one scratching without attribution. All it says is "I Love Tammy."

Maybe it's Ben Ballinger's ghost, still pining for his gal.

The company we keep

October 25, 1985

I don't recall the year, but I do know it was near the end of summer. A long, hot summer. East Tennessee had been without rain for weeks.

Lawns were brown. Crops were dying in the fields.

Naturally, lakes around here were much lower than normal. You don't have to be a whiz at hydrology, meteorology or physics to understand the relationship between rainfall and lake levels.

Yet the man standing in our newsroom had a different theory.

"The airplanes are what's dryin' up our lakes," he announced. "I sit on my front porch and watch 'em every day."

Come again?

"Happens all the time," he continued. "Those planes take off from the airport real fast. When they cross the lake, it sucks the water up. You need to write something about it, 'cause if this keeps goin' on, the lakes are gonna be plumb dry."

We took down the information and thanked him for coming by and showed him to the door. Then it was back to work like nothing ever happened.

Newspapers cannot exist without bizarre people and their offbeat stories. This is a fact of life in the communications industry, which is why you'll usually find the door of any newspaper office open. Including ours.

There might be a receptionist or security guard at each entrance. Someone to give directions or sift out the worst of the drunks. But even then, it's a daily game to see who's going to show up next.

Like the woman who came in carrying a large grocery bag. Said she had a gangbuster story to tell and asked to speak to a reporter.

So done.

"Nobody ever believes me," she started out. "My husband says I'm crazy, and so do the doctors. But I've got papers to prove I'm OK. Want to take a look at them?"

Certainly, said the scribe. Let's see what you've got.

With that, the woman produced a stack of papers from her bag. Each was a letter from a different doctor. And each clearly stated that she was as nutty as a pecan tree.

"Well, whatdaya think about that?" she asked.

"Yup," the reporter replied. "Everything looks OK to me."

"That's just what I thought," said she.

Then she repacked her bag and left, pleased as punch that someone had given her a forum.

Presidential campaigns always are fertile fields. A guy walked in here one morning and asked someone to get Walter Cronkite on the telephone. This was when Cronkite was a TV network newsman, not a spokesman for land developers.

"Tell Cronkite I'm announcing my candidacy," he said. "He'll want to have it on the 6:30 news."

And out he strolled.

Then one boiling day this past summer, another, uh, "candidate" showed up. Said he was hiking across America to kick off his campaign.

I'm not sure what his political platform was. Nor could I tell you his name or party affiliation. But it certainly wasn't difficult to notice one unique aspect about this character.

He was wearing at least six or seven coats, one on top of the other, each buttoned or zipped to the hilt.

Maybe he was preparing for nuclear winter.

A man of the soil

October 24, 1986

No fanfare.

If you have a friend, a really good friend, that's one way you can tell. There's no fanfare to the relationship. No ooohhing and aahhing and making over you like you were some sort of guest. They accept you and you accept them and that is the end of that.

What's more, there is timelessness to a good friendship. It doesn't matter if you see each other on a daily basis or once every 10 years. If the friendship is solid, it can be repeatedly interrupted, then restarted, just like a faithful old car.

Standing in line at an Athens funeral home a few nights ago, I did a lot of thinking about friendships. So did hundreds of other people — millionaires and mill hands, laborers and lawmakers. We'd all come to say goodbye to Charlie Browder.

Charlie was a farmer. A big-time farmer. In a part of the country where 50 acres is considered a vast spread, he worked 2,300 acres along the McMinn-Monroe county line. Dairy cattle, corn, tobacco, wheat, you name it.

"Agribusiness," they call it today. It means high-tech agriculture and Wall Street tactics blended into a fine-honed, sterile package.

I'm sorry, but that term and Charlie Browder simply did not compute.

Not that he wasn't a businessman or a progressive farmer. You don't supervise a huge farm, a wood products company and a dairy operation without knowing how to handle money. Nor are you named Farmer of the Year by refusing to change with the times.

It's just that Charlie Browder was cut from different cloth than your standard agribusiness baron. He was of the sun and the rain and the soil, not of the office.

He knew plants would grow not because a computer said they would but because he had learned the process, seed to harvest, by the sweat of his brow.

His boardroom was the dusty front seat of a dented pickup.

His trustees were family, friends and work crews.

His financial forecasts came from the weather bureau.

When he dressed for success, it was in Carhartts instead of Brooks Brothers. I knew Charlie Browder for over 15 years, and the only time I ever saw a tie around his neck was when I stood beside his coffin.

We were friends, Charlie and me. And I daresay our particular friendship was handled like all the others he acquired through farming, business, sports and community service. Strictly without fanfare.

When Charlie would call me on the telephone, he'd just start talking. It didn't matter if we hadn't communicated in months. Soon as the conversation was over, he'd hang up — thump — just like that.

When I'd see him on the farm and say howdy that's about as far as the greetings went. We'd launch right back into the conversation from our last meeting and never skip a beat.

If I stuck my head in the door within an hour of mealtime, he'd say, "You need to eat. Go get you a plate and sit down. Now listen, you know how. . ." And he'd be off into another session of homespun philosophy.

I knew when I saw him on Labor Day that time was running out. Cancer had weakened him, but he was still plain ol' Charlie. Still ready to climb into the pickup and drive his fields or sit in the shade and right the world's wrongs with his wry humor.

He was 77 when he drew his final breath last weekend. Tib Browder held her husband's hand, and he whispered, "I'm ready. I'll be waiting for you."

Then it was over. No fanfare at all.

But as I stood in line at the funeral home — a line that snaked down the hall, through the lobby, across the front porch, along the walkway and into the parking lot — I was struck with the notion that those who never dwell in fanfare usually end up generating the most of it.

Pint-sized Dr. Dolittle

August 18, 1985

For all you people who've had it up to here with daily assaults of news about nuclear warheads, bankrupt financiers, traffic fatalities, racial unrest and crooked politicians, this one's for you.

We have in our city a girl named Becky Cates. She is 11. When classes begin in a few days, Becky will be in the sixth grade at Gresham Middle School.

Like lots of little girls, Becky enjoys animals. She especially likes to nurse injured animals back to health.

Wild animals.

Veterinarians and wildlife biologists alike will tell you wild animals are difficult to work with, even for trained professionals. They will tell you laymen do not possess the knowledge or the equipment needed to heal a wild animal's injuries. They will tell you wild animals are not accustomed to being around humans, so even if a human provides proper physical care, the animal often dies from trauma.

And they are absolutely correct on all counts.

But what these learned people of science do not tell you is that 11-year-old girls know how to work magic.

Not long ago, Becky found a wounded butterfly in her yard. A yellow swallowtail. It was nearly dead. In all likelihood, it had been knocked from flight by a passing car. Such incidents occur thousands of times every day.

Becky picked up the butterfly and brought it inside. Her mother and father appreciated her concern, but told her it was too far gone. Surely it would die. Besides, who ever heard of nursing an insect back to health?

Becky paid no heed. She lined a plastic dish with leaves and sticks and put her patient to bed. She mixed sugar and water to simulate nectar and placed a small container of the food nearby.

Each day, Becky changed the leaves.

Each day, she positioned the dish in morning sunshine.

Each day, she gently picked up her patient and placed it upon the tip of her finger. Then she would dip a wooden toothpick into the sugar water and feed her butterfly. Drop by drop by drop.

And she would talk to it in quiet, soothing tones.

In a couple of days, Becky tried to get her patient to fly. But its wings were not yet strong. It fluttered feebly and crashed to the ground. She picked it back up and continued nursing.

Three or four days passed, and the butterfly was capable of short flights. After a week, it could fly around the house or the front yard. Sometimes, it would fly almost out of sight. But always, it returned to Becky and landed on her fingertip, just like a falcon to its master.

Two weeks after the rescue, Becky knew the time had come to send her patient back into the wild. She walked to the edge of her yard and stretched her hand as high as she could reach. The butterfly lifted, circled, and started to climb.

"It kept going higher and higher," Becky told me. "I watched until it flew out of sight. It was kind of sad, but I sure was happy for the butterfly."

So am I.

And just knowing there are little girls like Becky Cates makes it a lot easier to withstand daily assaults of news about nuclear warheads, bankrupt financiers, traffic fatalities, racial unrest and crooked politicians.

Sheer delight

December 4, 1983

You don't have to read Miss Manners' column to know letters must be written in black or blue-black ink. Not if you were a student of Miss Geneva Anderson, who died in Maryville last week at the age of 79.

You also know not to split your infinitives, dangle your participles, splice complete sentences with commas or (sin of sins) chew gum in class.

"Now cherubs," she would say, "someone in this room is chewing gum. We will stop our lesson until this matter is resolved."

That's when silence would fall upon her class. Like an anvil. And the tiny sliver of contraband Juicy Fruit in your mouth would balloon into a pumpkin.

But if you were lucky enough to be assigned to Geneva Anderson for a year of senior English, you came away with more than the basics of letter-writing and etiquette. Just ask the thousands of pupils who studied under her at Robertsville, Everett, Walland, Porter, Hixson and Young schools — many of whom kept in contact with her until late this summer, when she suffered a debilitating stroke.

In nearly two decades of formal education, I encountered countless dozens of teachers. Most were good, a few excellent and, alas, a handful so poor they gave tenure a bad reputation. Geneva Anderson was the bluest chip of them all.

We met in the fall of 1964, the start of my final year at Young High. English had never been a particularly difficult subject for me; but for three years, I had heard upperclassmen warn about nine months of enslavement if your name was included on her roster.

Mine, gulp, was. With fear and trembling, I entered her room.

What I happily discovered was not a female Simon Legree, but an utterly charming, humorous, knowledgeable and challenging tutor. Whenever Miss Anderson was particularly pleased with your work, she would write "sheer delight" at the top. I am here to tell you she was sheer delight from that first class in September until graduation in June.

Geneva Anderson could read Macbeth aloud, and you could smell the cauldron bubbling.

She could transform a vocabulary lesson into an exciting quest for new words.

She could show you how to decode Harbrace and use it as a road map into the world of communication.

And she could make a certain lad believe people would actually pay — yes, *pay!* — him to write. Then he wouldn't ever have to work for a living.

Firm? Indeed. But not strong-arm firm. I never considered it possible for this woman to raise her voice. Lord knows she didn't need to.

On rare occasions of civil disorder, all Miss Anderson had to do was cut her eyes and stare for a moment and calm was instantly restored. If you were never stared at by Geneva Anderson when she was in a testy mood, you never experienced primal fear.

That is why I hope St. Peter has everything in order. If that poor boy is chewing gum when Miss Anderson arrives, or if he tries to sign her in with green ink, he's going to wish he had applied for a transfer.

All in a day's work

July 24, 1987

"No, ma'am," the man from the wildlife agency was saying. "I don't believe a woodpecker is banging on your house at 3 o'clock in the morning. Woodpeckers don't feed at night."

The woman was not satisfied. She insisted the wildlife agent investigate. Which is why E.C. Higgins found himself crawling through her attic, trying to find the source of the fast-paced "r-r-r-r-r-r."

"Actually, it did sound like a woodpecker," says Higgins, "but when I got over the bathroom, the answer dawned on me. I crawled down and found the water line and followed it under the house. There it was — a water pressure valve that had gone bad. Whenever it would click on, the house would rattle. The lady asked me how much I would charge to fix it, but I told her we were in the wildlife business, not plumbing."

Tracking bogus birds is all in a day's work for a game warden stationed in an urban area. Higgins should know. He has just retired from the Tennessee Wildlife Resources Agency after serving nearly 30 years in the state's third-largest city.

"It's different than working in the boondocks," said the 55-year-old Higgins. "You get hundreds of calls from people who don't hunt or fish. Everything from how to keep bugs off rose bushes to getting rid of skunks in the basement. You get lots of calls about bears, too."

Bears? In Knoxville?

"Sure. Sometimes they do come out of the mountains. But most often, the 'bear' turns out to be an Angus calf."

A native of rural Unicoi County, Higgins grew up with a gun in one hand and a fishing rod in the other.

"I had coon dogs, rabbit dogs, bird dogs. We depended on hunting and fishing for part of our meat. Now that I'm retired, I'm gonna get back. I've missed out on a lot the last 30 years."

After high school and military service, Higgins was working as a railroad brakeman when a warden's position opened. He jumped at the chance. He served one year in Monroe County, then was assigned to Knoxville.

"The job has changed a lot," he said. "At first, all we did was game and fish law enforcement. Then came boating safety. Now, officers do it all — game management, fish management, surveys, hunter safety instruction."

Although his home territory was Knox County, Higgins often worked in the outlying areas. Frequently, he went undercover. Dressed as a good ol' boy hunter, he investigated everything from illegal duck shooting in West Tennessee to bear poaching near the Great Smokies.

"I got found out a couple of times and had guns pulled on me," he said.

"But I was always able to talk the folks into putting 'em down."

A natural storyteller, Higgins can hold his own around any campfire. With three decades of experience to draw upon, he has a wealth of material.

"Preseason squirrel hunting used to be real bad around here. One morning, I had slipped out this road where there was a lot of activity going on. I found a pair of shoes by the edge of the woods. I hid close by and waited. Counted 16 shots. Pretty soon, this guy walks out, barefooted, carrying 16 squirrels and a shotgun. He got his shoes, and I got him.

"Another time, we'd gotten a tip that some bear hunters had a live trap in Miller's Cove. Me and Ray Henry and Ed Witt had to lay out there for a week before we finally caught the men. It was awful — hidin' in the bushes with nothing but baloney and hot dogs to eat.

"A year or two later, the same thing happened. But before we staked out the trap, we drove to Townsend to stock up on good food. By the time we returned, the hunters had gotten back to their trap and taken the bear. They got clean away. All we had were bags full of groceries."

What's the most outlandish excuse he's ever heard?

"It was at North River, where you can only use artificial lures for trout. I sneaked up on this guy and caught him fishing with live bait. He had a wasp on the hook of his fly. The guy looked real surprised. Said he must have caught the wasp on his back cast."

No, the judge didn't buy it either.

A dog's life

April 26, 1987

Somewhere in the dark recesses of the J.C. Penney Life Insurance Co. in Dallas, way off in an obscure broom closet or down in a dusty cellar, I bet you can find a former policywriter who is draped with chains and shackled in leg irons.

And I wouldn't be a bit surprised to learn that when new policywriters are being trained, they are herded past the poor soul on field trips.

"Look closely, class," the instructor probably says. "This is what happens to policywriters who make us look like idiots! Do you want to end up like this? Of course not. Therefore, pay attention when you issue a life insurance policy. Otherwise, you can rot away the rest of your life like this fool."

Oh, well. Perhaps there isn't a dungeon at the company's headquarters. Still, I'll wager there have been some bloody chewing-outs in recent days, ever since the company realized who Sadie Sue Tarpy actually is.

For the record, Sadie is a dog. A nine-year-old English setter. Until J.C. Penney realized its mistake, she was the holder of a $40,000 policy.

"It never was a big secret," says Lynn Tarpy, the Knoxville lawyer who owns Sadie. "I never lied to the company. When they asked for information, I gave it to them. All I was trying to do was get 'em off my back."

This epic began in 1980 when Tarpy graduated from law school. The Penney company sent him a credit card. Within weeks, the firm also began bombarding him with requests for insurance.

"They were coming in every month, sometimes twice a month," he said. "So I finally filled one in with Sadie's name."

Tarpy completed every blank: Birthdate — Aug. 10, 1977. Occupation — bird dog. Job duties — raise and train hunting dogs. Height — 22 inches. Weight — 25 pounds. Beneficiary — Lynn Tarpy. Relationship to policy holder — owner.

"I even signed it 'Sadie Sue Tarpy by Lynn Tarpy,'" he recalled.

Surely someone at Penney's headquarters smelled a hoax, eh?

Nope.

It sailed through like a dose of salts. Within weeks, Sadie Sue Tarpy was insured for $20,000, and her owner began paying monthly premiums of $6.50.

This went on for s-e-v-e-n years.

"Twice, someone from J.C. Penney Insurance Co. called and asked to speak to Sadie," said Tarpy. "She was at my mother's house both times, so that's what I told 'em. They kept asking if she might want to increase the coverage to $40,000, and I finally said yes.

"It was great. I got $6.50 worth of pleasure each month just reading the mail Sadie Sue received."

A few weeks ago, the company wrote Sadie Sue to see if she wanted to change her term policy to whole life. Tarpy filled out the forms and mailed them to Dallas.

"Someone from Penney's called and said the application was being denied because Sadie Sue was too young," he said. "I wrote a letter and asked if she could be insured for accidental death, then why couldn't she get coverage on a whole life policy?"

That's when it finally happened.

Someone looked carefully at the original application and realized — in utter horror, no doubt — that Sadie Sue Tarpy walks on all fours and eats Alpo.

Within 48 hours after Tarpy had mailed his letter, J.C. Penney canceled the policy and issued a check for $512.46. That covered all the premiums, plus eight percent interest.

"They sent me the check by Federal Express," Tarpy said. "I believe that's the fastest an insurance company has ever moved."

Watch out, sister

June 3, 1986

It's not like Hazel Davidson needs a lesson in men.

After 40 years of catering to their needs and desires, she could teach a course in the psychology of the human male and teach it with more insight than all the Ph.D.s Harvard and Princeton could muster.

But she has just discovered what every other "working" woman has learned since Carleen Cavewoman accepted a raw fish for services rendered. It goes like this: When you're young and attractive, there's not enough they can do for you. But when the skin starts to sag and those age lines grow deeper, you better watch out, sister. 'Cause they're fixing to toss you out with the garbage.

Davidson refers to herself as a playgirl. That's a nice-enough title, I suppose. Whatever you want to call it is fine.

But play period is over. For the first time in her long and illustrious career, Davidson faces a stretch behind bars.

Right now, she's finishing a 10-day sentence for contempt of court. She got that for drinking in Judge Jimmy Duncan's court. Then comes a more lengthy stay — 11 months and 29 days for aiding and abetting prostitution and running a brothel. Three other prostitution charges are pending.

Yet weep not for Davidson. She knew the rules. She flaunted them for years. She played with matches and finally got burned.

Do feel sorry for her, though, because she's not the only one who should be staring from behind those bars. It takes two to tango. Or two dozen or 200 or whatever.

Any legend needs juicy stories to stay alive, and Davidson is no exception. It's difficult to separate fact from fiction about her and her choice of men. In her heyday, the list of her "friends" supposedly included a number of politicians, businessmen, law enforcement officers, entertainers and celebrities.

One of my associates at The News-Sentinel remembers the night he was searching for a high-ranking official from a professional football team. He knew the guy had come to Knoxville and desperately needed to reach him for a story.

"Call Hazel," someone tipped him. "Whenever he comes to town, he always goes there."

Yep, he sure was. Granted a bedside telephone interview, too.

And there are stories galore about Davidson's "gals." If legend is to be believed, her stable has contained everything from UT students to frustrated housewives to the wives of prominent physicians. So much for the guesswork and gossip of whoopie in Knoxville.

But one thing is certain: When Davidson was in her prime, she rarely had trouble with the law. Everyone conveniently looked the other way.

Now, thing's are different.

She's 62 years old. She's been married and divorced enough times to put her in contention with Hollywood's best. She drinks heavily — between a pint and a fifth of liquor daily, her doctor says. She has few friends, few family ties. And the protection she was afforded by this community for four decades is gone.

Sad? Of course it is sad.

But that, as they say, is life. No different today than it was 5,000 years ago.

What's sadder is knowing that out there somewhere is a new Hazel Davidson. Maybe a bunch of them. They're yukking it up with the guys and enjoying their fancy dinners and wearing their furs and flying in their jets and taking their money. And getting away with it.

At least until they grow old.

Plain ol' Andy

August 9, 1987

If you discount the fact that there is a lot of month left over at the end of the money, there are several benefits to being the son of a university professor. Especially a physical education professor at the University of Tennessee.

You have ready access to used equipment — old softball bats and boxing gloves and such — and instantly become the hero of the neighborhood athletic league.

On Saturday mornings, you can tag along while your daddy teaches class and play H-O-R-S-E on the same basketball court where the Vols will compete that very night.

Occasionally, star athletes such as Gene Tormohlen or Obie Lee Bowling will actually come to your house to talk to your daddy and then eat a meal with you. When you are a child, the bragging rights of such an encounter are worth 10 times more than someone else's grand slam home run in Little League.

Another benefit is that you get to know a man like Andy Holt.

That's who he was. Andy.

When he and his wife would come to our house, I never heard them called "Dr. and Mrs. Holt." They were "Andy and Mawtha."

All I knew in those days was that he was a friendly man who told funny stories in a deep, Southern accent that fairly dripped off his lips. Not until much later, after the used boxing gloves and the many rounds of H-O-R-S-E had been forsaken, did it actually dawn on me that Andy Holt was my daddy's boss.

As I look back on his life, which ended last week at the age of 82, I am confident the key to Dr. Andrew David Holt's enormous success was his ability to remain Andy.

Among his many accomplishments, he excelled as a university administrator, a politician and a speaker. Yet he defied the stereotypic image of an administrator, politician and speaker. He did it because he was Andy.

University administrators are supposed to be heartless old grouches who make faculty members toe the mark and keep students in their place, all the while billing and cooing the town's richest contributors.

Politicians are supposed to wear plastic smiles and cut secret deals that follow party lines.

Speakers are supposed to bowl their audiences over with fresh material, never once shoplifting from the past.

Not an Andy.

An Andy becomes president of a school that has 6,000 students and expands the enrollment to 22,000 not because he cares for numbers, but because he cares for people. And they care for him. Some would go so far as to call it love.

Yes, there was a bit of student unrest at UT in the waning days of Holt's presidency; there was student unrest throughout the country. It was easy to rebel against The Establishment in those days. But rebel against an Andy? Impossible.

An Andy can walk into the Legislature, pass the hat, and come home with millions of dollars for new buildings and programs. He can do it repeatedly. It does not matter to an Andy if the money is Republican or Democrat. It all spends.

An Andy can give you the same speech you've heard once before and make you want to hear it a third time. His "friendly faces" routine was delivered over tons of roast beef and mashed potatoes. But each time was a success.

He loved to tell the joke about the city slicker who stopped at a farm and asked for a drink of water. The farmer led his guest to the spring house, took a gourd dipper off the peg, ladled a cup of cool water and offered it to the man.

That's when the visitor noticed two dried streaks of tobacco juice running off the farmer's mouth. To avoid drinking from the same side of the dipper, he turned the gourd around and drank backward.

"Well, I'll be John Brown!" the farmer shouted. "You're the first man I ever saw who drinks water the same way I do!"

Andy Holt. Plain ol' Andy. He shared his dipper with the world.

The Titan of Trays

October 6, 1987

Slim Dickson is discussing the art of carrying cafeteria trays. When the master speaks, you listen.

"First, you bal'nce a tray on one hand like this," he starts out.

I look at his outstretched palm — a quarter-acre of brown skin radiating into fingers the length and shape of a fine cigar — and realize I'm already out of contention.

"Now, put the second tray on your arm. Let it set against the first tray."

He snakes out his left arm. It is approximately the same length as my left leg. From the waist down.

"Then all you have t'do is pick up the third tray with your other hand, and you're ready t'go up the stairs."

"Does it help to be right-handed or left-handed?" I ask.

"Neither. You gotta be both-handed."

Six-foot-four Walter Waltus Tennyson Dickson — a.k.a. Slim — ought to know. He is Knoxville's undisputed Titan of Trays, the Potentate of Platters, the Senior Statesman of Saucers, the Sultan of Silverware.

For nearly 60 of his 87 years, he has been ferrying Knoxvillians' vittles from cash register to table. His skills have earned him a legendary local reputation, a tidy income parlayed into real estate, and more acquaintances than any politician in this city's history, with the possible exception of Cas Walker.

Not bad for a man with a third-grade education whose first cafeteria job earned him $8 a week and all the bread heels he could eat.

For more than half a century, Dickson held sway at the S&W Cafeteria on Gay Street. He worked there from 1929, two years after the eatery opened, until 1981, when it closed because of declining business. Since then, he has been employed by Ramsey's Cafeteria on White

Avenue.

With tens of thousands of business people, office workers, professionals, TVA-ites and others in the downtown area every day, it is hard for me to imagine that the S&W could not afford to stay in operation. I suppose that explains why I am a broke newspaper columnist instead of a rich cafeteria owner. In any event, the death of the S&W Cafeteria — along with its shrimp creole, fried green tomatoes, coconut cream pie and other heavenly wonders — is a mortal sin against Knoxville I have neither forgotten nor forgiven.

"We used t'serve three meals a day, three lines at a time," he recalled. "When TVA came here in '36, the business really picked up. After the war ended, same thing.

"People would make a night of it. They'd eat here and then go see a picture show."

But as the city began to spread in all directions, downtown lost its luster. Shopping malls and free parking siphoned traffic off Gay Street. By the mid-'70s, evening and Saturday meals were phased out. When the revolving door was locked in 1981, a part of Knoxville died.

"Oh, yes sir, I cried the day I left," Dickson says. "Yes sir, I sure did. People called me for days and days and told me they saw me cryin' on TV.

"And they cried with me."

I know this is going to come as a shock, especially to journalists, but every now and then I have a serious thought.

Whenever this happens, I take a cold shower and hope it passes. If it doesn't, there's nothing to do but go ahead and write.

The trouble is, I've never been very good at righteous indignation. I know columnists are supposed to behave like TV preachers. We're expected to gnash our teeth and breathe fire and pound the pulpit of public awareness until changes are made.

Maybe that approach is effective in some circles, but it rarely works for me.

I'd rather poke fun.

Of course, this means I occasionally get poked back. But what the heck. If there wasn't supposed to be spirited debate between opposing factions, we'd have no need for tire tools and Band-Aids.

Chapter VII
The sermons of Chairman Venob

Proper perspective, please

February 23, 1988

President Reagan has proposed a $1.09 trillion budget for fiscal 1989.

So?

Except for mathematicians, statisticians, physicists, computer freaks and bureaucrats, the term "trillion" is purely imaginary. The rest of us cannot comprehend it.

We can handle hundreds. We can handle thousands. We can handle tens of thousands and hundreds of thousands.

Millions require a bit more concentration. But thanks to the federal government, we are learning to take this figure in stride. The same can be said of tens of millions and hundreds of millions.

Billions represent the upper limit of function for the normal human brain. Even with the help of Defense Department spenders, your average 9-to-5 American cannot grasp the reality of one billion dollars, let alone tens of billions and hundreds of billions. The only thing to do is take two aspirin and hope the pain goes away.

Government eggheads always try to help us understand, of course. They punch their calculators and feed us nonsense about how a trillion dollar bills, if laid end to end, would stretch from Earth to Venus.

As far as us hillbillies are concerned, those dollar bills could stretch from Earth to Venus to Pluto — and back. That's because we have no concept of distances in outer space. Newport to Del Rio by way of Highway 25, perhaps. But Earth to Venus? Forget it.

Which is not to suggest that we are ignorant. It's just that we see things from a different perspective than government statisticians do.

Oh, I suppose it helps to tell us that the precise budget figure of $1,094,200,000,000, divided by the January 1988 population estimate of 244,193,000, means $4,480 per man, woman and child. It's also very depressing.

We can better understand, and appreciate, if the budget is broken down into the units of measure East Tennesseans use every day. Here, then, are some easy-to-follow examples of what President Reagan's proposed budget will buy:

■ 45,591,670 executive skyboxes (at $24,000 per) in Neyland Stadium. This means that during a sold-out game (91,249 seats), every spectator would have 499 skyboxes apiece. With such spacious accommodations, you could invite all your friends and guarantee them a seat.

Obviously, it would be expensive as the dickens to feed that many people. We are talking tons of fried chicken alone. But thank goodness, you wouldn't have to buy liquor for them.

■ 36,473,340 bass boats, complete with the same number of four-wheel-drive pickup trucks to tow them to the lake. This estimate is based on a price of $30,000 for each boat-truck package.

Of course, things would get mighty crowded if those 36,473,340 bass boats and pickup trucks all headed to the same lake at the same time. In fact, tempers could flare in the heat of competition for casting room.

So let's say these boats were spread evenly across the combined surfaces of Fort Loudoun (14,600 acres at full pool), Douglas (30,400), Norris (34,200), Cherokee (30,300) and Tellico (15,860) reservoirs. That would mean a mere 290 boats per acre.

It also means 290 pickup trucks per acre at the launch ramp. Which is far less crowded than it was the last time I went fishing.

■ 60,788,900,000 front-row tickets ($18 each) to the Hank Williams Jr. concert this coming Saturday night at Stokely Center.

Once again, we can expect elbows in the face, for officials at Stokely tell me only 12,400 tickets have been printed for the entire event.

Big deal.

When it comes to Hank Jr. and his rowdy friends, it doesn't matter if 12,400 or 60,788,900,000 show up. There's going to be a fight, Bubba Joe.

Beating the system

May 1, 1987

Clearly, the man had tried to take his own life.

He was barely breathing when his limp, drug-ridden body was discovered. Nearby was a handwritten note asking that he be buried with some of his meager possessions.

This was not the first time he had attempted suicide. Only 30 days earlier, he had swallowed an overdose of pills. Between the two incidents, he had weakened his body by refusing to eat.

But this time, just like the last, his life was spared.

He was rushed to a hospital. Tubes were inserted into his nose and throat. His stomach was pumped. Within hours, he was conscious once again.

So what happened to the man who was plucked from the lip of the grave not once but twice? Funny you should ask.

Exactly one month later, he was led into a small concrete room. He was strapped into a chair. A hood was placed over his head. While 20 people watched, four steel-jacketed bullets were fired through his heart. At last, Gary Gilmore's death wish had been granted.

And in the eyes of the law, the deed had been the "right" way.

The "legal" way.

The "proper" way.

Gilmore was a confessed murderer, the first person to be executed in the United States after the U.S. Supreme Court lifted the ban on capital punishment. On Jan. 17, 1977, at Point of Mountain, Utah, after all the documents had been read, all the whereases and therefores pronounced, Gilmore calmly said, "Let's do it."

I didn't reopen the Gary Gilmore case to debate capital punishment. We'll postpone that until we've got five or six hours to talk — and then I'll probably change my opinion a dozen times. Still, I couldn't help but think about the last bizarre months of Gilmore's life when I read about Andrija Artukovic the other day.

Artukovic also is a condemned killer. He is imprisoned in Yugoslavia, convicted of war crimes and sentenced to die.

As interior-justice minister in the puppet Nazi state of Croatia during World War II, Artukovic controlled his own reign of terror. His methods of death were unconscionable, even by Nazi standards.

How bad?

Ask Aaron Breitbart, a senior researcher at the Simon Wiesenthal Center in Los Angeles. I interviewed Breitbart last year, shortly after Artukovic was deported from California where he had been living under an assumed name. Here is what he said:

"Hitler once sent officials to Jasenovac, Artukovic's favorite of the 20 concentration camps under his control. They reported how crude his methods were. Heads were put on anvils and smashed. Children were clubbed to death. People were fed caustic soda with their food. They even had throat-slashing contests — one person was said to have 'won' by slashing 1,250 throats in a single night."

Obviously, we're talking about a blue ribbon Nazi goon. That's why the Yugoslavs are eager, even 40 years after the fact, to see Artukovic stand before a firing squad.

That's the macabre irony of it.

Andrija Artukovic now is 87 years old. He is legally blind. He suffers from Alzheimer's disease and an aortic aneurysm. Because of his condition, a Yugoslav court has ruled his execution be postponed.

"A medical review determined that he is in no condition to be executed," the justices said.

So what officials hope to do is pump him full of medicine and get him well. Fatten him up, as it were. Then they will blow him to smithereens.

Sometimes, I wonder if the entire world isn't nuts.

Scaredy-cats and other party poopers

November 3, 1987

Here I am, a grown-up man, sitting in a grown-up office, typing on a grown-up word processor. And I'm eating a Tootsie Roll Pop.

Grape. I got the grape.

Berl Schwartz, my grown-up managing editor, wanted the grape. But when fellow staffer Susan Dawson held up the Tootsie Pops, I yelled first. Berl had to settle for cherry.

As I speak, he is leaning against a wall, a grown-up telephone in his ear. He is talking to another grown-up person while he licks a red Tootsie Roll Pop. If a stranger walks in, he's sure to think this place has been taken over by a bunch of cops named Kojak.

I have no way of knowing for sure, but I bet that in hundreds — nay, thousands — of grown-up offices across Knoxville these days, adults are eating Tootsie Roll Pops, Almond Joys, Milky Ways, Milk Duds and Sweet Tarts. They are polishing off the last of the Halloween sweets. These are the same sweets left in the bowl by the door Saturday night because only a handful of trick-or-treaters showed up to claim it.

I made a spot check about this matter over the weekend. Nothing scientific, you understand; just a question to several folks about the number of six-year-old spooks and goblins that came calling.

Almost to the person, they said the crowd had dropped appreciably. One woman, who said she used to give candy to 30 to 50 youngsters each Halloween, had not the first visitor.

Some of this decline is due to natural attrition. Obviously, as neighborhoods grow older, you can expect to see fewer and fewer children. But even in the heart of suburban Knoxville, I have a sneaking suspicion that trick-or-treating isn't as popular as it used to be.

Halloween is the one time of year when kids are perfectly free to behave like kids. They can dress in outlandish costumes and go from door to door begging for candy, and adults will laugh and give it to them.

At least that's the way it used to be.

These days, Halloween has been tainted. Ruined. And at the forefront of the assault are the very people who used to enjoy this holiday so much. We parents.

We have become a nation of scaredy-cats. We have taught our kids to mistrust others. We don't want them speaking to strangers. We are, in short, turning our children into a pack of paranoid freaks.

As long as there has been trick-or-treating, there have been ghouls who take advantage of the situation and prey upon children. Certainly, someone, somewhere has put needles into apples. Or given out Ex-Lax as chocolate drops. Or kidnapped trick-or-treaters. Or done any of the awful things we occasionally hear in the news on the morning after.

Nonetheless, I submit that the percentage of these barbarous crimes has not risen through the years.

Maybe we are more aware of the problem. Maybe more incidents have been reported. But when children's welfare is involved, I have enough faith in mankind to believe that 99 percent of the adults in this country would never intentionally lay a harmful hand upon a child.

Still, we panic. We catalog our children like prized bird dogs. We stamp identification numbers on their teeth. We keep their fingerprints on file. We fill them with awful stories about boogeymen who will snatch them off the street.

I am happy to report that neither of my children has been tooth- or fingerprinted. Nor any of my birds dogs, for that matter.

On the other hand, neither Venable child went trick-or-treating this year. I keep trying to convince myself they've grown too old to enjoy it.

Mum's the word

August 19, 1986

Let me see if I've got this straight.

First of all, research into "stealth" airplanes — ones that cannot be detected by radar and infra-red systems — has been going on for more than 20 years.

Second, the Soviets know we have a "stealth" fighter.

Third, something on the order of 40 of these super-duper F-19 jets are being tested in desert regions of the United States right this very minute.

Fourth, it quite likely was an F-19 that crashed in the mountains of California last month.

Fifth, the Testor Corp. has introduced a plastic model of the F-19 and is selling copies as fast as they can be delivered to toy stores.

OK. That much I understand.

So if the F-19 is such common knowledge, why does the Air Force keep insisting it does not exist?

It's like the emperor's new clothes, except in reverse. The peasants talk about F-19s and see pictures of F-19s and read stories about F-19s. But the rulers steadfastly maintain there ain't no such animal.

Just last week, the Pentagon's chief researcher ridiculed Testor's toy model. He said it was like nothing he had ever seen.

"My comment is that there is no F-19 program," Donald Hicks told members of Congress. "It does not exist."

Then how come Testor, the Illinois company which has been making plastic plane and car kits for years, knew enough about the aircraft to design a model of it?

"All the information came from public sources," Testor spokesman Steve Kass said in a telephone interview. "You can read reports on what's happening in magazines like Popular Science and Aviation Weekly. Our designer is an Air Force buff. He's been doing research in libraries. It's right there where anyone can find it."

The company makes a similar disclaimer on the box the F-19 model comes packed in:

"This authentic 1/48th scale F-19 Stealth fighter is based upon years of research. All specifications were obtained by the Testor Corp. from unrestricted public sources. Because it is a model, and critical full-scale internal components are not depicted, it does not expose any classified systems."

"We haven't had any problem from the government about this model," Kass added. "But this is not the first time a plane has been designed and flown before its existence was acknowledged.

"The SR-71 Blackbird spy plane was flying five or six years before the government announced it. We didn't introduce our model until 1983. It's still one of our most popular."

That is, until the F-19 hit the scene.

Kass became as tight-lipped as the Air Force when I asked him about sales. That was classified information. Competition from other toy makers, you know.

"Let's just say they're going to stores as fast as we can make them. If a store gets 24 today, they're gone tomorrow."

How well I know. Clay Venable, 13, is among the model airplane addicts who clamored for an F-19 of his very own. After finding empty shelves at several stores, he finally struck pay dirt at Kmart.

Clay's kit cost $6.87, plus tax. That's a total of $7.35.

Let's see, now. This is a 1/48th-scale model. So if I punch the price Clay paid into my calculator, and then multiply by 48, I should be able to determine the cost of a full-blown F-19, right?

(Clickety-click-click). That comes out to $352.80.

Gosh, no wonder those big cheeses in the Pentagon are mum. If I routinely wasted taxpayers' money on junk like $640 toilet seats and $435 hammers — and then discovered I could buy a jet fighter for a mere $352.80 — I'd be so embarrassed, I'd hide under my bed for a month and a half.

Effective communications

August 9, 1987

This occurred years ago, not long after I got married. My wife and I were driving down a road. I was behind the wheel.

Note use of the word "road" and not "interstate" or "highway" or "boulevard." The distinction is important, because what happened that day usually happens only on roads. It rarely happens on interstates, major highways, boulevards and other urban thoroughfares. Possible, but rare.

A car approached in the other lane. Just as it passed my window, Mary Ann said, "Why did you do that?"

"Why'd I do what?" I asked.

"You nodded at the man who was driving the other car. Except it really wasn't a nod. You sort of threw your head back and pulled it down. He did it back to you. What's that all about?"

"I was just saying howdy to him."

"Why didn't you wave?"

"You don't have to wave if you do this," I said, throwing my head back. "That's how you say howdy without using your hands."

"Then how come you don't do it all the time?" she said. "Sometimes, you don't do anything. How do you know when to nod and when not to nod?"

"You just do," I explained. "It's something good ol' boys learn as they grow up. It's like saying, 'Yes, ma'am,' and 'thank you' and 'Blue Ribbon.' You learn to say those things without thinking about them. It has to be a natural reaction or else it's no good."

"I don't understand," she said.

I could see this was not going to be easy. Knowing who to give the good ol' boy nod to, and when to give it, is involuntary. Trying to explain it is like trying to describe how your lungs know when to expand and contract.

"Maybe it has something to do with speed," I suggested. "People are going too fast on interstates and big highways. They can't establish eye contact. Out here on these small roads, it's easier."

"But I've seen you do it when you're not even in a car — like when you're walking on a sidewalk in town."

"Of course," I responded. "In fact, that's the best time. You can establish eye contact with another good ol' boy on a sidewalk. Next thing you know, your head is going back. His is, too."

"One more thing," Mary Ann said. "Sometimes, you utter a word. It sounds like, 'W'say.'"

"How observant you are. 'W'say' means, 'What do you say?' Sort of like when people ask, 'How do you do?' Is this making any sense at all?"

"Not really," Mary Ann replied. "But then again, there's a lot of things about you that don't make sense."

We drove on and dropped the conversation about good ol' boy nodding. But I felt it was necessary to relate that story so you could understand and appreciate what comes next:

A few days ago, I found myself at the King Street Metro station in Alexandria, Va. This is a subway stop where hordes of yuppie lawyers, business people and bureaucrats stand silently and read The Washington Post, The New York Times and The Wall Street Journal before climbing aboard and riding to their offices in Washington, D.C. We are talking a classic assortment of slicked-back, spit-shined humanity.

I was standing there, wondering how these people could live so bunched together, when something caught my eye on the railroad tracks behind the Metro station. It was over by the Amtrak depot, at least 75-80 yards away.

A slow moving freight train was passing by. I happened to glance up just as one of the engines cleared the depot. The engineer peeked out his window.

Without even thinking, I threw my head back.

He did the same thing.

If you don't understand the importance of that gesture, I'm sorry. But there, on the outskirts of our nation's capital, surrounded by a wall of concrete and chain link and adrift in a sea of pinstripes and brief cases, I found it very significant. And very comforting.

Nipping it in the bud

January 14, 1988

Officials of the Consumer Product Safety Commission are about to perform a feat that has stymied the best efforts of Congress, the American Medical Association, the American Heart Association, the American Cancer Society and the Southern Baptist Convention.

They're going to stop Americans from smoking cigarettes.

Read that last sentence again. I did not say these bureaucrats are going to "try" to stop millions from lighting their Luckies. I said they would succeed. You can bet the farm on it.

How will they accomplish this task?

By repeating the warnings about the hazards of smoking?

By publishing charts which show smokers live shorter, more sickly, lives than non-smokers?

By producing TV public service announcements illustrating the damage cigarettes cause to the heart and lungs?

Heavens no!

The people at the safety commission are taking a direct route. They intend to attack the problem at its source. Quite frankly, I'm surprised it took so long for folks, even if they do live in Washington, to latch on to this ingenious idea.

They're going to make a child-proof cigarette lighter.

Just last week, the safety commission announced an all-out campaign to make certain that cigarette lighters, especially the disposable butane ones, are constructed so they will be inoperable by a child.

Which means, of course, that no one over the age of 16 can work them.

Obviously, there is merit to the safety commission's decision. According to the federal agency, children playing with lighters caused 7,800 fires, 120 deaths, 860 injuries and $60.5 million in property damages in one year. Something has to be done.

That's the same sort of argument the safety commission used a few years ago when medicine bottles could be opened with a flick of the wrist. Too many children were being poisoned, the bureaucrats said. So with a stroke of the pen, medicine manufacturers were instructed to develop a child-proof container.

As we now realize, the resulting product was a miracle of engineering. If you have a headache these days, all you have to do is reach into the medicine cabinet and find a bottle of aspirin. Then you merely beat it with a hammer, twist it with pliers, gnaw on it with a hacksaw and run over it with your car. By the time the bottle coughs up two tablets, your headache is gone.

Of course, it will have been replaced by coronary arrest, stroke and nervous disorder, but that's a trifling matter. At least you don't OD on aspirin.

That's why I know the cigarette lighter campaign will be a huge success in just a couple of years. When that joyous day arrives, people all across this land will crush their Camels for the very last time. They'll have to do it because they won't have any fire.

You see, once the safety commission works its magic on cigarette lighters, not even an honors graduate from MIT will be able to operate one of the silly things. There will be so many elaborate steps in the torching process, people will say heck with it and kick the smoking habit.

Oh, I suppose a few old fogeys will revert back to matches; you can always count on a handful of survivalists to outlast anything. But since most of today's smokers grew up flicking a Bic, they won't realize that a three-cent pack of paper matches, or freebies from Joe's Diner down the street, will also do the job.

There's just one drawback.

Back when child-proof bottles came out, the only people who could figure out how to open them were six- and seven-year-olds. Once this law takes effect, the incidence of smoking among pre-teens is gonna skyrocket. Just you wait and see.

The nerds of '65

August 13, 1985

It was June 1965. Graduation time for some 325 seniors at "old" (it hurts to say that) Young High School.

Lyndon Johnson occupied the White House. Gemini astronauts James McDivitt and Edward White were walking in space. Knoxvillians were flocking to a World's Fair — in New York. And the Army announced seven servicemen had been killed in Vietnam, bringing the total dead to a staggering 403.

Here in Knoxville, Leonard Rogers was the mayor. Except we knew him as the husband of our algebra teacher.

You could buy a gallon jug of Weigel's milk for 73 cents, three pounds of Kroger ground beef for 99 cents, and three six-ounce packages of luncheon meat for 79 cents, friends and neighbors, at the sign of the shears and the name Cas Walker.

Rice Olds would part with a hot, new 442 for the outrageous price of $2,647.77. As the polyester plague had not yet struck, Penney's was stocked with all-cotton shirts for $3. Or you could get two for $3 at Kmart, even without benefit of a blue light special.

Not a single record in the top five featured a song by the Beatles. No. 1 was that classic toe-tapper, "Wully-Bully," by Sam the Sham. Others with high ranking included "Help me, Rhonda," by the Beach Boys and "I Can't Help Myself" by the Four Tops. Obviously, we needed a lot of help in those days.

Oops, pardon me. I didn't mean to wander off on such a random path of nostalgia. It's just that I've been in time warp the last few days. Twenty years of time warp, in fact. That's how long it's been since the Class of '65 flew out of the nest.

We got back together last weekend. And we behaved like Sixties reunionists everywhere.

We stared awkwardly at faces and glanced at name tags and shouted "Dennie!" or "Ann!" and hugged each other with a laugh.

We were shocked to discover how many of us have children in high school.

We poked fun at missing hair and bulging bellies.

We remembered the Optimist Bowl, the Jokers and Jivettes, the Biff-Burger, and that most-scandalous, scintillating song of all times, "Louie, Louie."

Reunions are great fun. When your number comes around, don't dare miss it. But in the excitement of peeling back the years, be prepared to have your emotions jarred. All of them.

You will bathe in happy times and sad ones. You will recall people and circumstances which make you laugh, also ones that make your palms sweat. Such is the nature of memories on the rebound.

From a 20-year perspective, what do I remember most about our class?

Probably how innocent we were. Really. I'm talking disgustingly squeaky clean. Idealistic to a fault. The kind of kids Norman Rockwell would have loved.

Drugs were something the doctor ordered, by prescription, when you caught a cold. There were occasional rumors of alcohol, but if the truth be known, I bet eight out of 10 had graduated before it ever touched their lips. Hair was cropped close and white-sidewalled around the ears. Shoes had a shine. Pants had a crease.

High crimes? Get serious.

Among the most heinous acts of barbarism you could commit were (1) puffing a Winston outside the smoking area, (2) blowing up a toilet with a cherry bomb, (3) rolling pennies down the aisle during study hall.

"You know what we were?" said one of my classmates. "We were nerds. All of us. Nerds! We were the people our kids laugh about today."

Yes, we were nerds. We were the last wave of conformists who crashed upon the shores of society. We missed out on Woodstock, bell bottoms, peace symbols, dope and free love. (Woodstock, bell bottoms, peace symbols and dope I can live without. But free love? Rats.)

Yet what is so crazy is that our parents, weaned on the Depression and full of Reader's Digest advice on the evils of modern teenagers, worried themselves sick about us. Now here we are, the Baby-Boomers, with children of our own. And we're worried sick about what might happen to them.

Weird, huh?

I just hope when my kids have their 20th reunion, they'll laugh at what nerds they were in high school. And I hope they'll be worried about my grandchildren.

A crisis a day keeps sanity away

March 29, 1988

It's not like I'm one of those survivalists you read about in magazines or see on TV.

I don't own an M-16 assault rifle or a Rambo knife with fishing hooks, matches and a compass hidden in the handle. Nor do I have an underground cache stocked with gold bullion.

As for feeding my face in a time of crisis? Forget it. It's hard enough for me to kill deer and ducks in the name of recreation. If I had to do it for outright subsistence, I'd starve.

Nonetheless, I still get chapped whenever I think how unprepared for emergencies we computerized, urbanized Americans really are. All it takes is one little glitch and our systems go haywire; then the only thing we know how to do is panic. It's enough to make Dan'l Boone's grave fairly quake in disgust.

I was reminded of this discouraging fact of life one summer afternoon when lightning struck a utility pole outside The News-Sentinel. In that instant, we were neutered.

Inside the building, nothing worked. We couldn't even sharpen a pencil because electric pencil sharpeners refuse to grind when the juice is off, no matter how much you scream and curse at them.

Our lights went out. Our phones went dead. Our desk-mounted computers went blank. Our air conditioner shut off.

Actually, that was a blessing, for we have a unique climate control system around here. In the winter, it blows cold air. In summer, it blows hot. So for once, we were comfortable.

There was nothing to do but wait. I walked outside and ventured up the street and happily discovered that the beer taps at the Buttonwood Cafe still worked. Thus, I was able to survive the situation in fine style.

The same sort of crisis happened a couple of days ago as I was driving to work. I had stopped at a gas station/convenience store for a cup of coffee. When I got inside, my steel trap mind told me something was amiss.

Frustrated customers were stacked up at the counter, money and goods in hand.

Bells from the gas pumps were going off everywhere, trying to remind someone to clear the switch so more gasoline could be dispensed.

And the poor woman behind the counter was in a mild panic.

She was talking to angry customers out of one side of her mouth. Out of the other side, she was speaking into the telephone receiver that rested on her shoulder. Both of her hands were buried in the bowels of the cash register, turning knobs and flicking switches.

"No, that still doesn't make it work," she said into the telephone.

The person on the other end gave her more instructions. She tried

them. For naught.

"You've got to get down here now and fix this thing!" she finally yelled.

Then she hung up the telephone and explained to everyone that the paper tape that feeds into the cash register was on the fritz. Because it wouldn't work, neither would the cash register. Because the cash register wouldn't work, the cash drawer wouldn't open. Because the cash drawer wouldn't open, she couldn't make change. Somehow, the gas pumps were also affected by this electronic illness and refused to yield so much as a drop. It was a madhouse.

Fortunately, most of us had correct change for our goods. The clerk had to record each purchase on a paper bag, just like they did 50 years ago at the general store. When I left, she was ready to hang CLOSED on the door until someone came to fix the stupid paper tape gizmo.

Now that I think about it, Dan'l Boone — who only had to worry about angry bears and warring Indians — didn't know how lucky he was.

The JACKWIF Syndrome

July 17, 1986

Twenty years ago this summer, I climbed aboard an airplane and headed for northern Idaho and a job with the U.S. Forest Service.

I was a sophomore at the University of Tennessee. A forestry major. I had been accepted by the Forest Service as a trainee — a.k.a. firefighter, tree-cutter, general laborer who would learn about his chosen profession from the ground up at minimum wage.

A holiday cruise to Cancun, it was not. I didn't need to worry about packing dress slacks and neckties. Instead, my duffel bag held the essentials for work: blue jeans, shirts, heavy socks, boots. Also included were two items for play: a fly rod and a deer rifle.

The duffel bag was so short, the rifle barrel and fly rod protruded from one end.

Surely they'll be damaged, I told the ticket agent. No problem, he answered. Just carry the duffel bag on board and stow it in the section where travelers hang their suit bags.

And that's precisely what I did — all the way from Knoxville to Idaho via two or three Midwestern cities, and then back again several months later when the job ended and I returned to school. I walked right onto all those airplanes carrying an exposed .30 caliber rifle, and not a soul so much as batted an eye. Fact of the matter is, I never gave it a second thought myself.

Impossible? Not in 1966. For this was before the JACKWIF Syndrome descended upon mankind.

Surely you've heard of the JACKWIFs. They're the Jerks, Airheads, Crazies, Kooks, Weirdos, Idiots and Freaks who have us by the throat.

The first thing the JACKWIFs did was stick pistols into the faces of pilots and order airplanes detoured to Cuba. Why Cuba, I never understood. Because soon as the plane landed, the JACKWIF in charge was whisked off to jail and left to rot amongst the cockroaches and rats, while the plane and passengers returned to this country.

Hijacking by JACKWIFs grew so popular, our entire air transportation system had to be changed. No longer could passengers simply board a plane. No longer could airports be peaceful depots.

To sift the one or two JACKWIFs from every 250,000 normal travelers, metal detectors were installed and security personnel hired. The price tag, passed along to passengers, has spiraled into the billions of dollars.

Then a few years ago, the JACKWIFs struck again. They poisoned Tylenol capsules. At least seven people died.

Once again, society was forced to undergo a complete change. Retailing would never be the same, thanks to tamper-resistant packaging of certain medicines. Chalk up a billion more dollars, and an equal number of fears, courtesy the JACKWIFs.

Now, this madness has spread to food products. In recent days, stores in many parts of the nation have been forced to clear their shelves of such items as gelatin mix and soft drinks. All of which means that packaging designers have new work cut out for them — at a cost of billions more dollars.

Where will it end? That's the awful part of this cruel story. There won't be an end.

That's because the JACKWIF "logic" runs like water flowing down an endless hill. It seeks the path of least resistance. If one avenue is blocked, it will merely find another.

Escape from the JACKWIFs is impossible. They will find new ways to haunt us, to terrorize us, to make us change our lifestyles.

And to think that 20 years ago, I walked onto a crowded airplane carrying a high-powered rifle and the only thing anybody said to me was, "Coffee or tea?"

The delights of autumn

October 9, 1986

I knew we'd make it.

No matter how long it took, no matter how many false starts flirted with us, no matter how many times we adjusted and re-adjusted the thermostat on the air conditioner, no matter how many gallons of sweat trickled down our cheeks, I knew fall weather would finally arrive.

Yes, there will be occasional backslides to August — the dying flutter of heat and humidity, as it were — from now until November. Indian summer it's called.

But that's OK. Let the mercury climb during the afternoon if it chooses. As long as I know the tropical grip upon our land has been broken, I can bear up just fine.

I like summer. Really, I do. Summer is a delightful season, one I could not live without. It's just that I don't need as much of it as a lot of other people.

My idea of a blast-furnace summer is for things to start heating up June 15, peak around the middle of July, then start cooling immediately. First frost by September 15 would be perfectly acceptable. And before you open your mouth, I've heard it from my wife a thousand times before: "So move to Minnesota, Slick. The kids and I will write often."

Why do I enjoy this season of the year? Simple. I can walk outside without wilting. I can breathe without drowning.

Autumn has many advantages over summer. Among them:

■ When the weather is cold, all you have to do is put on more clothes and you will warm up.

When the weather is hot, you can take off your clothes to get cool, but you run the risk of being arrested. Even worse, people will laugh.

■ When the weather is nippy, you can consume a breakfast of steak and fried eggs, hash browns, biscuits, gravy, jelly and gallons of coffee and feel great. Then you can split firewood, non-stop, until lunch.

When the weather is sultry, you nibble at watercress and feel too weak to lift a toothpick after the "meal" is through.

■ Old summer tennis shoes are a disgrace. They stink worse than a dead skunk. When the laces finally rot, you say good riddance and throw shoes and all away.

Old winter boots are a treasure. They smell like fine leather, an aroma enhanced by mink oil dressings. When the laces finally break, you spend half of the following workday searching through stores for another pair. Another pair of laces, I mean.

■ In fall, apples are real apples. They ripen on honest-to-God trees and have blotched skins. They pop when you bite into them, and they splash juice all over your face.

In summer, apples are made of wax. They ripen with the aid of chemicals and have unblemished, silky skins. They turn to mush when you bite into them, and they taste like Elmer's glue.

No, Elmer's glue doesn't taste that bad.

■ Grass must be cut in summer. Even on a cloudy day, this is sticky, nasty labor. It should not be visited upon humans, not even hardened criminals.

Leaves must be raked in autumn. This is a delightful chore, especially on a cloudy day. When little children have been exceptionally well-mannered, they should be rewarded by getting to help.

■ Certain summer sports — sailing and croquet, for example — move at the speed of the federal government. They're almost as exciting as watching bread dough rise.

Autumn sports — football and dove shooting, for example — are fast-paced and unbelievably exciting. Except at the University of Tennessee and when I'm behind the shotgun, respectively.

■ Summer is polyester slacks, a nylon shirt, a plastic raincoat and a film of vapor inside your sunglasses.

Autumn is corduroy jeans, a flannel shirt, a goose down jacket and a plume of vapor as you breathe.

Need more be said?

Is it broke?

April 25, 1985

"If you ever find something you like," my friend Ray was saying, "buy a gross of it."

"Why?" I asked.

"Because if it's any good, they'll take it off the market."

That discussion occurred one summer morning years ago. Ray was waxing eloquent on the virtues of a certain fishing lure. It was one he and I had caught a number of bass on.

I should have taken Ray at his words and purchased a lifetime supply that very day, for the next time I went to the store, those lures were missing.

"They don't make 'em anymore," the clerk explained. "At least not like the ones you're talking about."

He held up a lure.

"Here's how they look these days. They're supposed to catch bass better than before."

Which, of course, they did not.

I got to thinking about that incident the other day when I was in the grocery store. In the candy and cookie section of the grocery store, to be precise. There, amongst the Goo Goo Clusters and Little Debbies, was granola.

Granola? The trail food? The sensible alternative to junk snacks? The pine-bark-and-blackberry-briar mixture Euell Gibbons loved to munch?

You got it.

Except this "granola" bore scant resemblance to the product you remember from Earth Day 1970. It had been improved and Madison Avenue-ized. Which is another way of saying ruined.

Granola used to come loose, in a bag, and if you search through enough health food stores I suppose you can still find some like that. But years ago, packaging geniuses determined that more people would buy granola if it had a definite shape. So they added sugar, honey and corn starch and pressed it into a bar.

The metamorphosis did not stop there. Next came chocolate chips. Then peanut butter. Then marshmallows. Then graham crackers. Then the entire thing was dipped in liquid chocolate.

And before you could say "save the whales," the nectar of wilderness ecologists was transformed into a mainstay for zit-faced teenagers in Manhattan. At 200 calories a bar.

Nor is this an isolated case. Just look at the evolution of beer and soft drink cans.

When I was a boy, a hand-held implement — with one angled, pointed end — was required to punch holes in the top of cans. It was called, interestingly enough, a "can opener." Or, if you were bold and daring, a "church key."

Church keys were quite functional, but they had one serious drawback. They always got lost.

You'd be on a picnic, way up in the mountains, and pull a Schlitz from your trusty metal cooler. Then you would fumble for the church key, which was 47 miles away on the kitchen sink.

This left you with two options. You could pound the can with a sharp rock or try cutting off the top with a pocketknife.

Neither method worked satisfactorily. Either the beer spewed into a neighboring county or you sliced your fingers.

Then one day, a packaging genius — who obviously had grown weary of granola pursuits — devised the pop top can. Joy of joys! Church keys went the way of washboards and celluloid collars.

But wait! What about all those unsightly pop top tabs? The countryside was shin-deep in them. It wasn't even safe to walk barefoot to the mailbox.

No problem. Another genius, likely on the federal dole, designed a pop top tab that stays attached to the can.

Marvelous.

Well, almost marvelous. . .

The blasted ring is virtually welded in place. Unless you've got four-inch fingernails and the strength of a blacksmith, you cannot get the process started.

So how has technology solved the problem? By coming full cycle, of course.

I was struck by that fact not long ago while standing in the checkout line at WalMart. There, on the impulse item rack, was a small plastic device. Hand-held, slit on one end. The slit is so you can slide it under the pop top tab and crack it open.

The church key, redesigned for the '80s, lives on.

It's enough to make Levi Strauss spin in his grave every time some urban cowboy struts by in a pair of fancy Calvins.

Long green looks lovely

March 5, 1987

I used to make fun of old codgers who don't trust checks, credit cards, savings accounts or anything related to a bank.

You know who I'm talking about. They're the people who barely weathered the Depression and vowed never again to put their financial faith in anything except green paper that can be tucked into the pocket of their overalls.

These people always deal in cash. It doesn't matter if the purchase is a new car or a loaf of bread. They peel out a roll of bills, count off the proper amount and consider the case closed.

If they do accrue charges that cannot be paid at the time of purchase — say, a monthly telephone bill — they do not scribble a check and send it by mail. They drive to the phone company and whip out that same roll of George Washingtons and make sure they get a receipt stamped "paid in full."

Oh, and don't think for a minute their bankroll is stored in some vault downtown. Heaven forbid. They keep it between the mattresses or in a cookie jar or under a rock down by the springhouse.

Like I said, I used to get a kick out of their antics. I thought they were out of touch with the times, that their distrust bordered on paranoia. No more. Nor am I alone. Just ask anyone who put bucks in Southern Industrial Banking Corp. and ended up with a handful of dust.

The Butcher brothers and I never did business, thank goodness. But after what happened at the hardware store the other day, I have grown fond of our cookie jar for reasons totally unrelated to chocolate chips.

Actually, the hardware store was the final straw.

I had been harboring second thoughts about credit cards for the past few years, particularly since mail-order shopping became so popular. All you have to do is call a company's 1-800 number, place your order, read your credit card number aloud and hang up. A week or two later, UPS delivers the package and the tab shows up on your next MasterCard or Visa statement.

That's the way it works on paper, anyway.

But if the goods don't fit or you decide you don't want them half as bad as you originally thought, you have to send them back and hope your account is credited. The entire transaction might take a month — which means you must inspect each statement, line by line, month after month — until the matter works itself out. If a computer error is detected, it takes an act of Congress and the intercessory prayers of six bishops to right the wrong. Trust me.

So there I stood in line at the hardware store, about to buy grass seed and fertilizer with plastic money.

The clerk took my card. Instead of inserting it into one of those gizmos with a roller, she fed it into a telephone.

"It goes to Atlanta now," she said smoothly. "Your bill is automatically totaled down there."

The phone hummed and beeped. Then all of a sudden it ate my receipt.

The clerk said "drat" or words to that effect and made out another form. She fed my card back into the telephone.

"Wait a minute," I said. "All the machine did was eat my receipt. The numbers still went to Atlanta. How does it know this second form is a replacement and not a new purchase?"

"It just does," she replied.

My palms began to sweat. Common sense told me to throw a chair through the window and flee with my life. But, child of the computer

age that I am, I let her fill out a second form. This time, it was not eaten. I signed and left.

A few days later, I was back for some paint. The clerk recognized me.

"Remember when you were here and the machine ate your receipt?" she asked.

I nodded.

"I checked with the manager, and you were right! It *did* charge you twice after all, but we took care of it. Don't worry."

I smiled feebly and thanked her. Then I took the credit card I was holding, tucked it back into my billfold, paid with cash — and made sure I got a receipt.

My mattress may be a little lumpy from now on, but I'll just have to learn to adjust.

Big bro' is always watching

January 27, 1987

You may not be your brother's keeper, but USG Acoustical Products Co. certainly is.

USG Acoustical, a division of Chicago-based USG Corp., recently told its 2,000 employees they had to stop smoking. Or else.

We are not talking about puffing Pall Malls on the job. Since second-hand smoke has been proven harmful to those who don't indulge, many companies have instituted smoking zones or banned on-site smoking altogether. Which is great.

But USG Acoustical has launched a permanent, all-out war against employee use of cigarettes: off the job, at home, out on the lake, at the bowling alley, wherever.

The company says it made the stand to reduce the risk of lung disease among its workers. Those who don't fall in line "will be placing their employment in jeopardy," said USG Acoustical spokesman Paul Colitti.

Holy Benson & Hedges! All along, I thought only the federal government delighted in invading private lives.

This controversial order surely will wind up in court. And when it does — even though it pains me to side with smokers — I hope the company is told to deposit its crazy rule in a place where the sun don't shine. If not, here's what the nation's workers might expect one of these days:

(Knock-knock) "Uh, excuse me, Mr. Bigbritches. You asked to see me?"

"Yes, Zwieback. Come in and have a seat. I just got your report back from Health & Fitness. They pronounce you free from smoking. Good boy."

"Thank you, sir. I still don't think what the company did was fair, but my back is against the wall. Our third child is due and. . . ."

"Enough whining, Zwieback. We've been through that before. Now that we've cured you of smoking, there's a couple of other things we need to discuss if you expect to stay on board here."

"Beg pardon, sir?"

"It's that car you drive, Zwieback. The Pinto. Our boys down in Safety & Security have been checking statistics on the cars driven by employees. Don't you know if you get rear-ended, that thing's liable to blow to smithereens? That'll leave us to care for your widow and kids. We can't have it, Zwieback. Get a Buick by May 10 or you're out."

"But Mr. Bigbritches! You know I can't afford. . . ."

"Mind your tongue, son. You still value your job, don't you?"

"Yes, *(gulp)* sir."

"That's what I thought. Now, I understand you play softball on weekends, right?"

"Why, yes. In fact, I led the Midtown Giants in home runs last. . . ."

"That's history now. According to Health & Fitness, softball players incur 17.6 percent more lost-time injuries than the rest of our workers. You've got to quit the team."

"Quit the team? That's my only form of recreation!"

"You've never heard of checkers, son? Try it. It's calm and relaxing. But before we get into that, there's this matter of Sunday dinners at your mother's home. She's big on fried chicken, isn't she?"

"You bet, Mr. Bigbritches. She's the best cook in. . . ."

"Well, you and her both need to mend your ways. Our staff nutritionist tells me employees with a high cholesterol diet run a 38.2 percent greater risk of heart attack. You will eat yogurt and dried beans from here on out, understand?"

"Yogurt? Dried beans? Why, I'd just as soon throw . . ."

"Stifle it, Zwieback. That tongue of yours is about to get you fired. Now, there's one thing more. Your shirt."

"My shirt? What's wrong with a white shirt?"

"The color. The folks in Accident Prevention have come up with the latest numbers concerning clothing. They say white is too drab, that everyone needs to wear brighter colors so we aren't lulled into inattention and cause an accident. From now on, white is forbidden. You must wear red, orange or yellow."

"You mean I actually have a choice?"

"Of course, you idiot! Whatdaya think we're trying to do — run your life?"

Hard of hearing

December 5, 1986

Take it from someone who tried: Talking to God is not easy.

All along, I thought it would be a snap. Pat Robertson, Sun Myung Moon and Jim and Tammy Bakker seem to do it at the drop of a hat, for heaven's sake. But we mere mortals are not able to turn the trick without extensive training.

Brother Pat likes to discuss politics with God. In fact, the way Bro' Pat describes it, God is his personal political adviser. He provides sage counsel on when to call a press conference, what to say and how to rally the flock when signatures are needed on petitions.

Brother Sun and God dwell more on military matters. Just the other day, Bro' Sun said God had personally called upon him to straighten out the mess in Nicaragua. That stands to reason. Since Ronald Reagan & Co. fumbled the ball with the Contra slush fund, no one can blame God for taking his Nicaraguan advice elsewhere.

As for the Bakkers, God serves as a personal financial analyst. Personal, that is, in outlining what new and exciting fund-raisers to announce. The rest is up to those fine people in television land. Sister Tammy simply stands before the camera and cries a river. Then the money machine kicks into high gear.

But why not me? Just because I'm neither an evangelist nor politician nor cult leader nor TV preacher, does that mean God and I can't chitchat?

Apparently so. I tried diligently, but it just didn't work.

Right off the bat, I realized a busy newspaper office was not the best place to talk to God. Too many distractions — telephones and hollering people and the like. A quiet atmosphere surely would be better. A place, say, like a tranquil setting beside the lake. So I left my desk and walked straight to the car.

Well, almost straight. I saw two panhandlers coming down the street and had to duck into an alley until they passed. The nerve of those bums, shaking people down like that. They oughta be back in jail where they belong.

Then I had to sidestep a wino who'd passed out in the gutter. Sheeyew! Talk about gross. The guy was drooling all over himself. Smelled like he just fell off the meat wagon.

Finally, I got to my car and sped out I-40 for my long-awaited conversation.

Speaking of the interstate, have you noticed how the number of hitchhikers increases the closer we get to Christmas? There's everything from teenage girls to old geezers with scruffy beards; sometimes two men together, and you know what they have in mind.

I wouldn't dare pick 'em up, of course, because one of them's bound to put a knife in my throat. Besides, everybody knows they're diseased. I wish troopers would keep 'em shooed away from the roadsides. Sure as I'd hit one with my car, I'd get sued from here to eternity.

Anyhow, I finally reached the lake. I sat down on a stump and asked God how things were going. I also told him to advise me on matters personal, political and financial.

"Speak up, God," I said. "Lay it out like you do to Pat, Sun, Jim, Tammy and all the others."

He didn't say a word. At least if he did, I didn't hear it.

You see, the wind was whistling through the trees, and the waves were crashing against the rocks onshore. Overhead, a flock of crows twisted and turned, cawing noisily.

If that wasn't distraction enough, clouds started moving around in the sky. Every few seconds, sunshine would filter through and light up the place; then the cloud cover would close in again. 'Twas gorgeous, but it didn't help me hear God.

Disgusted, I gave up and drove home. By the back way, of course. Gotta stay off the main roads around Christmas if you expect any relief from those goody-two-shoes bell ringers at red lights.

So see there? I tried to talk to God. I really did. But I guess he was like some people I know.

Just not in a mood to listen.

One more time

August 11, 1985

Forgive me, readers and editors and journalism professors. With full malice aforethought, I am about to violate one of the basic tenets of our trade. I am going to address a timely topic after its timeliness has passed.

I am going to write about Hiroshima. Again.

I know everyone is tired of reading about Hiroshima and watching TV specials about Hiroshima and listening to radio reports about Hiroshima. I'm certain the world sighed happily when August 7 finally dawned so those of us in the news business world would start directing our attentions elsewhere.

That is precisely the reason Hiroshima cannot be forgotten. Aug. 6, 1945, is too important a date to stick back on the shelf and become lost in the dust of history.

It should be — it must be — branded onto the mind of every person on the face of this earth. If the events of that day are ever repeated, this tiny star we occupy will evaporate.

From a grisly, statistical standpoint, Hiroshima and Nagasaki were simply two events near the end of worldwide conflict.

Some 113,000 perished in the first atomic blast, an estimated 75,000 in the second. Five months earlier, Allied firebombs over Tokyo had killed 90,000, injured 125,000 and left 1.2 million homeless. Six months earlier, the non-military German city of Dresden lost an estimated 60,000 residents in two nights of bombing. Nor can we forget the terror of Dec. 7, 1941, when nearly 2,400 Americans died at Pearl Harbor, precipitating the United States' entry into the war.

Let those figures trickle off your tongue slowly. Say them aloud:

"One hunded thirteen thousand. Seventy five thousand."

Think about what these numbers represent. Think about the blood and flesh from an entire generation of human beings.

These were fathers and mothers, sisters and brothers. They were old men with wrinkled skin, laughing and telling stories. They were babies cooing peacefully in their cradles.

Was this horrendous loss of life necessary?

Given the unfortunate circumstances of the time, of course it was; if for no other reason than to show mankind, vividly, he now had the means to destroy his planet.

A friend and I were talking about Hiroshima the other day and imagined ourselves inside the "Enola Gay." Knowing what we know today, would we still pull the lever to open the bomb bay?

Yes, we agreed, we would. In war, it is thee or me, and may God have mercy on our souls.

But now, we are not at war. The United States and other superpowers of this globe sit atop mountains of megaton nuclear devices, cautiously waving the flag of peace. We speak softly, but, oh, what a stick we carry.

How can we ensure the stick is never swung again?

Harold Agnew offers a novel approach. At age 24, Agnew flew on the instrument plane during the Hiroshima mission. He later was director of the Los Alamos Scientific Laboratory. Read what he told "Time" magazine:

"Most of the decision makers have never seen a bomb. These guys talk about bombs — so many kilotons, so many megatons — but it doesn't mean anything to them. So I say maybe every five years every world leader should have to strip down — Mrs. Thatcher in her bikini and the other guys in skivvies — and watch a multi-megaton bomb go off.

"What'll impress them is not the flash, not the size of the cloud and not the boom. It's the heat. If they're 25 miles away, they will get very antsy, 'cause they'll get hotter and hotter, and they will worry that maybe somebody's made a mistake. The heat. Really scares the bejesus out of you. After that, the chances of their ever using a bomb would diminish rapidly."

Aug. 6, 1945. Let us keep writing about it and reading about it. And let us keep thinking about it.

If we do not, I fear God will peer down some day, watching his earth flicker, and shake his head sadly and sigh.

"Oh, well. Maybe things will work out better next time."

The breaking of a hero

December 20, 1985

Sometimes I think life would be a lot better if adults turned everything over to kids. I mean everything. Business, politics, religion, jobs, sports. The works.

That's because kids have not been tainted by knowledge. Their ignorance, indeed, is bliss. Maybe with a bunch of ignorant kids in charge of this globe, there'd be less red tape, far fewer ulcers, and two tons more goodwill. And maybe Roger Maris would have enjoyed a happier life.

I was barely out of grade school the summer Maris started his assault on Babe Ruth's home run record. That was 1961, about the time baseball's magic grip upon my life was over.

I still followed Cincinnati because it was my pappy's favorite team.

And I still played a few sandlot games with my brothers and friends. And I still went to see the Smokies at Bill Meyer Stadium every now and then. But truthfully, after Don Larsen pitched that perfect game in the '56 World Series and Yogi Berra jumped into his arms, everything else was anticlimactic.

Yet Roger Maris rekindled my interest.

At least he did enough for me to occasionally turn to the sports section of the newspaper or watch the 6 o'clock news on TV and see how he had fared. On October 1, 1961, when he stroked his 61st homer during the final day of the American League season, I was both happy and envious.

I was happy because he had done something no other person had done. Not even Babe Ruth. I was envious of him because he was, and would always be, a famous baseball player. A hero, loved and respected by all. Just like Babe Ruth had been.

Or so I thought.

It wasn't until Maris died of cancer last week, and I read stories of his career, that I really understood what a two-edged sword this honor had been. What should have been the happiest years of his life were stained with regret.

"It would have been a helluva lot more fun," he once told an interviewer, "if I had not hit those 61 home runs."

Maris' crime — and to some baseball fanatics, that's precisely what it was considered — was to have the audacity to challenge the record held by a legend.

Instead of being cheered, he was booed.

Instead of being the champ, he was the chump.

Perhaps Maris brought part of it on himself. He and sportswriters were not on the best of terms from the start. Add the cheerleading and booing which commonly flowed from press boxes in those days, and it's easy to see why the sores continued to fester. Maris certainly didn't help matters when he pushed aside autograph hounds, the very people who paid his salary.

Or maybe Maris' problem was his inability to handle success. Maybe he never could adjust to getting pricked by the thorns whenever he plucked a rose from the bushes.

Whatever the reason, it's obvious Roger Maris was far from the happy hero I always had pictured in my mind.

Oh, I know I'm being simplistic. I know there's no way life will ever be a smooth, happy trip. I know this truth, unfortunately, because I am an adult.

But it sure was a lot more fun back in the days when reindeer could truly fly and jolly fat men slid down the chimney with ease. And baseball players who broke home run records were heroes, loved and respected by all.

Now you're talkin'

February 28, 1988

If I had not read it with my own baby blues in my own hometown newspaper, I would not have believed it. But I saw it in The News-Sentinel. Thus, I know it is so.

A diction teacher in Detroit has offered to help ("hep," actually) people in Texas learn to speak.

Yup, podnah. You heard me right.

For a mere $225, Margo Manning will give six weekly lessons guaranteed to de-twang a Texas accent. She says she can teach people to drop their regional dialect, get rid of their drawl, pronounce words more fully, speak in a more clipped fashion and breathe from the diaphragm.

This, says Manning, is "efficient communication."

Bull.

It is teaching unsuspecting people how to talk like a Yankee, that's what it is. Anybody who would consciously pay $225 to sound like someone from Dee-troit has money to waste. Or else works for the federal government.

Certainly, there is merit in learning to tell one dialect from another. I wrote a column several years ago about a diction expert from here in God's country who was teaching other Southerners to be mindful of their "y'alls" when conversing with those from the shores of Akron, Toledo and beyond.

But this woman wants to teach Yankeeze, which everyone knows is a foreign language. What's more, she wants to teach it to Texans!

As we would say on the farm, that beats the hens rootin' in concrete. Next thing she'll probably want to do is change Davy Crockett's name to Bruce.

I used to have some wonderful neighbors from Detroit — Jim and Nancy McDonald. We remain good friends to this day, despite the fact they took leave of their senses a few years ago and moved to California.

When the McDonalds first arrived in Knoxville, we both faced a serious communications barrier. Fortunately, I was able to break down the wall by learnin' them to tawlk good.

It was tough at first. If Jim was thirsty and I asked if he wanted a drink, he was bad to say something like, "Yes, do you have any pop?"

Except he wouldn't say "pop" as in pop goes the weasel. He would say "paap," like he was holding his nose.

Under my gentle tutelage (I called it the ridicule method), Jim ceased this gross misuse of the Lord's chosen language. He learned that if you got thirsty and it was too early in the day for a beer, like before 6 a.m., you asked for an RC, a Coke or a Big Orange bellywash. You would die of a loathsome disease before you'd ask for a "paap."

Next, I learned him good about food.

Until Jim and Nancy moved to Tennessee, these people — I am

embarrassed to mention it — had never tasted okra. They weren't even sure what it was.

Think about this for a moment. Here were two people, both college-educated, who had lived 30 formative years and had begun a fine family. Yet not once had this nectar of the gods passed their lips. And people have the nerve to call us disadvantaged in Southern Appalachia.

But I changed all that. Or I should say Mary Ann did. One mess of her fried okra and the magnolia blossoms fairly drifted from the McDonalds' fingertips. Jim fell so deeply in love with fried okra, he started putting it on his pizza.

I have not talked directly to the McDonalds in several years. We converse by letter from time to time, but it's hard to tell if they have started backsliding and returned to that awful Yankeeze in daily communication. Even worse, I'd hate to find out they were now speaking the valley talk of California.

You know, like it would totally bum me out. I mean, like gag me with a spoon, man.

The farce of Fido's food

May 22, 1988

You gotta wonder about a country where the people go hungry and the dogs are pampered with special diets.

I think about this every time I pick up a newspaper and read where some richer-than-sin pet owner has kicked the bucket and bequeathed $2.7 million to Fido. Invariably, the will specifies that the mutt shall live in luxury until its dying breath.

C'mon. Do you really believe it turns out like that?

If I were named executor of such a will, I would set aside $50 a week for choice cuts of meat. Then I would spend the remainder on a far more worthy cause. The Venob Equitable and Laudable Fun Fund and Traveling Ministry, for instance.

But even if they don't wind up with a major inheritance, most dogs in this country — cats, too — live better than human beings in many parts of the world. Of course, in countries where dogs and cats are frequently served as the main dish, I suppose these animals are happy to simply see another dawn, but that's neither here nor there.

I have just finished reading a full-page advertisement for dog food. It was the kind of food for old, overweight dogs. I didn't know whether to laugh or cry. So I did both.

I'm sure some Ivy League economist could calculate how many billion dollars the dog and cat food industry pumps into the American billfold each year, but I'm really not interested. All I know is that ads for porky pooches are the most laughable export from Madison Avenue since testimonials by hemorrhoid sufferers.

First off, these commercials violate every rule of diet food marketing. They depict a fat dog. If I were an animal rights activist, I would make up a bunch of ugly signs and protest this cruel exploitation.

When have you ever seen a diet food ad for humans that shows a two-ton Tessie?

Never.

That's because the big cheeses in foods and advertising want to give you the impression that using their products will make you slim, not fat. Wouldn't you think twice about buying a six-pack of Tab if you saw Chef Paul drinking it with his seven-course supper?

Second, why all the fuss about how great a dog food tastes?

Do you think, even for a half-second, that a beast which rolls around in dead carp and sniffs where it and other dogs have recently sprinkled the shrubs gives a flying flip whether his supper tastes like real beef?

Which brings up another point: If taste is such a big factor, what is the purpose in telling humans? We don't eat the stuff, for Pete's sake.

Telling humans how marvelous a Bark Burger tastes makes about as much sense as the sign I recently saw on a restaurant door: "We have braille menus." Fine. But if you are blind, how can you read the sign?

I would love to talk to the people who actually taste-test dog food. On second thought, maybe not. I bet they'd have a worse case of bad breath than the winner of a ramp-eating contest.

Finally, the choice of dogs used in commercials continues to perplex me. These animals are always so cutesy and obedient.

Why don't the ad makers weave some truth into the script and show us a mutt that chases the mailman, chews up your best pair of golf shoes, digs in the garden and leaps on your new tan suit just as you leave for work?

Oh, one more thing. How come you never see a pit bull in a dog food commercial?

Heavy Chevy rides again

April 7, 1988

I saw a 1955 Chevrolet for sale the other day and immediately spotted a number of things that were amiss.

First, it was the wrong color. It was candy apple red. A '55 Chevy should be midnight metallic blue.

Second, it had an automatic transmission. How utterly tasteless. Anyone with an ounce of class knows that a '55 Boss Hogg Heavy Chevy should not come equipped with one of those sissy transmissions that says "P-R-N-D-L."

Instead, it should have a three-speed Hurst shifter, preferably mounted in the floor and fitted with a chrome-plated knob. That way, when you pull out of Babe Malloy's parking lot, the stub of a Lucky Strike dangling from your lips, you can squall your tars and impress all the girls. They love it.

Third, it had the wrong price. The owner had originally asked $12,500, then carved it down to a cool 10-grand.

The last time I checked, which doesn't seem like more than a year or so ago, you could buy all the '55 Chevrolets you wanted for less than $750, plus maybe an extra hundred or two for a new engine that you and a friend could install on Saturday mornings.

The reason I know so much about these matters is that I used to own a '55 Chevy. This was long before a 1955 automobile qualified for antique license plates.

It was midnight metallic blue, of course. With dual exhaust. And a 283 cubic-inch engine with a four-barrel carburetor that made this car so fuel-inefficient it may bear sole responsibility for launching Ralph Nader's career.

Why own such a beast?

Bite your tongue, stranger. You ain't from around these parts, are you? Otherwise, you would know it is the patriotic duty of every teen-aged male from the clay hills of East Tennessee to own a redneck car.

This is drag strip country, son. Dirt track country. A land where grease and oil and loud engines make the man. This truism has particular application to those of us who matured (I use the term loosely) south of the river during the Sixties.

All I have left of my midnight metallic blue '55 Chevy is a faded photograph in an old shoe box. I'll never know what happened after I regained my senses and exchanged it for a Corvair. When I go for culture shock, I go all the way.

It wouldn't surprise me to learn it had been crushed and melted into steel for another car. Maybe two, considering the length of time since Back Then.

Which is fine. I am quite content these days to putter around in my old pickup truck or Mary Ann's sewing-machine-of-a-compact-car. Speed and squalling tars are not nearly so important as they used to be, and for that I repeatedly thank my blessed guardian angel — even though I was too young to appreciate it at the time.

But when you are 18 years old and Miss Baby Cakes is cuddled beside you in the front seat (usually) of your souped-up '55 Chevy and the Four Tops are blaring from the radio, you are king of the road.

And then when you travel deep into the outer reaches of Pennyrile or Neubert Springs and unscrew your cut-out pipes and blast the peaceful surroundings with the undiluted exhaust of a V-8 engine . . . well, Heaven simply knows no sweeter sound.

The guy at the car lot where the $10,000 Chevy is for sale told me I could take it for a spin.

I didn't have to ponder at length. Thanks, I said, but no thanks.

All my '55 Chevy happenings took place a long, long time ago in a land not-so-far away. Much better to leave things well enough alone.

But dang if I didn't have a sudden craving to fire up a Lucky Strike and turn on the radio.

Baaaby, I need your lovin'; got t'have all your lovin'. . .

Ain't that jest like the govermint!

August 29, 1985

Dear Cuzzin Clem:

Thangs is fine here in jail. Oh, the food ain't too good. But hit's free, and they's enough of hit where I don't go hongry. Which is more'n I can say fer vittles around home. But that ain't why I'm ritin.

This is the 12th time I been throwed in the jailhouse for makin likker. Seems like ever time I git my still set up in the holler, some fool revenoor or sheriff comes along with his ax and chops the thang all to Hale and hauls me to jail.

Then the jedge, he tells me how bad hit is to make likker and how much hit eats your guts and how hit's agin the law to run hit. Well, the jedge, he orter be an xpert, 'cause he's drank enouf of my likker to know. But I didn't rite this letter to talk about that jedge or any other jedge. Shucks, they's my best customers.

I been readin some newspapers here in jail. And son, I done found us a way to make likker and not be bothered by the govermint. In fact, the govermint will pay us to do it!

Here's the way it works: All along, I thought the TVA was in bizness to take streams and make lakes outter them. They musta run outter streams to make into lakes. 'Cause hit sez rite here in the newspaper I'm a-readin that the TVA is givin $50,000 to Grundy County to help set up a winery. One of them high-fashion "community development programs," they call it.

And that ain't all. The state's done put up another $150,000. Cash dollars. That $200,000, son! To make likker!

And that's jest the start, Cuz.

The govermint wants to make a turist attrakshun out of that winery. They want to plant grapes along Interstate 24 up near Monteagle so's the people from the flatlands can stop by and ax us to talk funny. And they want to build a gift shop so's the flatlanders can give us their cash dollars for them thangs we git from Japan.

Son, with a deal like that, you can't lose. I don't care if the govermint is behind hit!

Yeah, I know that ol' sissy wine ain't got the punch of my likker. But when you stop to thank about hit, I never did hear of nobody gettin jake laig from homemade wine. So I reckon thangs ain't all bad.

Besides, Clem, you gotta admit they's a lot bigger market out there that we ain't been a-tappin. They jest ain't as many likker drinkers as they used to be. Everbody's drankin white wine and them fancy wine coolers and stuff like that, so mebbe we orter get our share of the sellin.

Shucks, Clem, if the govermint's puttin up the money and not tearin thangs up with their axes, hit don't matter to me if I make white wine or white lightnin.

So you jest lay low til I get outter this jailhouse. Ain't got but four more months to serve. Mebbe less, if the jedge gets the jug Aunt Sadie was supposed to deliver over by the courthouse.

Lissen to what I say, boy. Don't you be messin with no more likker til you hear from me. I'll do some more readin and'll try to figure how to go bout gettin some of that govermint money.

And whatever you do, Cuz, stay outter the mariwanna patch. If you don't, some fool sheriff'll bust you up side the haid and burn the crop and you'll end up in the jailhouse with me.

Jest bide your time, boy. Afore you know hit, they'll be a-payin us $200,000 to grow dope, too.

I wanted to name this particular chapter "Woe Be Unto Anyone Unfortunate Enough To Be Related To A Columnist."

But then I realized that unless the book is large enough to hang off both sides of a card table, that sort of title wouldn't fit.

Nonetheless, it is true that the families of writers lead miserable lives. They are subjected to lengthy periods of moodiness, depression, anger, despair, rage and hopelessness. And that's during the good times.

Even worse is the fact that members of a writer's family have no private life.

If Pearl Culveyhouse, wife of truck driver Roscoe Culveyhouse, makes an embarrassing mistake or says something sickeningly cute, it is tucked away in Culveyhouse family history and never paraded around except during small family gatherings. But if the same thing occurs to the people in a writer's family, they can expect to see it revealed to hundreds of thousands of total strangers.

Perhaps this helps explain why I occasionally spend the night curled up beside my bird dog.

Out in the kennel.

Chapter VIII
A family affair

The Venable look

August 15, 1986

If I can round up enough candles, I just might bake a birthday cake for my dear ol' Grandfather Brown.

Aaron V. Brown, that is. If Gramps Brown was still with us, he'd be 191 years old today.

Brown was governor of Tennessee from 1845 until 1847. He's the man who set the stage for Tennesseans to earn their nickname. During the Mexican War, he issued a call for 2,800 soldiers. Instead, some 30,000 showed up, and we've been known as Volunteers ever since.

How come I know Aaron V. Brown and I are related? Because of his middle name. The "V" stands for Venable.

When you own a weird name like Zweinstein, Ruskenwalter or Venable, you notice things like that. You assume anyone else named Zweinstein, Ruskenwalter or Venable is kin to you somewhere along the line, because there are so few of your breed in existence.

Over the years, I have learned that we Venables earn our livings in closely related vocations.

When I was writing outdoor news, I discovered that back in merrie olde England, there was a Robert Venables who was an advisor to Izaak Walton, the father of sport fishing.

About the same time, I stumbled upon the byline of Clark Venable. It took some probing, but I found out he was a deceased outdoor writer who had followed the bird dog circuit shortly after the turn of the century.

And although there are only a handful of us, we Venables strive for excellence in our chosen fields.

In Atlanta, for example, there is a James Venable. He is Grand Wizard of the Ku Klux Klan. And in Cincinnati, there lives one Max Venable. He is an outfielder with the Reds.

I would pay $50 to see those two Venables meet at a family reunion. In all likelihood, Cousin James would jump right out of his sheet when he found out Cousin Max is black.

Sometimes, having the name Venable can be a real liability. Like the night I got a call from Hank Hill, a lawyer in Chattanooga. He was representing a man charged with murder.

"I need to get a statement from you about it," he said.

"About what?"

"The murder you witnessed."

"C'mon, who is this?"

"I assure you this is not a joke," Hill replied. "You are Sam Venable with The Knoxville News-Sentinel?"

"Yes."

"Well, the Chattanooga police tell me you're the one who gave them the information."

I told Hill I hated to spoil his case, but I didn't know anything about a murder in Kookamonga, let alone Chattanooga. How the cops got my name, I'll never know.

Hill hung up and never called again. Out of curiosity, I phoned him a year or so later.

"The Sam Venable we were looking for turned out to be a salesman who lived in Georgia," he told me. "Someone in the police department knew your name and figured you were the same man. Sorry for the mix-up."

Whew!

But even when there is confusion about the name Venable, there is a sure-fire way to clear it up. All of which brings me back to dear ol' Gramps Brown.

In most history books, Gov. Aaron V. Brown's middle name is Venable. But in one — "The Governors of Tennessee" by Margaret Phillips — the "V" stands for Vail.

A phone call to the State Library in Nashville settled the issue once and for all. It's Venable, they said.

But nobody had to tell me that. Because the more I read about Gov. Brown, the more I was convinced he and I had to be related. Straight blood kin, in fact.

How come?

Because the Honorable Aaron Venable Brown — Congressman, postmaster general and governor of Tennessee — was known to his friends as "Fat."

Footprints in the sand

August 4, 1985

ST. AUGUSTINE, Fla. — When first she came to the ocean, she was two.

She tottered awkwardly along the beach, leaving tiny baby footprints that quickly disappeared in the cool, wet sand.

She was afraid of the ocean then. It was too awesome a body of water for one who scarcely had seen beyond the confines of a bathtub. Its waves, even the gentle ones, swept her off her feet and ground her into the sand. Its brine stung her eyes and she cried.

But even the mighty ocean is no match for a daddy's hand.

So she would cling to her daddy's fist, and they would dance together in the surf. He would hold her to his chest and let the waves pound against their bodies and she would not be afraid.

The brine still stung her eyes, but she cried no more. For her daddy could make it all seem like so much fun.

"Do 'gin, daddy!" she would shriek. "Do 'gin!"

And so they would. Again and again and again.

When next she came to the ocean, she was eight.

She left girl-sized footprints on the beach and giggled gap-tooth, little-girl giggles as the outgoing current melted sand from beneath her feet.

The ocean was just as awesome as it had been before, but now she was not afraid. Not even from the start.

She and her daddy still danced together in the surf. She still clung to his chest and laughed as the waves pounded against them. They would swim offshore and catch the tops of the breakers and ride the foamy roller coaster back to the beach.

The brine hardly stung her eyes this time. All she could think about was laughing and shrieking and playing in the waves with her daddy.

Again and again and again.

And now she comes to the ocean once more.

It is daybreak on a stunningly beautiful summer morning. Her daddy stands on the balcony, five stories above the Atlantic, and watches his little girl walking alone on the beach.

Except she is not a little girl any more.

She is a young lady, blossoming into full womanhood almost by the minute.

No longer does she totter, leaving awkward baby footprints in the cool, wet sand. Hers is a graceful gait. So delicate, so feminine.

Her daddy stands there in the morning breeze and sips his motel coffee and watches the waves devour his lady's footprints, one by one.

He knows they will dance together in the surf this day and let the waves pound against their bodies. And that they will swim offshore and catch the tops of the breakers and ride the foamy roller coaster back to the beach and laugh and shriek as always.

And that they will do it again and again and again.

But he also knows little girls don't stay little forever.

Perhaps that explains why this time, the brine is stinging his eyes.

Shy Sammy

February 14, 1984

All I wanted was a set of cap pistols, one of those double-holster Hopalong Cassidy outfits like all the other boys at Mooreland Heights School wore around their waists.

I had lobbied hard at Christmas. But when you are eight years old and possessed of parents who frown upon toy guns, Santa Claus is forever fresh out of firepower.

But Christmas was now history. Valentine's Day was nigh. Which meant there would be another opportunity for gentle, subtle hinting.

Such as, "I want a double-holster Hopalong Cassidy outfit for Valentine's Day."

As I contemplated the package on Valentine's morning, I knew additional pistol pleas would be required before my birthday. The present before me was heavy enough, but it was short and dumpy. A set of pistols should be long and flat.

Clinging to my last vestiges of optimism, I decided they had bought me a single-holster outfit. Better than no gun at all, I reasoned. So I closed my eyes and tore into the red paper.

It was a birdhouse.

How do you slap leather with a birdhouse? Who would reach for the sky if you were wearing a birdhouse on your belt? Geeez.

Unfortunately, I seem to step square into the paint bucket nearly every time February 14 rolls around.

Oh, not at first. I was always big into giving valentines in grade school. So was everyone else. The system operated smoothly.

We'd each tote 30 cards to class, stuff 'em into the box, dole 'em out at the party that afternoon and tote 30 new cards home.

Then in early high school, Cupid's arrow pierced my hide. . .

Shy Sammy rode home on his bike and waited for that cute little Hill girl in Mrs. Runion's class to call and coo her thanks.

The phone never rang.

"Did you give the deliveryman her name?" Shy Sammy's sainted mother inquired.

"No, ma'am."

"Did you give him your name?"

"No, ma'am."

"Did you write her a sweet note?"

"No, ma'am."

"What *did* you write?"

"The address."

"Boy," she said, "you got a lot to learn about the process."

After two hours, Shy Sammy called the cute little Hill girl.

"Did, uh, you get, I mean, did it, uh, did the, you know, the candy, did it get there?"

"Oh, *that's* what it's all about!. . . Hey mom! I found out where this stuff came from!"

"Didn't you, uh, realize it was, I mean, didn't you know I, uh, sent it to you?"

"Heck no! Nobody could figure it out. Mama thought it was from Daddy and he thought it was from her and I thought it was from them. We've all had a good laugh out of it. You know, boy, you got a lot to learn about the process."

Fortunately, Cupid was in a benevolent mood. The cute little Hill girl has been a Venable for nigh unto 15 years.

Yet embarrassing as it was at the time, that incident pales in comparison with Valentine's Day 1983.

On that fateful day last year, dear hearts, when you were sniffing roses or fingering through a Whitman's Sampler, love was the farthest thing from my mind.

Teams of radiological technicians had me broken down across a metal table in the basement of University Hospital. They were introducing all manner of vile instruments and solutions into a very private and sensitive portion of my chubby little body. They were trying to determine what had gone wrong with my digestive system.

At the same moment, several miles to the east, teams of bank examiners faced Jake Butcher across a walnut table on the top floor of the UAB Building. They were introducing all manner of writs and warrants into a very private and sensitive portion of his chubby little ledgers. They were trying to determine what had gone wrong with his financial system.

I may have been in a gown and Jake in a three-piece suit, but we both experienced the same sensations.

A night at the ball park

June 21, 1981

My old man called 'em right every time.

No matter if it *was* the bottom of the ninth, bases loaded, two men out, Knoxville down by three. No matter if the crowd *was* standing and clapping. No matter if the pitch *was* a sluggish drifter that hung in space and begged to be slapped across the fence.

At the crack of the bat, my old man would watch the arc begin. Then he would rise to his feet for the walk to our Studebaker.

"Too high," he would shrug.

I could never understand his logic. Here was a baseball that was surely on its way into orbit, and he was not even excited. I would watch it sail into the night, confident it would not fall to earth for an hour and a half.

Then the centerfielder would trot forward and calmly pick it off.

Twenty-five years of summer nights have elapsed since then. The South Atlantic League is history. The crew-cut Smokies of the Fifties withered on the vine, died, were reborn as long-maned Sox, and now play as Blue Jays. The kid brothers who shared my belief that every pop fly was a home run have scattered with families of their own. And our old man is gone.

But I wish he could have been with me the other night at Bill Meyer Stadium, Knoxville versus Charlotte. I know he would have loved it.

You see, I turned the tables on tradition this year. Gave myself an early Father's Day present. I took my own son to see his first baseball game. And I can hear my old man laughing now.

"Who is Bill Meyer?" eight-year-old Clay asked as we walked from the truck to the gate. "Is he a baseball player?"

"Can't remember," I replied. "I think he might have been. There's a plaque about him inside. We can read all about him."

So much for good intentions. The popcorn line was more inviting. And much too long. I finally persuaded Clay that we would try again after the game started.

It would not have mattered to me if they were giving out hundred dollar bills for every other seat in the house that night. My son and I were headed for the same place where my old man and my brothers and I used to sit.

Near the top. Just to the left of home plate. I could find it in the dark.

No sooner had we plopped down that Clay announced that he had to visit the john. Back down we went. Yes, the popcorn line was still too long.

It was top of the second when we returned. Time for me to start tutoring.

I told Clay to watch the pitcher and how he would look for a signal from the catcher. He asked why the fence had advertisements painted on it.

I told him to watch the infield and outfield and see how they reacted to each play. He asked if the pigeons ever pooped on anyone.

I told him to watch the third-base coach and see how he licked his fingers and touched his cap and patted his knee to signal the runner. He asked if the popcorn line was still too long.

I told him to watch all the action carefully, that there would be no instant replay to show what he had missed. He asked if we would get back home in time to see "The Dukes of Hazzard."

We took our seventh-inning stretch a bit early. Halfway through the third, to be exact. I left Clay to see the game or watch the pigeons or whatever else he might be interested in and said I'd go fetch us some popcorn.

I walked downstairs, savoring the smells and sounds of the old concrete stadium. Here was a place that had not changed one iota during the last quarter-century. Alas, the line had not changed either. After 15 minutes, I finally made my way to the front and learned they were sold out of popcorn.

Back upstairs, I told Clay that we didn't have long lines to worry about when I was the son at baseball games. All that wholesome junk food was sold in the stands by a guy my old man used to call Friend. My brothers and I called him Orange Drink because that's what he was yelling all the time.

Once, Orange Drink was standing close to us when a Knoxville player did something spectacular. I forget whether it was a diving catch or a last-inning home run or what. But I do remember that Orange Drink was watching and got caught up in the excitement. He started waving and jumping and cheering right along with everyone else — except that he never quit hollering *"orange drink!"* at the top of his lungs.

Tell me why an incident so brief and insignificant can be branded onto the minds of children. I cannot fathom the rationale. But I will promise you this: I have a brother who lives in New York City. I will bet you a beer that I could get within 50 yards of him on the noisiest street in town and holler *"orange drink!"* and he would know that big brother had come to visit. Such are the good and noble things you learn when your old man takes you to the ball park.

Enough nostalgia. Clay wanted to climb to the top of the stadium and look down upon the cars. When you are eight years old and are standing at the top of Bill Meyer Stadium, you are gripped by the same emotions Sir Edmund Hillary must have felt when he reached the summit of Mount Everest.

I know. So I turned in my seat and watched him peer out across the world.

The crack of a bat brought me back to reality. Willie Royster of Charlotte was sending one over the fence. Clay missed the whole thing.

That one bothered him. He had wanted to see a real, live home run. He scampered back to his seat — over the chairs, not via the aisles — and kept his eyes glued to the action for at least half an inning.

No homer — and "The Dukes of Hazzard" was drawing close.

"Wanna go?" I suggested.

"Yeah," he answered, "I guess so."

No matter the outcome. The man on TV would tell us later — after "The Dukes" had gone off — that Knoxville had dropped another one, 5-0.

We started down the steps, hand in hand, a king and his prince on an honorable mission in life. About that time, someone else walloped a pitch with a lick so loud it must have been heard on Magnolia Avenue.

"There it goes, Dad!" Clay shrieked. "A home run!"

"Nope," I shrugged, "too high."

Killer toothbrushes

November 21, 1985

Technology is a lot like salt. You need a touch of it every now and then to improve the taste of life. Too much, though, is disastrous.

That is why I haven't bought toothpaste in a pump dispenser.

Until just a few years ago, toothpaste came packaged in a metal tube. The first few times you squeezed it, everything was OK.

But the longer the tube was milked, little creases would start to develop in it. In a few more days, one of these creases would rupture and send a curl of toothpaste onto your hand. When you put the tube on the shelf, toothpaste would start drooling out. By the next morning, you had one fine mess.

Then someone perfected the plastic toothpaste tube, and happiness reigned throughout America. No more Gleem creases. No more Colgate hands. No more Crest pools on the bathroom shelf.

You'd think people in charge would leave well enough alone. But they didn't. They had to invent the pump.

On the surface, a pump toothpaste dispenser makes sense. With one finger, you can deliver a carefully metered dose to your toothbrush. No more mess. No more unsightly, curled tubes on the shelf.

But what the toothpaste people didn't realize was that the soap people had already beaten them to the punch. Since bathrooms across America already are filled with pump dispensers of hand soap, who would want to run the risk of also having one for toothpaste?

With pumps of toothpaste and soap sitting side by side, it would just be a matter of time before someone stumbled in half asleep and squirted Ivory onto his or her toothbrush. Or tried to scrub his or her hands with Aim.

Trust me when I issue this warning. Such a mixup gave my Grandpop Spencer a horrible case of bad breath.

This occurred more than 50 years ago, when pumps were located outside the house and dispensed neither toothpaste nor soap.

Grandpop was an L&N railroader who lived in the tiny Campbell

County community of Chaska. He went to brush his teeth one night, but he didn't bother to light a lantern.

Instead, he just patted along the shelf until he located a metal tube. He squirted something on his brush and shoved it into his mouth. That's when Grandpop Spencer discovered he had grabbed his shaving cream tube by mistake.

He spat and rinsed his mouth. Then again. And again. Nothing would remove the soapy taste. Nothing, he reasoned, except Lavoris. So he patted around some more until he located the Lavoris bottle.

Being a railroad man, Grandpop Spencer was quite conscious of safety. He did not err often. But when he did, it was a doozy.

Before he unscrewed the bottle cap, he had the foresight to strike a match. Sure enough, he did have the Lavoris bottle. And sure enough, the stuff inside was red.

So he blew out the match, opened the bottle, took a long pull and started to gargle.

That is when Grandpop made his second shocking discovery of the day — that Granny Spencer had filled the old Lavoris bottle with red cedar oil for polishing furniture.

Bad as it was, I suppose Grandpop should have been happy for small blessings. At least he blew out the match first.

If not, the house might have gone up in flames.

The Big Four-Oh!

May 22, 1987

You will do one of two things when you read the second paragraph in this column. I just know you will. So get ready:

The day after tomorrow, I turn 40.

If you are older than I, you will click your tongue against your teeth and sigh wistfully, "Lord have mercy. What's that boy fretting about? He ain't nothing but a child. I wish I was 40 all over again."

If you are younger, you'll click your tongue against your teeth, too. And you will also make an utterance. But instead of a wistful sigh, it'll be a statement of shock. Something like, "You mean he's 40? Gad, what an old goat! Reckon they make him drink prune juice every morning before he leaves the rest home?"

That's the way we all react to news of someone else's age. We cannot help ourselves. It's the nature of the beast. None of us — not one single, solitary person — is immune.

When we were kids, we hated it when Aunt Maudie pinched our cheeks and gave us one of her slobbery kisses.

"Ooooh, how you've grown!" she would coo. "And how old are you now? Is it 10? Lawsy sakes! I remember when you were still crawling around on the floor. And to think you're 10 now."

Sound familiar? Of course it does.

And as soon as Aunt Maudie turned her back, you'd wipe her drool on your sleeve and make a solemn vow that you would never, ever, not-under-any-circumstances say something stupid like that when you got to be an adult.

So what happens these days when your nieces and nephews come for a visit? You hug 'em and plant a kiss on their cheek and blurt out, "Ooooh, how you've grown! And how old are you now? Is it 10? Lawsy sakes! I remember . . . ." And the instant you turn your back, their shirtsleeve starts to drip.

Oh, well. Since we're on the subject of birthdays and repetitions (a redundancy if there ever was one), I might as well follow tradition and give you my thoughts on crossing the great divide into hardcore middle age.

■ Does the Big Four-Oh! bother me?

Yes. As a card-carrying, first-wave Baby Boomer, my initial reaction upon seeing the numeral "40" after my name is to think there's been a mistake — mathematical, typographical or otherwise.

I had an aunt (not Maudie) who told me she cried the entire night before she turned 30, but that 40 was a piece of cake. This same woman, I might add, chain-smoked Parliament cigarettes and lived well into her 80s.

Her birthday theory is not working for me, however. In my case, No. 30 was just another day. But 40? Gulp.

I better get used to it, though. Because the thought of that milestone waiting 10 years hence is enough to make me faint. (If your 50-year-old tongue is beginning to click against your teeth, go back and read the first few paragraphs. And hush.)

■ What great mysteries of life have I solved in four decades on this earth?

Not many; maybe none. In fact, there's one heck of a lot more mysteries than I ever imagined.

What's weird is that I'm not as driven to solve them as I was 20 years ago. Instead, I strive for peaceful coexistence.

■ Have I changed significantly — besides waistline and hairline?

Only in one respect: Believing the notion that it's noble to "grow up."

Horse pucky.

When I was young and impressionable, I thought being an adult would be neat. And it is a marvelous experience, despite the 10,000 strings of job and family that pull at me in unison.

Nonetheless, I don't ever want to "grow up."

I have seen 22-year-olds who are "grown up." And I have said last rites over 85-year-olds who never "grew up." I pitied the former, envied the latter.

Because as each day passes, I realize Peter Pan had the right idea all along.

Her side of the story

May 24, 1987

by MARY ANN VENABLE
Long-suffering wife of Venob

It must be true. His mother swears it's so. Sam Venable's birth certificate lists his date of birth as May 24, 1947. Thus, today he is 40 years old.

I have reason to doubt it. I live in a household with three adolescents. Their ages are 13, 14, and 40. The air is filled with loud rock music, roughhousing and squabbling. And that's just from Sam. Add in the other two and it gets worse.

I have to sit between Sam and the children at church. They get the giggles too bad. Around home he is in charge of teaching culture, such as drinking milk directly from the carton and catapulting peas on a spoon.

Let me tell you the truth about Sam. What you see is a smiling face by his column. I'll reveal the real man under the kinky hair.

Sam, of course, loves to hunt and fish with his good buddy, Rollo Ray McKenzie. All week long they get ready for an upcoming trip. Equipment is purchased, discussed, processed, personalized and installed. Trips are made back and forth to be sure everything is prepared. Their planning makes a space shuttle launch seem spontaneous.

The appointed day starts early. They get up long before dawn to cram dogs and equipment into the truck. Off they go, sloshing coffee everywhere, with high hopes for plenty of game. They drive hundreds of miles.

Of course, they stop frequently to replenish their supply of Little Debbie cakes and Snickers bars. After spending a few short hours afield, they drag home without anything to show for their efforts. The remainder of the evening they spend on the phone discussing and analyzing the day's events . . . and planning for the next jaunt.

After Sam and Rollo complete the discussion, Sam calls another buddy to tell him about the hunt. Then another. And another. So I get to hear again and again how many mallards came in or how many quail flushed or how hard the rockfish bit or how high the bass jumped or how many times the bluebills circled or who shot first.

I can tell if he is talking to a sporting buddy or someone else by the words he uses in conversation. When he talks to his mother, he is Mr. Virgin Lips. "Yes, Mother . . . how was your volunteer work today? . . . yes, ma'am . . . "

I won't repeat what he says to his buddies. He does use a variation of the word "mother," however.

Sam likes to eat — not just Little Debbie cakes. His idea of gourmet food is sliced hot dogs in pork 'n' beans. Admittedly, this makes cooking for him very easy. It doesn't matter what you put in front of him; just be sure you have plenty.

Whenever we make a meal of some of the game he has brought in, the dinner conversation revolves around the trip that provided the meal. He can tell the entire episode — when, where and how it was shot with a side story on the weather that day.

I realize a lot of men are messy. They just don't seem to notice disorder. It must be in the genes, and I don't mean their Calvins. But Sam elevates it to a fine art.

After I was in the hospital a few days when our first child was born, Sam picked up my mother, then Clay and myself, and drove us home. Inside, I picked my way gingerly around the heaps of clothing, mail, dishes and food to go upstairs.

My mother refused to let me go into the kitchen. "It will send you back to the hospital," she said. And get this — he had cleaned up!

Another time, Sam received a letter noted "copy for your files." I just about choked. Sam's files consisted of a mound of correspondence and other papers about 3 feet wide and a foot high on the floor of the spare bedroom.

We don't need a calendar at our house. Instead of months, we have "seasons." Night-fishing season, then follows dove season, deer season and so on. Not to mention such exotic activities as bow-hunting gar and grabbling for catfish.

"Sam, can you wash the outside windows for me?" I might ask. "Sure, I'd be happy to! Right after duck season." After duck season: "Sam, can you wash the outside windows for me?" "Sure, right after turkey season!" After turkey season: "Sam, can you wash the outside windows for me?" "Sure, right after crappie season!"

Needless to say, the windows are awfully dirty.

Of course, there is another side to this. Do you remember several years ago a woman who put an ad in the paper offering to trade off her husband along with 50 pounds of deer meat, two dogs and five shotguns? After several days and numerous offers, she decided to keep him.

I feel the same way about Sam. I would like to chuck out every chest wader and spinnerbait in our garage . . . but then, maybe not. After all, this is the man who said he would rather have me than a six-pound smallmouth bass. How can I resist such sweet talk?

He is a kind, sensitive, generous man who remembers birthdays and anniversaries. He is a great father to our children. I'll keep him.

Even if he is much older than I.

True grit

June 26, 1986

It is one of those dreadful summer afternoons. Hotter than a depot stove. Sticky. The sort of day that makes asphalt bubble and gardens wilt.

But relief is on the way.

A stiff breeze has rippled the surface of Fort Loudoun Lake. From my vantage of 11 stories, the reservoir looks like a shimmering, serpentine washboard. Moments before, it was slick as glass.

The wind races toward me. It strikes land, leaving tiny tornadoes of dust in its wake. In rapid succession, it engulfs a highway, a pasture and a wooded ridge where maples and oaks respond by curling their leaves upward. Their silver undersides shine.

"It's going to rain," my mother would say. "Whenever the leaves turn silver, that means it's going to rain."

Perhaps it will. But I am concerned with neither heat nor humidity nor wind nor silver leaves nor rain at this moment.

Rather, I am standing in the air-conditioned comfort of a hospital room. And what concerns me is my mother.

She turns slightly in her bed. The hint of a grimace streaks her face. Her eyes remain closed.

"You need more medicine?" I speak into her ear.

"Yes," she whispers, almost in a croak.

"Then push the button. Remember what the nurse said? You won't get any more than you need."

"You're sure I won't get too much?"

"No, mama. It's preset. Whenever you feel pain, push the button."

She does. The machine beeps. A metered dose of morphine enters the tube attached to her arm.

"Feel better?"

She nods her head yes. "Amazing, isn't it?" she whispers before sliding back into slumber.

I watch her sleep and a flood of memories sweeps over me. How could the tables have turned so quickly?

It was 25 years ago. I was the one in the hospital, manacled with tubes. She was the one at the foot of the bed, worried as only a mother can be, discussing the operation with the surgeon. He was that "nice young man" her sister-in-law had taught in school.

Now, she lies in the bed, and I am the one who maintains a worried vigil. The surgeon who has worked his magic is another nice young man. He and I were in school together.

She stirs momentarily. I reassure her it's OK to push the button and receive another jolt of painkiller. The machine, I reiterate, will not let her get too much. Convinced at last, she mashes the button again and the machine beeps again and she starts to drift off again.

"Amazing, isn't it?" she whispers again.

When doctors run out of tests to conduct, but yet the pain persists, there is nothing to do but go inside for an inspection. "Exploratory surgery," they call it.

Sounds simple enough — unless you happen to be the exploree. She knows the doctors will discover what's wrong. That's the fear. "What" they might find is the word we are hesitant to even speak.

She stirs again. Her eyelids part slightly.

"Are you sure there's no cancer?"

"I promise, mama. Nothing but a worn-out gall bladder you don't have any more. You're gonna be good as new."

Then I reassure her it's OK to push the button again. It beeps again and she says, "Amazing, isn't it?" again and drifts back off to sleep.

I gaze at her and shake my head in awe.

She is 73 years old. She has just had her guts carved apart. She has weathered two world wars, a devastating economic depression, four childbirths, the deaths of her father, mother, husband, brother and countless other relatives and friends. And she is worried about becoming dependent on a crutch to give her strength.

Amazing, isn't it?

Goodbye, Ol' Paint

September 20, 1987

I can't explain why I behave this way. But I've done it before, and I'll do it again.

I get hopelessly sentimental about inanimate objects, particularly objects that have served me faithfully. When the time comes to banish them to the trash can, I feel as if I've betrayed a friend.

Make no mistake: I don't get weepy with each and every item that dies in my hands. In fact, I have hastened the death of many a tool and machine, laughing maniacally while it writhed in pain.

Once, I owned a radio that steadfastly refused to stay on the proper wave length. No matter how much I twisted the dial and fine-tuned the station, that hateful radio would issue clear signals for no more than 15 minutes, max. After that, the only transmission I heard sounded like a World War II newscast from the front lines.

Like a fool, I put up with these shenanigans for years. Then one day the torture got to me and I cracked. So did the radio when I smashed it with my fist. Cracked right down the middle, in fact.

It didn't dawn on me at the time that I could have been electrocuted. Minor details like that never matter when I take a fit. At least I would have died happy.

But when it comes to loyal equipment, I fall to pieces. So, it seems, do others.

"Being sentimental about a car or a pair of pajamas or a refrigerator is ridiculous and I know it, but I can't help myself," Andy Rooney wrote in his bestselling "Pieces of My Mind."

"I have this irrational notion that the refrigerator has feelings and will be hurt when I cast it aside after it's given me 17 years of good service," he continued. "It will want to know what it's done wrong to deserve ending up in the dump. The car I drive for 91,000 miles before I trade it will be heartbroken at being turned over to a new owner who will abuse it."

That's precisely the way I felt not long ago when I pulled into Goodwill Industries to drop off my son's old bicycle.

This was Clay's first real bike, purchased after the days of kiddy toys and training wheels had passed. It was a 16-inch model of Star Wars vintage, although Luke Skywalker and R2-D2 had long since been buried under "customizing" layers of black spray paint.

Face it; this was just another old bike, another piece of metal and fiberglass to be pounded back into shape and re-sold. I do hope that's what happens, too. I hope some other little boy will own this bicycle and ride it and love it the way my son did.

But even though Clay is now in high school and hasn't straddled that bike in years, even though it had been gathering dust in the garage, even though Star Wars was a long, long time ago in a galaxy far,

far away, I still felt awful. It was like I was leading the gentle family pony to the glue factory.

"Want a receipt for it?" the Goodwill man asked me.

"A receipt?" I thought to myself. "Will a piece of paper give me back those years? Will it help me hear the laughter again? Will it show me skid marks on the driveway? Can I take that receipt and use it to inflate flat tires or kiss a strawberried knee?"

"No receipt," I said, ducking my head and walking away. "Just take good care of it."

The man assured me he would. I suppose when you work at Goodwill, you get used to situations like this.

The Chair

June 21, 1987

Sometime this weekend, maybe even before you read these words, I shall drive to my mother's house and find The Chair and bring it back where it belongs.

The last time I saw it, The Chair was stacked atop mounds of other family memorabilia in the attic above my mother's carport. We Venables are notorious memorabilia collectors.

(Would you like to see my boyhood display of bird nests? I have a blue-gray gnatcatcher's that is simply the berries. And my Baltimore oriole's, despite its age, will knock your knickers off. But for the moment, let us concentrate not on chickadees but on chairs. The Chair.)

I am preparing myself for an extensive search, for Mother has spent most of the summer straightening her attic. This could spell trouble.

Quite possibly, The Chair is still where I left it years ago: on top of a roll of used-but-not-abused living room carpet. Or maybe it has worked its way to the rack of vintage dresses and suits. No matter; I am determined to find it.

The Chair needs to be brought home for two reasons.

First, Mary Ann and I recently added on to our house. Before the new storage space gets filled with other important junk, I want to give The Chair its rightful place. But the other reason, the more important reason, is because this is Father's Day.

A few weeks shy of Father's Day, 1972, an ordinary piece of furniture wrote a chapter in our family's history. It was transformed from "a chair" into The Chair. And its birthing was among the last moments my dad and I shared.

This was a moment of laughter. Good laughter. The way things used to be.

My old man and I were close when I was young. Tight. Pals who could make each other laugh at a glance.

But teenage years and higher education can sometimes hammer wedges between parents and children, a truism I am re-learning from the other side of the fence. When you take an opinionated father who grew up during the Great Depression and match him one-on-one with an equally opinionated son who grew up during the Wild Sixties, the sparks . . . well, you understand.

But all that was changing by the time The Chair came to be.

I was several years on my own by then. Married. A child on the way. Well into my career with different jobs and different cities under my belt.

A wonderful thing happened when I moved back to Knoxville. I discovered that my father had grown in wisdom and insight during my absence. By some quirk of coincidence, he perceived the same about me. Best of all, we were starting to share our zany sense of humor with each other. Just like before.

So there he is at my house one day and lunch is over and we've all gone into the living room and we're sitting around talking and I rock back in my chair.

I always rock back in chairs. It's a habit I picked up — and was continually scolded for — as a kid.

A scowl flashed across Dad's face. "Put the four legs of that chair on the floor!" he shouted in mock anger.

I did. And with all the deliberate cockiness of James Dean, I picked up a fine, straight-backed, wooden kitchen chair and headed toward the basement.

Everyone was struck speechless. They knew what was about to happen. Mary Ann, who is prudent about matters of wholesale destruction, even jumped up and tried to stop me.

She did not succeed.

You see, for all those years when I was a kid and was getting yelled at for leaning back in chairs, I had sworn when I grew up, I'd invent a chair you not only *could* lean back in, you *had* to lean back in. And my invention was far behind schedule.

So I dragged the chair through the basement door and grabbed a saw. In a virtual tornado of sawdust, front-leg amputation was performed.

By the time the operation was completed and I was re-seated — or re-leaned, as the case may be — in the living room, the house was shaking with laughter. Pappy and I were the worst. We were into wheezing fits.

The Chair was still leaning against the wall some weeks later when I was awakened by the telephone and heard the voice of an old family friend:

"Come quick. He's had a heart attack."

We buried him on Monday. The day after Father's Day.

Trouble on the line

September 23, 1986

Normally, I don't engage in lengthy conversations with people who don't want to identify themselves. I have to sign my name on everything I do, so why should someone else get to hide behind the cloak of anonymity?

But the woman persisted. No way, said she, was her name going public.

"Why not?" I wanted to know.

"Because I've just done something awfully stupid," she replied. "I can't believe I did it. I don't want anybody to know it was me — even though nobody in this town knows me in the first place."

By now my mind was racing. What crime had this poor soul committed? Killed someone in a fit of rage? Run over a dog and left it in the ditch? Defaced a library book? Ripped the label off her mattress?

Nothing that bad, she assured me. But it didn't matter by now, for I was hopelessly hooked. I had to hear the details.

Go on and tell me, I said. No names.

So she launched into her story.

The deed occurred a few days ago in Sevierville. The woman had driven from her home in Atlanta to visit her sister-in-law in Knoxville.

"Then what were you doing in Sevierville?" I probed.

"Oh, I didn't actually do the driving myself," she said. "I rode with a neighbor from Atlanta who was traveling to Sevierville. I had arranged for my sister-in-law to drive from Knoxville to Sevierville and pick me up when my friend dropped me off."

"That makes sense. But how was your sister-in-law going to know where you were and when to come get you?"

"I was going to call her as soon as we reached Sevierville," she said. "That's when this whole dumb thing started."

The woman told me she had gotten out of the car, walked to a phone booth, and prepared to place a long-distance call to Knoxville. She carried a fistful of quarters to plug the machine.

"I have been using telephones all my life," she said. "I am retired from a large government office that was full of telephones. I know how to place a telephone call. But when I glanced up and saw where the directions said to dial '1 + number,' that's exactly what I tried to do."

"What's exactly what you tried to do?" I begged, struggling to keep pace with her story.

"Dial the '+' " she said. "But I couldn't find a '+' anywhere on the dial."

"There is no '+' on the dial," I said.

"I know that!" she replied. "I had a mental block or something. It just never registered in my head."

"So what did you do?"

"First, I tried pushing 1 and the '*.' That didn't work. A recording came on. It told me my call could not be completed as dialed and to check the instructions. So I did. Sure, enough, it said to dial '1 + number,' and I started looking for that crazy '+' all over again."

I told her not to worry, that we all have little mental lapses from time to time. They're what make life so interesting.

"But that's not the end of it," she said. "No matter how hard I looked, I still couldn't find that '+' sign. So I asked my neighbor to get out of the car and come help me.

"The same mental block hit her. She started looking for the '+' right along with me. Finally, we agreed that dial faces on phones in Tennessee must be different from those in Georgia. We drove off to get some help."

I was chuckling to myself by now. "When did the mistake dawn on you?" I inquired.

"It didn't," she said. "That's what's so awful. All the phones were the same. We finally stopped at a motel and asked a desk clerk how to call Knoxville from Sevierville. He looked at us kinda funny and said, 'Just dial 1 plus the number.' That's when it hit me. I've never been so embarrassed in my life. Ooooh! Wasn't that dumb?"

Yes, I agreed. It most certainly was.

And that's why I promised my Aunt Delphy I wouldn't use her name.

The Evil Eye

August 11, 1987

It sneaks up like a sneeze, but the result is not nearly as pleasurable.

You know what's about to happen. You know because it has happened so many times before. That's why you try extra hard to resist the urge.

But your fight is in vain — as you knew it would be — and 10 seconds later, you are mired in the tar pit of embarrassment. Again.

I speak, of course, of inopportune laughter: the uncontrollable, crying, shaking, hoo-haaing fits of laughter that invariably strike when you'd rather be in Philadelphia.

It happened to my daughter in church last Sunday. I don't know what got her started, but that doesn't matter. It never does. Take it from an expert.

When I was a kid and got the shakes in church, my pappy could drive them from me with The Evil Eye. You probably never saw a Big Sam Evil Eye, but it bore striking resemblance to the Big Fred Evil Eye, the Big George Evil Eye and other frightening facial expressions administered by fathers everywhere.

What it means is, "When we get outta here, I'm gonna burn you a new one."

But now that I am a father, I find myself unable to give The Evil Eye. At least not one that drives the laugh bug away from my kids in church.

What usually happens is that they get me tickled and we all start hoo-haaing. Perhaps that explains why our pew is rarely crowded. Also why wife Mary Ann, sitting way up there in the choir, keeps her Evil Eye on red alert. Properly delivered, a long-distance Evil Eye is just as effective as one from four feet.

It is comforting to know other people have been smitten by this horrible disease. One of them is Kenneth Wilson, a law enforcement supervisor for the Tennessee Wildlife Resources Agency.

I have noticed game wardens universally are overtaken by laughter when I start making excuses about unplugged shotguns, running lights that don't work, no boat cushions, extra ducks in the game bag and other minor offenses, but that's neither here nor there.

Wilson once told me about the time — he will strangle me for retelling it — when he was sitting in the Polk County Courthouse, waiting for his cases to come up. On the witness stand, in a totally unrelated matter, sat this woman. The judge and lawyers were quietly conferring among themselves. The room was silent as a tomb.

That's when the woman — oh, gosh, how do I say this? — was, uh, "smitten" by a touch of intestinal gas.

She unsmote herself in a loud manner.

"Every person in the courtroom started shaking silently," Wilson told me. "We squeezed our knees till our knuckles turned white. Our faces were red. After what seemed like six hours, we regained our composure."

That's when the woman unsmote herself once more.

Louder.

"The entire courtroom — I mean *everybody* — stood up in unison and walked out. About the time we hit the halls, the laughing started. It was awful."

Another time, I saw Pete Gardner totally lose it on TV. This was years ago when he anchored the evening news for WATE.

Apparently, something off-camera got Gardner started. But as I said earlier, the reason never matters. I don't recall the story he was reading, but it went something like this:

"Two people were killed — *snicker, excuse me* — today when the car in which — *chortle, snicker, I'm SO sorry* — they were riding smashed

into a tree — *hooo-haaa, please do forgive me* — on Highway 11W near Knoxville."

It got so bad, the station switched to a commercial. When the news resumed, Gardner apologized profusely and began another story.

Then the laugh bug bit him again.

I don't know when I've ever felt as sorry for another human being. Having been there myself, I knew poor ol' Pete was laughing on the outside, but dying on the inside.

What he needed was a dose of the Big Sam Evil Eye.

The homecoming

December 24, 1985

They were in a hurry, the young Army officer and his wife. In a hurry to go home for Christmas, to share the holidays with their families, to show off their new baby girl.

The call to home is strongest at Christmas. Almost instinctive. But this particular year, it was more intense than ever, for the nation was at war and the young Army officer had been assigned overseas. "Next year" in a war is light-years away.

So with a 48-hour pass in his pocket, he drove his young family through the cold Georgia night to Tennessee. For the moment, at least, they would get away.

Away from the infantry. Away from M-1 rifles. Away from orders and drills and regulations. Away from the business of making war.

They were going home. Real home.

Not just to the town where they had grown up, met and married. Not just to any old house. Rather, they were going to their own home. The home he had built in the pines at the top of the hill.

The entire family gathered that Christmas Eve in 1944: uncles, aunts, brothers, sisters, cousins, nieces, nephews and friends thereof. They ate and sang carols and exchanged gifts, and in an eyeblink it was over. Back to the horrible business of making war.

The young officer spent the next Christmas Eve in Europe, but the rest of the family gathered just the same. They ate hot dogs instead of turkey and ham this time — because "good" meat was still in short supply — but they ate heartily nonetheless. And they sang carols and exchanged gifts and thought about the soldiers half a world away.

The war ended, and the young officer came home. Back to his home in the pines at the top of the hill. Home to stay. And for every Christmas Eve thereafter, he brought his own family together with uncles, aunts, brothers, sisters, cousins, nieces, nephews and friends thereof. By the dozens.

The crowd grew larger each year. Those who had originally attended as children began arriving with boyfriends and girlfriends. Then with husbands and wives. Then with a new generation of children. They all came to eat and laugh and sing and celebrate the eve of this most hallowed of holidays in Christendom.

Wars have an awful habit of interrupting such fun. Nearly 25 years after the young Army officer missed the Christmas Eve gathering, one of his own sons was absent. Vietnam.

Perhaps that Christmas Eve hurt him the most. For he, more than any of the others in the crowd, knew how the heart aches when it yearns to go home and yet cannot return because there is a war to be fought.

But that war ended, too. And the son came home. And the Christmas Eve celebrations continued.

Father Time started taking a toll on the original cast. Every year or so, an old face — a familiar, laughing, loving face — would be gone for good. In 1972, the face of the young Army officer, who by now was no longer young nor still in the Army, turned up missing. Missing forever. Yet new faces continued to appear, as a third generation of babies was at hand.

So now it is Christmas Eve, 1985. And the family will gather once more.

The young officer's wife from that first celebration is retired from a lifetime of teaching school. Her children have children of their own.

The baby girl from 1944 is 41 years of age. Her son is 15 and stands two inches taller than his mother.

They and all of the others — all the brothers and sisters, wives and husbands, children, cousins, uncles, aunts, nephews, nieces, in-laws and friends thereof — will gather tonight to eat and sing and laugh and exchange gifts and remember the good times.

All of us.

Back to the home in the pines at the top of the hill.

The home my father built.

The art of giving gifts

December 13, 1985

It is better to give a Christmas gift than receive one.

Trust me.

I am reminded of this truth 96 times a day, 672 times a week, 35,040 times a year. And before you start dividing, that comes out to once every 15 minutes.

That's how often the Westminster chimes strike on our grandfather clock.

The grandfather clock stands in our living room. You will find it just to the right of the front door. The same door Mary Ann would have loved to pitch it through the day it arrived.

This problem stems from the fact that I am a master at giving people gifts I would love to receive.

When I was a boy, I sometimes would take the bus to town to see a movie. Before starting home, I would stop at the bakery in Rich's and buy my mother a jelly doughnut. Never a cupcake or a sweet roll. Always a jelly doughnut.

Why?

Because I liked jelly doughnuts and figured everyone else would, too. Even my mother's subtle hints — "I don't like jelly doughnuts" — failed to stop these gestures of goodwill.

So it was only natural, years later, that I would be buying a grandfather clock for Mary Ann. After all, hadn't I always wanted one?

Not just any clock would do. I wanted a grandfather clock like the one that stood in the old Russell Hotel in LaFollette. That's where my grandfather used to live. And from the first moment I saw that clock and heard its slow, rhythmic ticking, I started wishing for one.

By Christmas 1979, I had done enough wishing.

Christmas 1979 also was the time Mary Ann had her eye on a Tennessee pearl ring. Knowing my penchant for missed cues, she began dropping subtle hints.

Such as, "I want a Tennessee pearl ring. Listen up, Fat Boy. Read my lips: R-i-n-g."

As always, the message soaked in like rain on concrete.

Throughout November and early December, I searched furniture stores and specialty shops. Nothing suited my fancy. Then my mother, who had surfaced for air after 8,176 jelly doughnuts, told me about a custom clocksmith. I paid him a visit, found what I had been looking for and made a down payment.

Now, the plot thickens.

I was in Louisiana when the clock was delivered. When the appointed day arrived, I called home, fairly quaking with excitement.

Mary Ann answered. Quietly.

"MERRY CHRISTMAS!" I shouted.

"Thank you," she replied. Quietly.

"WELL!" I yelled back. "WHADAYA THINK? REALLY NEAT, AIN'T IT!"

"It's nice," she said. Quietly.

"NICE? IT'S JUST NICE?"

"We'll talk about it, quietly, when you get home."

Which we did.

That's when I realized after 10 years of marriage — 10 years of open, frank discussion on any matter, no holds barred — not once had we broached the subject of: (1) my love of grandfather clocks and (2)

Mary Ann's loathing of same.

I thought the ticking sounded soothing and relaxing. She thought it was depressing.

I thought the chimes were delightful. They made her cry. Literally.

Lest ye worry, the hatchet has long been buried — and not in my head. She has her ring, I have my clock, and we've both had several good laughs.

So what's on tap for Mary Ann's present this year?

S-s-sh! Just tiptoe down the hall and peek into the closet. Over there behind the raincoats.

Isn't that the prettiest little shotgun you ever saw?

Through a mother's eyes

May 12, 1985

It had started as a square of congealed salad, a dinner party leftover banished to the back of the refrigerator for more than a week. By the time it was discovered, the forces of nature had been at work.

The surface of the salad once was glossy. Now, it was fuzzy with mold. Closer inspection revealed that each individual growth in this tiny jungle had sprouted a minute stem and red "flowers." Not at all unlike a wee field of scarlet tulips.

This was just the sort of goo most folks would pitch into the trash with a disgusted "yuck!" Then they'd reach for the Lysol.

Not my mother.

"Look real close," she was telling me. "Hold it under the light. Isn't that the most beautiful thing you ever saw?"

Yes, it was. And in so admitting, I knew the apple had not fallen far from the tree. That's also why I understood completely when mother gently placed the dish back into the refrigerator to see what other colorful fungi would sprout in coming days.

Mothers sow a variety of seeds as they ferry their broods across the river from infancy to adulthood. For some, the resulting harvest is money. For others, a plucky spirit. It could be the skill to cook the finest stew or sing a song or any of 10,000 talents.

Mine gave me the ability to perceive beauty, no matter where or when it is found. For that, I will be eternally grateful.

Flowers grow all over the hill where I was raised. Especially irises. In particular, there is a purple iris, a violet so deep and pure, it almost hurts your eyes to gaze upon it for long.

But I'm not certain mother isn't more fond of what she calls her Concrete Garden. You'll find it in a section of the driveway sealed from auto traffic when a carport was added to the house years ago. The pavement is cracked and broken. Over time, the fissures have been reclaimed by wild flowers: black-eyed Susans, Queen Anne's lace and ironweed, to name a few.

Inspectors from "Better Homes and Gardens" might deem the place an eyesore and prescribe massive doses of 2,4-D. Heaven forbid! In late summer, that stretch of driveway is absolutely dancing with color.

Oh, as long as you're touring the Concrete Garden, you might also want to take in mother's redwood table. It's at the rear of the carport, just below the hanging baskets.

In its first life, this served as a picnic table for humans. These days, it is the hallowed picnic ground for insects. Some sort of winged wood borers the size of bumblebees.

I don't know how long it's been since the first bugs arrived. Three years at least. But not once has mother offered to chase them to another feasting area. Rather, she has watched in amazement as tiny grains of sawdust dribbled into mounds beneath the holes.

"Isn't it just marvelous how they can do that?" she asks.

Of course it is. And a few days ago — while I held my lunch in my lap — I, too, was watching the spectacle and pondering just how the devil they do it.

Beauty is everywhere. Some of it's just more perceivable than others. Often, the best is camouflaged from the eyes of casual viewers.

It takes someone skilled enough to unlock this wonderment, to free you from the bonds of conformity. Then you can see it, too. And with a bit of luck, you can pass the gift to your own children.

Already, my kids show encouraging signs.

East Tennessee was under siege from a heat wave several summers ago. We'd gone for weeks without rain. It was hot, muggy, sticky. (Yes, my mother can even see beauty in the haze of a steamy day — something I devoutly refuse to do.)

Then late one afternoon, the sky turned black as a crow's wing. The wind freshened. The temperature dropped. Way off in the distance, filaments of lightning began to tickle the heavens.

Mother Nature can really put on a show when she throws a fit like that. I announced it had been quite a spell since I'd seen a fierce storm brew, and I was going to make the best of it. With that, I marched across the backyard, climbed into a hammock, and swayed in wide-eyed peace as the concert started.

Mother happened to telephone the house about that time. Daughter Megan answered.

"Sorry, Grandmommy," she laughed. "Daddy can't come to the phone right now. He's outside baying at the moon."

What's so wonderful is that all three of us understood perfectly.